The CROWNS of CROSWALD

D.E. NIGHT

The Crowns of Croswald by D.E. Night
Published by Stories Untold

Editors: Jessie Chatigny & Miriam Lacob Stix
Cover design and illustrations by resn.co.nz

Publisher's Cataloging-in-Publication Data

Names: Night, D.E.
Title: The Crowns of Croswald / D.E. Night.
Description: [Pembroke Pines, FL]: Stories Untold, 2017. | Series: Croswald series ;
    no. 1. | Summary: Ivy Lovely's powers awaken when she enters a school where
    students learn to master their magical blood and the power of mysterious gems.
    When her magic — and her life — are threatened by the Dark Queen, she must
    unearth her history and save Croswald before the truth is lost forever.
Identifiers: LCCN 2017936188 | ISBN 9780996948654 (pbk.) |
    ISBN 9780996948630 (hardcover) | ISBN 9780996948623 (epub) |
    ISBN 9780996948616 (mobi)
Subjects: CYAC: Magic -- Fiction. | Coming of age-- Fiction. | Private schools --
Fiction. | BISAC: JUVENILE FICTION / Fantasy & Magic. | JUVENILE
FICTION / Action & Adventure / General.
Classification: LCC PZ7.1.N54.C76 2017 | DDC [Fic]-- dc22
LC record available at https://lccn.loc.gov/2017936188

Manufactured in the United States of America

STORIES
UNTOLD

To my husband, who has proven
fairy tales aren't only in books.

CONTENTS

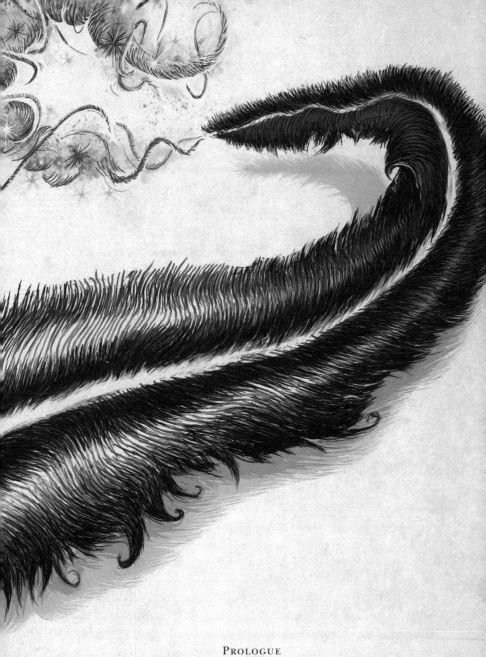

THE SCRIVENIST

T HE village, well, it had a lot of secrets. And its secrets need to be kept safe. So, the town's name was like a key—those who knew the name could find the village. Let's call it The Town.

It was early winter, early morning. Snow flurries swirled in the dry, inhospitable air. They made a soft white covering over The Town's crooked angles, thick roofs, and dark buildings cut from porous stone. On the cabby roof deck, a thick mist covered what the snow didn't. The hairies were still glowing in lanterns dangling from lamp posts, their little fairy bodies almost hidden under their colorful, illuminated hair. Beneath a particularly bright lantern on a roof deck overlooking The Town, inside of which a curious pair of hairies mashed their noses against cold glass, stood a young man: Derwin Edgar Night. He was small framed, but held his body rigidly at its full height, chin high and shoulders squared. His pride was well deserved: he was the most promising student that anyone in The Town had ever encountered. Even the hairies were curious about him. What adventures in magic lay ahead for Derwin?

Leaning on the iron railing and looking over the enchanted, forbidden town, Derwin wondered what his assigned castle would look like. He was sure that he would be a world-renowned scrivenist, but would his royal family be kind to him? Which family would it be? Just visible through the cloud that seemed to sit on the ground he could see a dreary street paved with uneven cobblestones. Other scrivenists began to assemble around him, mauve umbrellas floating above their owners and protecting them from the flurries. In the warmer season the snow turned to rain for a few moons, but other than that the snow was as much a resident here as the scrivenists who came to study. The trickle of people grew steadily until a crowd rushed past the tailor, the pie shop, the potion apothecary, and the other stores that lined the street that lead to the cabby roof deck. Each wore a crisp, new uniform. These uniforms had been around as long as scrivenists had been writing, exploring the magic of Croswald, and serving the royal class in their cavernous castles.

Derwin was lost in his thoughts and distracted by the crowd that pressed in on the platform, eager for their own adventures. He made his way through the line, his satchel heavy with books. The rooftop deck was just beginning to steam as the warmth of morning broke through. He directed his gaze toward the newspaper he held but had not read. The *Scriven This* headline, highlighted by the paper's built-in roving spotlights, read, "Wandering Family Still Lost!" He skimmed the first line: "Selector scouting scrivenists for..." The article attributed the disappearance to a suspected, at-large dwarf who had cursed the family seven generations ago. All these words went perfectly undigested by our young scrivenist. Strangely, since he'd received his Deed of Service, he'd had a problem focusing on anything for very long. This was very uncharacteristic. He'd chalked the haze in his brain up to the excitement of finishing his studies.

It was the Day of Ordination for newly minted scrivenists. Having completed the requisite training and apprenticeship in The Town, these bright scholars were off to ply their trade for the royal families to whom they had been assigned. Standing pressed together on the platform, their energy was palpable. It was no wonder that their newly acquired quills were quivering in the special pocket of their plum-colored, tightly buttoned, tweed jackets. The air hummed. One small scrivenist practiced turning snowy slush to a sweet delicacy, looping his quill in tiny circles. Another was reading the stars (through the thick cloud, no less) to determine the ease of their cabby travels.

"I can't believe it!" A tall, slender scrivenist's face was alight with anticipation. "See you, books and class! I'm off to do real magic."

Though she had addressed no one in particular, a bearded scrivenist responded with a sly smile. "Careful—you may not have to study books now, but you do have to write them!"

She laughed. "Ever since I felt the magic in my bones at eight, I knew I'd be more the doing type of scrivenist and less the writing type." With that she drew her quill from her jacket and swooped a large arc, her many-layered tweed skirt twirling around her knees. Tiny, yellow sparks turned into flowers with a lovely fragrance that fell on those around her.

"I can hardly believe that this—" he said, unrolling a vellum scroll, "—this small thing holds my future! Embossed letters telling me where I'll reside and serve the rest of my days."

"I hope the Royal Family Lichen appreciate flora!" The female scrivenist continued to send flowers out over the crowd.

To Derwin's left stood a scrivenist reading her copy of *Creaking Caldrons: A Self Yelp Book for Leaks & Squeaks*. The fellow pressing into his right shoulder was deeply interested in *How to Tame a Scrivenly Beard*. Though young, Derwin was assured of his superior skill—his performance and confidence had surely guided him to a posh position. As was his nature, he noted with a slightly proud smirk that he was by far the brightest person on the platform.

As he made his way up through the line, Derwin rocked on his heels, his Deed of Service clutched at his side. The anticipation, the urge to cast spells and invent, was almost too much to bear. Derwin patted his pocket. *Ahhhh.* His quill—a scrivenist's most prized possession—was exceptional. Silver nibbed, its rare handle was one-of-a-kind, a cross between a rapier and a writhing snake. It fit his grip perfectly and practically spat out ink in excitement. Its academic vigor matched his own: it represented the perfect cap to his completion of scrivenist studies and a marker of his voyage into service.

The crowd may have looked like a bunched-up jumble, but it actually formed a snaking line toward an ornate ticket window. Winnowed from a solid piece of brass, the whole booth was polished to a golden sheen, including the delicate bars that ran up and down the window that occupied its top half. The ticket booth was almost entirely filled with a corpulent woman, the ticketing agent.

Finally, the line snaked far enough along that it was Derwin's turn. Bright, gold bars were about the only thing that stood between him and his dreams. Finishing a wide-mouthed yawn, the ticketing agent hollered, "Next in line, please! Let's keep it moving!" He handed her his deed and she unrolled the document. She saw the family crest inside and stopped abruptly. Noting his confidence, she said, "Not much for reading the news, are you? Or history? Makes every bit of sense that you'd be headed back there, doesn't it?" She smirked, her lips curling too easily. Derwin could smell her breath, sickly sweet from too much pie.

"It does, doesn't it? I've been promised one of the most prestigious families in all of Croswald—cousins to the Queen, let's hope. I'm sure their library is quite extensive, needs a lot of magical management—and the acreage! So much to explore!" Derwin's eyes glowed. It *was* strange that he couldn't hold the family's name in his mind, but he was sure it was a good one.

She removed her quill from her walnut inkwell and jabbed at Derwin's Deed of Service in a forcible fashion, inscribing something practically illegible across its entire width. The second she stamped his deed, the writing began to fade as if the letters were disappearing in mist.

"Aren't you afraid you'll get lost on your way to the cabby? Don't wander off now," she teased. But Derwin was already lost in his thoughts, wielding his quill and casting spells and creating magical beasts—all to great applause—in his mind. Even now, just directing his thoughts to his quill made it leap to life. He patted the quill pocket, conscious of its detection of magic beyond the town's cloud cover. It was scanning for potion ingredients in the dark forest, itching and twitching to write.

Derwin was so preoccupied that he missed the cabby's approach but the usual crash landing and the snorting of the giant, rhino-like beast jolted him from his reverie. The cabby station's deck bore many deep scars in its wood from rambunctious, barely-made-it landings. The drivers and beasts fairly careened in and out of the sky. Distractedly, he stepped into one of the three house-like carriages that the beast towed through the air. Like all wheel-less cabby carriages, its small wooden door opened to what appeared to be a tiny, eccentrically decorated living room. Mismatched chairs and wicker benches were jammed inside leaving little in the way of legroom. By now, with several seasons of scrivenist training under his belt and cabbies being the only way in and out of The Town, he was quite familiar with the rocking and jolting of cabby air travel. The takeoff was always the roughest part—or was it the landing? Both were highly uncomfortable.

Derwin was careful to get a spot on a bench near a port-hole-like window, not that there would be much of a view. As dozens of scrivenists crammed inside, Derwin looked out on the hindquarters of the five-thousand-pound beast that towed the carriage. Soon enough, even that vista would be obscured.

The flowery scrivenist had managed to wedge herself next to Derwin and was looking out the porthole as well. "Oh, I wish that I could see my castle from the sky. You know, before we land. What fun! This blasted cabby storm. I nearly always need stomach-bestill from Quinton's Brews and Hodgepodge after each ride! So terribly cold and one just can't see anything!"

Derwin was a little annoyed to be taken away from the richness of his daydreams. "Don't you know, the cabby storm is the only sort of disguise that—"

"I know, I know," she sighed.

To protect the coordinates of The Town and the riders, all cabbies created their own mobile weather systems to conceal their journey. Derwin didn't bother telling her about the intricacies of the cabby storm spell and the peculiarities of the beasts. Even now he could feel the storm whipping itself into freezing existence. He took comfort knowing that all anyone on the ground would see was the roiling, cabby-created squall. With a jolt and a snort from the beast, they took off.

I have surely landed one of the choicest positions in all of Croswald, Derwin thought to himself. He sighed happily in his daze.

"What's that?" a young man asked Derwin.

"*Grumph.* He's just thinking about how magnificent he is," said another in a less charitable tone.

Derwin only smiled.

They traveled for hours. Just as the sun set, a strange treetop in the forest appeared through a momentary clearing in the cabby storm. This tree rose above the rest, its foliage darker and somehow metallic-blue and angular. Derwin caught glimpses of its eerie outline cutting through the haze like glass, twinkling as lightning ricocheted in the sky. His quill now practically burst from his jacket. The cabby continued its descent, tumbling closer to the tree's spire until brush scraped the sides of the carriage and jolted the riders even more than the stormy ride. Finally, in a tumble of wicker benches and plum-colored pillows, they stopped.

"Derwin Edgar Niiiiight!" trilled the cabby driver.

He straightened his jacket, gathered his satchel, lifted his trunk, and ignored the hushed whispers of the other scrivenists. Lastly, he double checked his quill and set out.

The tree, of course, was the tallest spire on what had to be the grandest structure Derwin had ever seen. He felt his knees tremble from the jolting ride—or was it nerves? Derwin approached his new family's castle and his new home. Suddenly the castle shimmered as if it were neither solid nor real. Derwin felt a wave of recognition roll over him. He knew this place! He had spent many hours here! He tried with all

8

his might to remember the name of the family on his deed. But, not only could he not recall the name, his feeling of recognition had disappeared as well.

He came to what must have once been a clearing, perhaps a garden. An enormous wrought iron gate stood at the end of a winding path lined with lavender oranstra trees in full bloom. The gate twisted in a floral pattern and rose to at least four times Derwin's height. Behind the castle was a large gray mountain—the castle was built up against the rock face of a cliff. Standing in front of it, in awe, he felt impossibly small. The shadowy form rose up, equal parts beckoning and foreboding.

Derwin paused. Grand though it was, the castle seemed unkempt. Looking closer he realized it was in a shocking state of disrepair. As he approached, the ivy that hung all about the castle seemed to grow before his eyes, creeping along as he walked. Rust corroded the blue metal roof of the turrets and ivy was enshrouding the dark stones at the same rate. As Derwin reached the door, he saw the final swath of beautiful sapphire metal was encased in a layer of rust. In contrast to every other castle he had ever seen, this one was perfectly unlit.

Derwin stepped through the doors, left ajar, into a massive entry. As he did, billowing clouds of dust rose up from the castle's marble floor.

"Hello?" he called out tentatively, his voice echoing in every direction. Cobwebs spun and spiraled from the foyer's enormous chandelier. The creaking door closed behind him, leaving Derwin alone in sheer darkness. The room was empty. More than that, it appeared entirely deserted and forgotten.

He stepped into the center of the grand entryway, over a gray-and-white family crest. From the circle inlay that surrounded the emblem a dark fog began to swirl around Derwin, plunging the room further into darkness. The image of the castle around him began to waver like a mirage.

"What the—"

But in a puff of marigold, Derwin was gone and the room and abandoned castle disappeared into the twilight.

o   o   o   o

The strange fog dumped Derwin onto a path that clung to the side of a cliff. His cartwheeling came to an abrupt halt as his rump bumped into the wheel of a decrepit carriage. For a moment, all Derwin could see was the night sky and the trees overhead. Shaking his head, he sat up to gauge his surroundings. The carriage was totaled: it had veered off the path and crashed into a tree several yards down the slope. He surveyed the scene. The carriage was empty and the wood was quiet. If anyone had survived that crash—which seemed impossible—they were gone without a trace. Derwin gulped as he looked down beyond the carriage.

Suddenly he felt a tickle in his pocket. It was his quill, twitching in response to some magic inside the carriage's splintered frame. Cautiously Derwin inched closer to the opening. He murmured a spell and the small bits of debris at the bottom of the carriage hovered with a sparkle and moved away. Just beneath was a finely crafted box, unharmed by the crash. Its dark wood was well oiled. As Derwin lifted the box with his quill, bringing it out of the wreckage and into his sweating palms, a pulsing white light seeped from its edges. With the box in his left hand, Derwin made a swirling swoop with his quill, organizing the light into a halo. The illumination shone on a slip of folded parchment attached to the box's lid with a wax seal. It was a letter. The only things Derwin could focus on were the first and final lines: they were written in a hurried hand and read, *To the One to Whom This Box is Entrusted.* It was signed, *The Hand That Left Her.*

THE
SLURRY

THAT evening Ivy was, as usual, lost in her sketching. This was Ivy's favorite place to dream: the hill on the Plum acreage overlooked the notched valley and a vast purple sea of slurry blossoms. The farther away from the castle, the taller the stems of slurry grew. What made this spot so special, more important than its beauty, was its distance from the castle's kitchen—the furthest that Ivy had ever ventured. It was a steep enough climb that the castle's head cook, Helga, would never attempt it. Helga was the type who considered eating the best sort of bodybuilding.

A resounding *thump* jolted Ivy from her reverie. The vision that she had been drawing gave way to the affectionate face of her old (and only) friend. Rimbrick leaned against an old oak with his thick, short arm, his warm brown eyes meeting her hazel ones. She smiled up at him. Lying down was practically the only way she could look up at Rimbrick, an ancient woods dwarf—at least he seemed ancient to fifteen-going-on-sixteen Ivy. She loved his books and stories more than anything, tales of deep magic that were so far from her reality. Ivy would gladly give up sketching to hear his raspy voice spinning yarns about trolls and dragons, princesses and castles, scrivenists and their quills. Rimbrick was the bright spot in the scaldrony maid's life of drudgery.

"Hello there, Ivy! I'm interrupting you." Rimbrick returned her smile, a little out of breath from his hike up the opposite side of the hill.

She stretched and said, "The best kind of interruption."

As the castle's scaldrony maid, Ivy was solely responsible for managing the kitchen's fire-breathing cookers from dawn till dusk. Despite being the oldest breed of domesticated dragon, scaldrons were creatures that needed quite a bit of care. But Ivy spent each evening at this crest, dreaming. In the warm moons she spent entire nights out here to escape the tiny windowless room where she slept. Whenever the moon was full, Rimbrick would meet her here. Her earliest memory of him was when she was about five, but Rimbrick told a story about her baby blanket magically changing colors so he must have known her even longer than that.

Now she drew a deep breath of night air into her lungs—the fresh, sugar-sweet scent of the slurry fields was good for that. Ivy was lucky it was Rimbrick who had found her. Even though the House of Plum was an honorable, generally nice lot, royals didn't take well to their servants loafing about.

"I'm so glad you came! I didn't know if you'd be able to. You're a bit later than usual," Ivy added with tenderness. He was the closest thing to family that she had.

"My legs, whew! My legs nearly gave out!" he panted. "Brought you some books. Finally some about what you've been nagging me for—the ancient art of scrivenist studies." Rimbrick was the only one she'd ever met who understood her thirst for knowledge and love of reading—everyone else at the castle seemed dull and muted, uninterested in anything beyond their work and the latest servant gossip. That he brought her books was a small miracle; after all, books were luxury items not intended for the help.

Rimbrick kicked off his pointed hickory boots and untucked his loose shirt, getting comfortable and catching his breath. He stretched out, though his form in the grass still wasn't all that big. He tossed a coarse sack to Ivy who squealed with exhilaration. She counted one, two, three books.

"Oh, Rimbrick. They're beautiful."

He smiled, "A little birthd—er, Moonsday present for you, Ivy."

Ivy kneeled, gently holding the books, these valuable yet mysterious gifts. She read the gilded words on the spines, and skimmed the flowing script within, each book sounding more intriguing than the last:

The Whiz and The Weasel by Derwin Edgar Night

Wanda Wetzel The Wise by Derwin Edgar Night

A Scrivenist's Guide to Quills by Derwin Edgar Night

"These books here are unlike those you find in a royal's library, Ivy."

Her thoughts swirled. Scrivenry—just the thought of magic exhilarated her. "Rimbrick, Old Rim, you've brought me books before, but this! Books about *magic!* I can hardly thank you. I know it is ridiculous but sometimes I even imagine that I myself am a scrivenist. Ha!" She laughed and waved an imaginary quill about, nearly losing her footing on the steep hill.

Rather than chuckle at his favorite daydreamer's antics as he usually did, Rimbrick coughed and looked away, almost as if he were hiding tears.

"First editions. Collector's items. Glad to know you like them."

"Like them? I love them! I mean I loved Collette Crumb's *Charmed Chai and Crumpets*—I use it every day in that kitchen—and I've almost finished Monda Meade's *Magical Stones*, but these take the cake, Rimbrick. I know every castle has a scrivenist, but ours here at the Castle Plum…doesn't he seem a little, a little dull? I've never seen him do anything. Anything but nap, that is."

"Well, the Castle Plum is a special place in that it is very unspecial. The Plum family has historically prized predictability over imagination, routine over discovery. Hence the slurry fields. I suppose Theodore Thumb, their scrivenist, was sent to Plum because he would appreciate the family's philosophy. Or lack thereof," Rimbrick added ruefully.

"What do you mean about the slurry fields?"

"You'll read about it in there." He jabbed an old finger at a book. "Slurry dampens the effect of magic. Wanda Wetzel's the one who discovered its properties. Oh, what's that you have there?" He unfolded the vellum at her side to reveal a detailed sketch of an ancient, deserted castle, rotting away. "I can see in your work a little spark of the old magic, despite these flowers. You know, it's best not to let Helga find you with any of these."

"You forget I work with the castle's fire squad. I keep only my favorites hidden in the inside pocket of my skirt. The rest help to heat up breakfast."

"Just be careful, my friend. Someday you'll meet others like you, Ivy. The scrivenists we were just talking about. Their memories are photographic and their fingers unstoppably fast at sketching. Just as yours are. Another, more important thing you have in common with them is their powerful, inter-connected memory. It's something that they practice for years. Your visions, your dreams…there's magic in you. You're dif-ferent. The slurry is fighting it. But even the slurry can't win every time."

Ivy bit the side of her lip, intrigued.

"But I'm stuck here. Can't I go with you? I'd rather be with you."

"Here you are safe, Ivy. But the time is coming when—" Rimbrick swallowed and looked away as if he didn't know what to say next. "Today you are safe but things are changing in Croswald. You need to be ready."

Ivy thought of the dank larder that was her room. "It doesn't feel safe. The only thing keeping me from being eat-en alive by rats are the castle's cats!"

"You always said you wanted a pet! Cats *and* rats, how lovely you have lots of them," he smiled wryly.

"Ha! And scaldrons."

"Well, would you look at this," Rimbrick chirped, holding the pocket chime clipped to his beltless belt loops. "It's almost midnight."

"Which means I really should get some sleep in," Ivy muttered, a little annoyed. She grew quiet, as her closest friend—though they were separated by decades and their species—still gazed closely at her sketch. The majority of her sketches were of this very same mysterious castle. He drew in a long, wheezy breath. "Listen, I have to ask you before I go, is this, this castle still appearing in your dreams?"

"I visit there almost every night. A shame I can't visit one less overgrown," Ivy smiled, trying to lighten the mood and the weight of this apparent obsession. Then, growing serious, she added, "But the castle's library. You should see it, Rimbrick. Just like in your stories, vast with rows and rows of shelves and countless books, but when I go to open them, it's a whole lot of blank pages. And there's always someone there—the same man. Not scary, but, but weird. He's intent, like he has to tell me something, but I can't ever see his face or hear him say anything. I can't explain it. Every night I visit this strange place, exploring its dark, dusty halls," Ivy shook her head, baffled, "only to wake up in the Castle Plum's kitchen larder."

"Hmmm. It reminds me of a story. I've been saving this one. Would you like to hear the tale?" Rimbrick asked.

"Would I? And after, I should get some sleep. Tomorrow's the holiday. A big day, feast and all."

"Moonsday. The biggest day," he grinned.

"I'd invite you if I could. I'm not even invited myself."

"Thank you for the thought, dear girl. Now, where was I? Oh yes. The story I'd like to share is of a castle lost."

"A lost castle? Who could lose a thing like that?" Ivy giggled.

"Well, it all started with a petty prince and surly dwarf. This prince set off to get a pint and stepped on the beard of a dwarf. His beard was as long as the tavern's floorboards. 'Give it a good cut,' the prince suggested to him snootily. 'Do you expect me, a prince, to shuffle along walking, sweeping the floor with my feet? Your hair is longer than that of my horse!'

"Out of malice, the prince sneakily swapped the dwarf's drink with another as red as the dwarf's excessively long ginger beard."

"Like yours!"

"Ah, this was a much, much younger, less cautious dwarf. After taking a swig (a volume of five human sips!), the dwarf turned into a donkey, a common reaction for dwarves who are, of course, allergic to beet ale. The prince laughed, but it was the scrivenly dwarf who had the last laugh. He cast a forgetfulness curse over the prince and his family, causing them to wander away from their castle, never to find it again."

"And the family's scrivenists, did they go too?"

"The whole lot of them," Rimbrick said woefully. "For generations, I'm afraid."

Ivy scoffed. "But, Rimbrick, honestly! Who loses track of a castle? Perhaps you are taking your art of storytelling a bit too f-fa-aarrr," Ivy ended her sentence with a sleepy yawn. "I'd love to meet a real scrivenist one day. Besides plain old Theodore."

"They, I am certain, will come to find *you* soon."

THE SCALDRONY
MAID

I VY watched as Rimbrick's small figure shuffled through
the slurry—she could only see where he was by the way
the plants swayed in the moonlight. Then he was back in
the forest beyond.

Ivy turned her gaze to the pearlescent full moon, which
cast a shimmery glow across the Castle Plum. The moon,
though gorgeous, was only a shadow of what the Moonsday
holiday celebrated: a strange double moon (twice as large,
twice as shimmery) that used to occur once a year. Oddly,
after two centuries of celebrating the double moon, it had
disappeared sixteen years ago. It was said that the double
moon's advent marked the time when magical stones began
to flourish in Croswald. Or so Ivy had been told. Its absence
had been one constant in the confusion and civil unrest since
the death of Princess Isabella, the last in the Queenly line.
Now only the Moonsday festival and its feasts remained. She
knew that some people celebrated all day and through the
night, lighting the darkness with lanterns and colorful hairies, but for Ivy, Moonsday meant work.

Gripping her sketches, Ivy let the moon wash over her as

she made her way back to the castle. She almost always slept outside during the full moon but the thought of an early morning spent prepping for the Moonsday festivities propelled her to her dark, windowless room. It had been a grain larder complete with a grain mill, but was so damp that everything in the room mildewed. She stashed her vellum and new books next to the only thing that gave the dank room some life and color: her forever-fitting dress, the same one that she had been found in as a baby.

Once nestled in a makeshift bed on the hewn stone floor, Ivy drifted. She was again transported to the castle in her dreams. She stared at a door, cracked ever so slightly. Vast and silent, the castle stretched upward and outward forever, impossibly grand and tall. Her curiosity propelled her to peek through the small crack. Before opening the door fully, she knocked lightly. A whisper reverberated in her dream. But she couldn't quite catch it.

Suddenly, there was a sharp sound on the other side of the door. Peck. Peck. She held her hand still at the door, knowing the rap wasn't her own. Then with a gasp, Ivy jolted from her makeshift pillow. It was a woodpecker on the outside wall. Then came a clatter from a small cat as it knocked over Ivy's canister of ink.

Can it possibly be morning? She saw a sliver of light through the crack where the stone wall met the stone ceiling, her only sign of the world outside the castle. *Breakfast! Moonsday! I overslept! Helga will be furious.* She leapt up, banging her head on the low ceiling.

"Ow!" Ivy rubbed her head. Now *that* would be a real dragon's egg, probably purple and everything. She scrambled out of bed. Hunched over, she hastily pulled on the scaldrony uniform: a loose dress made of rough material, belted at the waist with an apron that was worn thin with washing and bore the stains of many smoking scaldron burps. A headscarf, made of the same material as the apron, kept her long chocolate-brown hair swept up away from her face and the beastly little cookers.

Ivy's daily reality began in a dark room below the kitchen in the scaldron scullery. That hot, fragrant room was home to her earliest memories. Now, she rushed down the stone steps, descending down, down, down. It must have been a dungeon at one time before people began using the scaldron dragons—winged but flightless, large-mouthed and pot-bellied—to cook food. Ivy could feel the customary pulsing heat rising up the narrow stairwell to meet her. This was why the castle kept the multi-colored fire breathers apart from the other kitchen functions: they were incredibly hot and needed considerable attention. Every kitchen in Croswald had a scaldron. The Plum kitchen had nineteen. They were peculiar dragons and only grew to the size of their cage.

Just as expected, Helga Hoff stood at the entrance of the kitchen, hands on her overly wide hips, steaming mad.

"And you, Ivy, just who do you think you are sleeping in later than these lizards?" Her voice was shrill and unpleasant. "Lucky! You are lucky, little orphan, to even have a job. And at such a castle as this! Spoiled little brat. And on this of all days? Attempting to ruin the party, how dare you?" As Helga went on she took several steps closer, as if to ensure that her piercing voice penetrated Ivy's eardrums. So close, her putrid breath filled Ivy's nostrils. *Wretched.*

Helga muttered, almost to herself, "I should throw you out but working with those scaldrons is punishment enough."

"I'm sorry, I overslept. It's so dark in my room. Perhaps if you allowed me some light inside—"

"Light? And what, allow you the honor of reading and sketching during your time off? What a waste of time. For your poor behavior, you'll snack only on scaldron scraps today and tomorrow. Not a lick of Moonsday delicacies! Do you understand?"

Helga was as unfortunate looking as a scaldron's back end. Perhaps her horrid personality had seeped out and shaped her appearance. Underneath her frizzled hair, her face was full of scars because she scratched her face incessantly. Nothing about Helga was quiet. Not her voice, not her actions, and certainly not her bodily emissions.

"I should get rid of the lot of you. Look at them! Lazy little lizards. Now get to work!"

The door slammed immediately behind Ivy, but not even the metal door's bang roused the sleeping dragons. Soft black smoke curled up from their cages as they snored, sleeping in as usual. *Honestly,* Ivy thought, *it's a wonder that anyone can get these beastly little dragons to cook anything.* Despite being bred as living ovens of sorts, scaldrons had the well-deserved reputation for being persnickety and prone to lazing about. Even as she had that uncharitable thought, Ivy's demeanor softened and she smiled slightly. She really did like them, unlike anyone else on the kitchen staff. They might bite, but at least they didn't talk back. Doubtless that's why Helga Hoff put Ivy in charge of the scaldrons: Ivy was just ambitious and tomboy enough to be part beast keeper, part baker, and one hundred percent kitchen drudge.

Ivy began whirling about in a flurry of productivity: mixing flour, sugar, berries and more to make the castle's favorite blueberry griddlecake. Then onto warming up the stacked scaldrons, waking the slumbering beasts using the tickle feather that hung from the basement's beams.

"Come on, wake up," Ivy said kindly. "You got some extra sleep, too, didn't you? Come on." She continued to tickle them. "Of course, it would be nice to sleep through a Helga huff."

The scaldron's belched their fiery greetings and stretched their jaws, readying to cook up the morning's delicacies in their warming mouths. Ivy knew exactly how each scaldron liked to be treated, which ones ran hot or cold, which ones did better on the first or second tier, and even which cages were due for a tune up.

She distributed the buttery batter amongst the wide pans and then popped them into the scaldrons' mouths, where hot breath would roil over the dish for a few moments before it reached a caramelized golden brown. (The wideness of the pans kept scaldrons from eating everything whole.) As she put the last pan in, giving the beast an affectionate pat on the head while taking care to avoid its fangs, a certain wheezing caught Ivy's attention. Any other maid in the house would have passed the wheeze off as the typical scaldron snore. Not Ivy. She knew that shallow, high-pitched breathing could mean only one thing: flue flem. The sickness was highly contagious amongst scaldrons and the bane of a scaldrony maid's existence.

She dashed in the direction of the noise and found the

smallest of the scaldrons lying flat at the bottom of his cage, listless. This black-and-white creature—scaldron number 19—was one of the scrawniest of the crew, a bit of a slow cooker, and one that Ivy had been training and building his capacity. Number 19's eyes were dull and rheumy and the only movement he made was for his labored breathing. The telltale pink smoke was seeping out of his nostrils. This was not good news. Helga was the type of head cook whose specialty was flying off the handle in a rather violent, eruptive manner. She hated anything unexpected, especially unexpected nuisances.

"No no nonononono! Please. This can't be happening! Not today!" Ivy's mutter turned into a wail. "You heard Helga! She said she'd put you out if you so much as burnt the morning muffins again! Come on. You're okay, aren't you?"

He wasn't. The scaldron shot a pathetic look at Ivy, clearly feeling sorry for himself. With some encouragement and a bit of gentle prodding the scaldron managed to get up. Berry batter dripped out of his mouth, uncooked and runny. Looking around in horror, she saw that there was a considerable pool of the uncooked blue mess around the scaldron and seeping out of the cage.

Ivy panicked. She whirled around to scramble for a mop, a rag, anything and ran smack into Helga's generous bosom.

"Girl! Where are the griddlecakes? They are late and you know how I feel about late and—"

"So sorry, ma'am, I'll bring everything up in one moment," she interrupted, spreading her hands wide in a gesture of apology and conveniently hiding the mess that number 19 was rapidly becoming.

Just as Helga advanced, number 19 made a small sniffling noise. Then, "Ah-ahhh-CHOOOO!"

Number 19 sneezed massively, spewing the contents of its oven mouth onto both Helga and Ivy. Helga took the brunt of it and was covered in blueberry batter (and even a bit of last night's dooger stew) from the wart on her forehead down to her pointy black boots. Helga nearly slipped. She whirled around and when she spotted Ivy, her face changed from its usual disagreeable pink to a surprising shade of lilac.

A complete silence fell on the room. Number 19 and Ivy made eye contact, the scaldron looking nervous and guilty. The short-lived silence was pierced by Helga's shrill scream, reaching decibels new even to her. Both rows of scaldrons shook in their cages as Helga unleashed.

"Ack! What is this? Disgusting!" she screeched. The goop, like slippery glue stuck to her body, smelled worse than her horrific breath. Ivy hurriedly started mopping the floor, hoping that erasing some of the mess would help bring Helga out of her rage orbit.

"You stupid, stupid twit! I'll have that scaldron executed! I've always sensed that you were a good-for-nothing!" She chased Ivy around the room, taking swings.

"But I've only just discovered the flue flem! Please don't hurt him. I'll take him outside. If I clean up thoroughly, and I will, the others won't get it! I swear it!"

"Not a chance!"

"The griddlecakes! They're burning!" Ivy pointed behind Helga, where gray smoke was rising up. While Helga yanked pans out, Ivy ran to jiggle number 19 free from his cage.

"Get out, I said! GET OUT!"

Helga lurched at Ivy, who was half her size. Picking up a heavy cast iron skillet she ran toward her, knocking over pounds of flour on her way. Eyes bloodshot and furious, Helga slipped on the batter pool and this time fell back on her bottom, her stocky legs flying up over her head in a whoosh of petticoats. Ivy gave a final yank on number 19, but instead of pulling the dragon out of its form-fitting cage, the whole row of scaldron cages came tumbling down. Now Helga was irate, her cheeks as fiery-red as a scaldron gone wild.

Ivy saw her chance for an exit: she grabbed number 19's cage and skirted around Helga's flailing body as she struggled to get up. Even though she was trembling with fear, Ivy found it hard not to smile at the gloopy batter dripping from Helga's pinched face. She backed up the rough stone stairs as quickly as she could—dragging the cage, tripping once and catching herself—and left Helga squirming on the floor.

She dashed out the first door she could to safety. A gust of cool air pushed back her headscarf and blew her tangled hair gently. Looking down she saw the scaldron's gloomy little face. She couldn't help but feel sorry for him—after all, even though he was no longer in a dungeon, his cage was prison enough.

"Sorry about her. She's awful, isn't she? She shouldn't treat you like that. I'm sure she's had her sick days. If it weren't for you she'd be putting out a cold meal, wouldn't she?"

The scaldron lifted its head and batted his pale yellow eyes.

"Are you feeling better? You've never been outside, have you? Poor thing. It's a lot less dingy out here." *It's beautiful*, Ivy thought, knowing she had never witnessed daylight directly either.

"Number 19. You deserve a name better than that after putting up with Helga all these years. Can't imagine if they called me by a number. How about I call you Humboldt?"

Their tender moment was interrupted by the sound of carriage wheels spitting out gravel: one of Miss McCorkle's Forever Filling Carriages was pulling up to the Castle Plum. It swerved right, then left, veering a little too wildly for even the scaldron's comfort. The carriage came to an abrupt halt just outside the grand entryway, bobbing forward because it was so top heavy.

A profusion of bright, sparkly dresses burst from the carriage doors, carried by lady's maids. Miss McCorkle's roving fashion trunk was here for young Princess Alianna who was about to enter her third year at the Halls of Ivy, the prestigious school of magic where young royals learned to wield the magical stones in their crowns and young sqwinches practiced for the day when they would receive their own quills as full-fledged scrivenists.

As a mere scaldrony maid, there was no reserved spot for Ivy at the school. In one of Rimbrick's books, Ivy had learned how ancient magic was distributed between the royal families through crowns encrusted in magical stones. Each royal family anticipated with joy the day their child would receive an enchanted crown from the Crownerie, a small token of magic traditionally given on sixteenth birthdays, a custom since the would-be-queen Isabella's death. It was either by crown or by magical blood that one was able to attend the Halls of Ivy, and every time Ivy thought of the place her heart sank knowing she'd never be able to visit, let alone attend.

That's when Helga Hoff came stumbling out the side door, jolting Ivy out of her reveries and reminding Ivy where she really was.

"Get lost! And take that little hooligan with you! If I ever hear the name Ivy Lovely again, I'll throw the cages at you!"

She tossed Ivy's apron toward her, now ripped and even more stained as Helga had clearly used it to wipe her face. She slammed the door behind her and the force made dirt fly up into Ivy's face.

"Where am I supposed to go?" Ivy shouted back in a panic. There was no reply. *Whatever's beyond the Plum acreage, it must be better than here,* she told herself. On some level she felt relief that the decision to leave was made for her—but she had nowhere else to go.

"Rimbrick," she called softly, looking toward their spot on the hill, knowing that he wouldn't think to meet her at this time of day. The slurry fields looked different in the daylight. The purple was somehow harsher but the candy-sweet scent was the same, and that small thing comforted her.

Rather than finding her old friend at the top, she found the imprint in the grass that her body had left the night before. She set the cage down in the imprint and saw a large rucksack and next to it a folded letter held down by a little leather pouch. Ivy was curious but had also never felt so terribly lonely as she did in that moment.

"What's all of this?"

She felt her stomach sink as she opened the letter and read:

Dearest Ivy,

You ought to know the comfort watching over you has brought me all these years. I have come to love you as if you were my own kin. I find it hard to let you go even though I know the times demand it. I need to repay your family a debt of sorts—that's what's in the pouch.

Ivy glanced down at the small pouch tied with a leather strap. It was heavy, like a bag full of rocks. She opened it and found more coins than she had ever seen before. Ivy counted six silver ketzels and 96 bronze brums—just short of the 97 needed for a ketzel. And in the larger satchel were all three of the new books Ivy thought she had left behind, her sketches, and her dress, too! Ivy continued reading in awe.

This, and watching over you, in no way atone for my mistakes, but I hope that you'll remember me with fondness. The best advice I can give is to leave the slurry fields, Ivy. Leave them now. Like you always wished. You'll unlock many mysteries, Ivy. Even mysteries within yourself! Trust the magic in you and know I will forever be in the shadow of its light.

Your dear, dear friend,
Rimbrick

Ivy reached to cover her face as tears sprang to her eyes. As she did so, she dropped the scaldron's cage and its door flew open. Humboldt sprang to life—perhaps inspired by the outdoors or his new name—and with a wheeze and spray of flue flem hurried down the backside of the hill. If she needed any more encouragement to cross the slurry boundary, Humboldt's jailbreak was it.

Ivy wiped her tears, stuffed the letter and pouch into the satchel and chased after him. She leapt over the stream that separated the slurry from the forest and as she did an enormous sonic boom shook the landscape. For a millisecond, it seemed as if everything had bent toward her, the trees and rocks bowing inward before stretching back up. It felt as though someone had stopped the world in its tracks. The silence that followed was almost as deafening. Even Humboldt froze.

"What was *that?*" Ivy wondered aloud. She bit her lip then shrugged. *No time for that now,* she thought and without a second glance behind her, ran and jumped on top of the wayward scaldron. He made a noise like a giggle and then wriggled out from under her to shimmy up an old tree. Who knew scaldrons could climb?

"Are you going to keep playing around or are you going to come down?" Ivy called to Humboldt who was skittering about the branches, camouflaging himself with gritty bark. "Fine! If you want to stay up there, I'm leaving! You can fend for yourself!"

She took a deep breath of morning air and began walking toward the vast open fields where horses grazed. Where Ivy was really headed, she had no idea; anywhere that wasn't

Helga's kitchen would do. She took a moment to take in the Plum acreage, more open land than a unicorn could fly in an afternoon. Ivy let the cool breeze wrap around her skin.

Nothing but sunshine today. Well, except for that low little cloud over the forest, Ivy mused. Then to her surprise, that low little cloud grew closer and larger. It seemed to be rolling like a giant ball, leaving a distinctive trail of saturated forest and earth in its tracks. Dark gray and decidedly wet, the miniature storm was about the height of a barn and moved faster than a horse could gallop. Ivy froze as it barreled toward her, knowing there was no way she could outrun it.

LIONEL
LUGG

THE cloud crashed into the tree where Humboldt hid and came to an unexpected halt directly in front of Ivy. She jumped back in fright. Enclosed in a blanket of fog, she could see only a few feet in front of her. *So much for sunshine.* The dampness in the air mixed with the sweat already on her face. Ivy felt frustration rising to meet her fear.

"Great. As if things couldn't get any worse. Let's cap it off with a rain cloud just for me," she shouted to no one in particular. And just like that, thunder growled as if with laughter and a torrential downpour to match dumped down. In the flashes of lightning, Ivy saw a great beast illuminated, its gigantic, gray feet crushing the bushes and felled tree beneath it. *What is this?* The beast seemed to wear a harness, but what it attached to Ivy couldn't see. As the torrent tapered to a light rain Ivy could hear the beast breathe.

Helga. Flue flem. Cast out from the castle. Losing Rimbrick. Some strange beast. As Ivy stood there damp and cold, shivering in her maid's uniform, she couldn't hold back the tears anymore. The flood of emotions consumed her.

"Humboldt? Where are you? Are you okay? Helllooo?

Is anyone there?" Ivy cried. No one replied, but she caught sight of a shadow moving above her head.

The mist slowly lifted and a scrawny fellow with freckles dotted across his fresh face appeared on top of the giant beast's back. The man wore a large blue umbrella as a hat and a matching rain-soaked coat. He jumped nimbly down from the creature's back and then cranked a small wheel on the side of his hat, reeling in the umbrella: now it looked as if he sported a plastic pole on his head.

"Any luggage, Miss?" he asked, his manner stiff.

"Um, not exactly," Ivy replied as she struggled to hold the weight of both the satchel and the empty scaldron cage. "Excuse me, but, if you don't mind my asking, where did you come from?" She wiped her nose dry.

"Ravenshollow, of course," he said matter of factly.

Ravenshollow? Ivy had never heard of the place. Then again, one doesn't hear much of anything growing up in a larder.

He nodded toward the cloud. "Please excuse our landing—not always predictable. We've been searching for you. Follow me."

Ivy trailed cautiously and curiously behind him. She watched as he swung the satchel and cage easily over his head, taking athletic strides that belied his rail-thin frame. "You must have the wrong girl."

The man didn't respond, leaving Ivy no choice but to follow him around the side of the beast. Ivy peppered him with questions as she hopped over fallen branches. "Excuse me, but how did you even know I'd be here? And this beast? Will it bite us? It looks *huge*! Is he friendly?"

The man stopped in his tracks, nearly causing a two-person collision. "I must warn you, Parsley is very sensitive. He might hear you questioning his character and referring to him as an 'it.' He might travel hundreds of miles in the wrong direction in retribution. Or worse. He may choose to, um, relieve himself in your presence. Consider it a greeting from him personally should he choose to do so."

"Relieve himself? That's absolutely revolting. I mean, I beg your pardon, Parsley." Ivy nodded with deference toward the great big beast, slightly distracted.

"My name's Woolem. I'm your cabby chauffeur on this gloomy morning. Rather, *in* this patch of particular cabby gloom this morning."

A cabby, Ivy pondered, while taking in Parsley. The beast's head, while wider than any arms could reach, was rather small in proportion to his enormous body. His head tapered from a thick neck and ended in a strong curved horn between his eyes. Parsley shuffled his feet as if eager to get moving. Like steam from a horse's back on a cold morning, Ivy could see the cloud emanating from Parsley—he was the origin of this tiny yet powerful localized storm! It was magnificent, pure magic. As the cool breeze passed and ruffled the leaves, the five-thousand-pound creature stood still, his slate-gray skin and harness shining in the rain. His large hooves turned in slightly, ready to propel back into the sky.

Ivy followed the line of the harness with her eyes to three small houses that were towed behind Parsley. Their pointed roofs were clad in shingles that were weathered to a stone color and appropriately covered in lichen, given all the moisture. The convoy had turned up the dirt upon its abrupt landing but didn't seem any worse off for it. Despite the steep angle of the roofs, luggage was tied on top. And like an ornament hanging off one gable, there was Humboldt, blowing steam on the slippery roof in fear. After retrieving and caging him, Woolem led them to the nearest little house, a faded midnight-blue cabby compartment, and set down Ivy's things. He opened the front door and bowed slightly, motioning her in. Still unsure, Ivy lingered at the threshold. Inside a small candle flickered on the sill of a crooked window and the diminutive chimney sent small tendrils of smoke rising into the sky.

Then in the not-quite-square doorway a strange man with a welcoming smile appeared. He removed his hat, revealing a terrible case of hat-hair, and cried, "Ah! There you are! Not at all what I expected. Though I will admit I have picked up others in worse condition. Still, never with that pull of magic! What a resonance. Clearly it's not what's on the outside that counts—" he gestured to her muddy clothes and matted hair with some humor, "—but on the inside." He tapped on her forehead.

The older fellow's eye sockets were shaded by a heavy brow and deep creases surrounding his light eyes. A large bushy beard dominated the lower part of his face. His completely unbuttoned scrivenist jacket swallowed his small shoulders. His purple, plaid bow tie was tied primly underneath his chin and exactly matched the color of his tweed pants. He was thin and tired-looking and had to hunch to fit in the doorway.

"I'm sorry, but do I know you? To which castle do you belong?"

"Lionel Lugg, here." He straightened his bow tie, pulled on his lapels and reached for the bronze-dusted trunk at his heel, initialed LOL. "Lionel Ohlander Lugg. Longtime scrivenist, at your service. As to which castle, I must say I'm a bit of a freelance sort of fellow." He cleared his throat. "And this cabby here is the Halls of Ivy's traveling admission office for promising sqwinches, young ones studying to be scrivenists at the Halls. I suppose it's also my personal library and thinking laboratory and home and, well, just about everything else."

Ivy looked at Lionel blankly.

"You seem spellbound. Have I cursed your voice, girl? Do say something. Perhaps we should get started on a bit of paperwork."

"Are you out of your mind?" Ivy burst out in a peal of laughter. "Is this some kind of joke? Me? The Halls of Ivy? You can't be serious."

Apparently Ivy's laugh was contagious as the gentleman laughed heartily, too. "It is funny, isn't it? A potential scrivenist who has spent her younger years as a chambermaid surrounded by all that slurry."

"Scaldrony maid, thank you."

He lifted the scaldron's cage, twirling it in circles, examining Humboldt's black-and-white frame.

"Yes, well, and I see you've done a fine job with your traveling companion here—I can tell that he likes you very much. He's suffering from flue flem, isn't he? Poor fellow's embarrassed. Very unpleasant business. Nothing a little magical massage and country air can't cure."

"Yes, but how could you tell?"

"My job may be admissions but my passion is dragons. All

sorts. This is the best luggage I've had onboard in a while. Not the sort to strap to the roof," he smiled. Lionel put down the scaldron and then brought his quill out from his jacket pocket; it looked to have about as much verve as a sloth. The feathered end was so worn it was nearly bald with hardly a barb left. He gently waved it back and forth, coaxing it to life. Slowly a small light formed at the quill's feathered tip. The light grew brighter and brighter. Ever so gently, Lionel sent the beam of light over to Humboldt, which wrapped itself around the poor beast. In a sparkle, Humboldt was cured of his ailment. As the light faded, the scaldron became instantly perky. Not only was he well, he and his cage had grown about three inches in size. *No longer the runt of the bunch!* Ivy thought with admiration.

"That's genius! How did you do it?" Ivy asked, her eyes glowing like the tip of Lionel's quill.

"No doubt magic is a mystery to you. I dare say that Plum's scrivenist must have a decidedly uninteresting job: all writing and no magic." He nodded slowly. "I should have guessed that's where you'd be, in the slurry fields. Good place to hide magical blood, it is. Although, I'm afraid to say that even though it was my duty to find you, I thought I never would. Been searching for days now and I just knew you were somewhere around here. Couldn't pinpoint your location until you left the fields. And you're just in time!"

"I don't have magic. I don't know what you're talking about." Ivy thought about her letter from Rimbrick.

Lionel sighed. "Perhaps you think that now. Look here," he pointed to an elaborate machine with several cogs. Brass and mounted on the wall, it looked as if the innards of several old chimes had been mounted on an ancient sword. "Anytime I came near that blasted slurry, my compass had me spinning in circles! It stopped working!"

"This all sounds very lovely, but I, I can't be the girl you're looking for. Look at me...I—I'm just, just a girl. A nobody. Maybe you're looking for Princess Alianna?"

He peered over his enormous, round spectacles, his face softening. "Some scrivenists start out as nobodies. We're different than royals, who are, by the way, relative newcomers to the Halls. Sqwinches work their way up—their merit is a twinkle of magic in the blood compounded by dedication. Why don't you come in? There's much to talk about. Much to sign."

Remembering the crash landing, into a tree no less, Ivy asked warily, "In there?"

"Have you somewhere more pressing to be?" The gentleman's point was a valid one. Ivy had nowhere to be.

"Perhaps I should inform you that if you choose not to join me on our ride, the Cloaked Brood is sure to assist you to a destination of their choosing, and not a good one. In fact, I suggest we leave quickly. They are due here any minute. In fact, they are coming now."

"What?!"

Even in Ivy's little world she had heard of the Cloaked Brood—Helga had often threatened to throw her to them. The name of the roving band that served as the nefarious Dark Queen's henchmen stirred in Ivy's heart a dark shadow of fear, almost like a memory.

At the swish of Lionel's quill, a tiny segment of cloud cleared to expose the Dark Queen's Cloaked Brood traveling fast across the ground in the cabby's direction, their hulking, not-quite-human bodies nearly crushing the unicorns they drove.

"Now or never." Lionel motioned her into the compartment.

Ivy looked toward the Cloaked Brood and raised a brow, then scurried after him. Woolem swung the compartment door shut behind her. Parsley snorted with pleasure then took off with a jolt, the surrounding thunderstorm a clever and chilly disguise. Brittle branches scraped the windows and twigs broke in half as they flew through the thick forest, above and beyond the crown of trees. Ivy's stomach lurched as they flew along inside the cabby's storm behind Parsley.

The compartment was empty but for the two of them, not to say that it was roomy. The small patch of ceiling that did exist was painted a deep indigo and laced with gilded paintings of feathered beasts. The ceiling was lined with over-head compartments, all odd dimensions and not one section alike, fighting for space along the angular roof. In the far corner was a narrow brick hearth burning sweltering hot wood, tended by a pint-sized, fiery red dragon flitting about. Humboldt scurried over, curious.

Lionel now slouched at his desk, patrician and antique. He removed his orange and tan scarf, scrunching it and us-ing it as a pillow beneath his rather bony rear end. The desk's wood was stained dark with use, age, and the characteristic cabby dampness. It was flanked by windows as tall as the com-partment would allow, and floor-to-ceiling bookshelves stood on either side of the leaded glass. The shelves curved around the cabby's rounded walls, coming closer together near the top of the room to almost form a perfect sphere of books.

"Take a seat, please." Lionel gestured to the wingback chair opposite him.

As soon as she sat, the voice of Woolem, the cabby driver, projected down through the chimney. "Welcome aboard, ladies and gentlemen. We are expecting a bumpy ride due to a wicked wind set against us. Lucky for us, the Brood has been left in our drizzle!"

The cabby rattled wildly both from the incredible speed and the wind. Ivy couldn't believe that such a stocky, lazy-looking beast could reach this velocity. Even more amazing was the formation of the storm. It seemed as if Woolem was whipping swirls of hail and launching them at the Cloaked Brood for fun. Rain pelted the windows until they could no longer see anything outside but fog.

Woolem's voice sounded again, "For those of you taking your first ride, note that the compartments overhead open every ten minutes, always with something delectable to keep your stomachs from protesting your journey!"

"Does he mean food?" she asked with excitement. Ivy was never sated but had never felt so starved as she was just then.

Woolem continued, "Your first pairing will be a cup of clobber coffee—it quite literally clobbers you with energy! And a bite-sized peach pecan pie—warm and flakey!"

"I swear I could eat a pie the size of the beast pulling the cabby. My mouth is watering already."

And just like that warm, artfully plated food was lowered from the compartments overhead by little accordion arms.

"Isn't this pie just the perfect complement to a rainy day," the scrivenist remarked. "A lovely way to celebrate Ivy Lovely being found!" He laughed at his little pun and then took a swig of his overflowing mug of clobber coffee.

Woolem's voice rang out again: "Please enjoy the warmth of your fire, as it will keep the inside of your cabby compartment from freezing over. Help yourself to the complimentary witchy warmupps!" Two sets of lumpy, cozy socks dropped from a hatch in the ceiling, right into their laps. "These massaging socks can't be beat!"

Ivy's feet were instantly more rested and warm than they'd ever been—she hadn't noticed how chilled she was. Damp clothes, warm knee-high socks, wet hair, and a mouth full of pastry. Ivy didn't need a mirror to confirm that she was a mess. She noticed Lionel's feet below his desk, layered in more socks than she had ever owned, his ankles padded inches thick.

Ivy sipped her clobber coffee, the first she'd ever had. She could feel it coursing through her veins. Lionel was quite clearly effected, too, having downed his cup in a large gulp. He was a man with work to do and rolled his wingback chair to the tall boy with impressive speed. He opened a drawer and a towering stack of silver envelopes popped up. He pulled one from the middle with an air of certainty and then gestured to the shelf with his quill. One small volume floated into his hands from a shelf at the top of the sphere. Then with a swoop of his quill he crammed the rest of the tidy stack back into the drawer.

"Ah yes. Yes. Here it is. To one Miss Ivy Lovely."

Ivy recognized it immediately—it looked just like the letter Princess Alianna had received two years ago. It was an official invitation to the Halls of Ivy; even now she could hear the festive music carrying on inside the envelope. She broke the seal and opened the card to reveal bright lights, a spray of confetti, and the music of an energetic marching band. The light show inside flickered and spelled out I-V-Y. Her eyes widened to the size of the miniature pies.

"There must be some mistake. I—I can't, I mean, I..."

"Do be careful not to spill your drink. It's hot," Lionel said, a completely worthless piece of advice as both of their cups sloshed all over from the bumpy ride.

Ivy put down her cup of clobber coffee, gazing at the invitation and wondering if it was just a figment of her imagination.

"In this book, your personal Compass Startus," he continued, holding the volume from the shelf, "you'll find your official welcome letter from the Selector into the Halls. As you may well know, the Selector is a highly influential scrivenist; it's a post that lasts a lifetime. The Selector is both guardian of magic in Croswald and the only avenue through which scrivenists can communicate to the Queen. The Selector is part ambassador, part dean."

Ivy read the first line: *Dear Miss Lovely, I am so pleased to extend this invitation. You have been selected—*

Lionel pulled the book out of her hands. "And so on and so forth. Critical information regarding your schooling—your schedule, school agreement, etcetera—are in here. As you go, you'll take your notes, write your essays, and do other assignments in this volume. Don't worry! Pages will add themselves as you go. Then at the end of the year it'll be graded and emptied for the next term. If you've been very clever, any new discoveries will be added to the Compass Collectis..." Lionel saw Ivy's eyes glaze over. "We'll leave that to Mr. Munson, I suppose. Please use my quill to initial each page and claim ownership of this book. You'll carry it with you wherever you go should you make a discovery anywhere, including school restroom facilities."

At this juncture, Lionel's ratty quill nearly grabbed Ivy's hand, not the other way around, and Ivy found herself bewilderedly initialing each page. Her fingertips tingled.

"This page, well these next six pages, contains the Halls' Code of Conduct. The invitation to the Halls is extended to youth who show magical aptitude and a love of learning, but the invitation may be revoked for behavior that is not fitting for a royal crown or quill. The Queen is especially specific about this—she does not care for youth who wield magic of their own accord." At this point, Ivy thought she saw a look of disdain flit across the scrivenist's face.

"You'll find that there are many rules, but I suppose all in efforts to protect you from unintended consequences of your budding magic and also from, er, the Queen. There's a…a tricky balance when it comes to performing magic in her kingdom. Don't fret too much—that's part of the reason the Selector is at the Halls. Our first and most important rule is that you must never under any circumstance mention your cabby travels or all memories will be revoked and manipulated. Any chance of turning scrivenist revoked. Got to keep The Town safe, you see. Consider this your first test."

"The Town?" Ivy wondered.

Lionel moved on quickly. "The rest is basically, 'Don't do magic outside the Halls,' 'No visiting floors in the dormitories or halls above your grade level,' 'Only leave the campus on chaperoned school assignments,' 'Do no harm,' 'No roaming the halls naked,'" Lionel finished. Ivy giggled at the silliness of the Halls' last request. The quill was still guiding her hand, signing away.

The rest of the signing flew by. The only pages that stuck out in her mind were her class schedule and a map of the Halls, perhaps because she was allowed to keep them. Her mind was aflutter with thoughts: could it really be that she was going to the Halls of Ivy? That she was to be a scrivenist? She looked out the window wishing she could tell Rimbrick.

She watched glimpses of landscape flashing through the fog. A lush forest gave way to a marshy valley. She was beginning to see glimpses of what looked like a town aglow in the mid-morning light. The fog closed in again, and the ride became as bumpy as ever. Lionel dozed. With Humboldt curled warmly at her feet, Ivy gripped her Compass Startus, turned the page and read:

CONGRATULATIONS ON YOUR ADMISSION!

Please Arrive in Time for the
Ravenshollow Moonsday Festivities

FIRST YEAR CLASS SCHEDULE

Minor Magic   **First Hour**
Professor Royal: Be prepared to leave all fears outside the door as you become your magic's master and discover your own strengths and weaknesses.

Fenix's Finest Glanageries **Second Hour**

Professor Fenix: Explore your own powers within the magic of a glanagerie bottle. Filled with charmed spring water, the bottle is a stage upon which to act out imagined scenarios with real skills.

Art of Ink & Memory **Third Hour**

Professor Petty: Develop the connection between your ink, porcupel, and mind as you practice the ancient art of scrivenist drawing. This class is a challenging combination of theatrical tableaus, life drawing, and honing photographic memories.

Luncheon **Fourth Hour**

Enjoy a magically prepared lunch of your choice served to you by a ghostly trio, professors emeriti, or our wild-eyed Jester.

Creatures of the Night **Fifth Hour**

Professor Wheeler: Discover the world of night creatures. Learn their habits and behaviors well.

Hour of Discovery **Sixth Hour**

Venture, discover, and learn on your own. Let the halls lead you whichever way they wish. Choose to explore as much as you see fit or not the slightest bit. Do remember to stay on floors appropriate to your grade level.

READING LIST

Poems and Musings for the Budding Magic Practitioner
by Walt Winter

Perfectly Imperfect Potions by Lois Squibb

Worst Case Glanagerie: A Somewhat Survival Guide
by Filbert Fenix

How to Sketch (With a Bit of Magic) by Priscilla Petty

Stones and Sorcery by Laverna Royal

A Guide to Identifying the Lesser-Known Magical Creatures
by Whersit Whump

Nocturnal Creatures: What to Fear and What to Revere
by Igmar Ingrich

The Compass Collectis: A Collection for Collaboration and Comprehension
One million authors and counting

Find all required reading (and more) at All Things
Scrivenist or borrow from the Den.

FIRST YEAR SQWINCH SUPPLIES

You'll find your magically fitted uniform in your dormitory
closet, compliments of the Selector and Miss McCorkle.

Ivy looked down at her soaked, stained, and overall wretched scaldrony uniform. It had never properly fit her anyway.

* 1 Porcupine for practice quills called porcupels (available at Pines and Spines)
* 1 or 2 Hairies for a bit of evening light in your dorm (available at Pairies of Hairies)
* 1 Inkwell (available at Boulliquiste's: All But Your Quills)
* 2 Refills of Visiblink, preferably blue (available at Boulliquiste's: All But Your Quills)
* 1 Potions Starter Kit (available at Mr. Munson's: All Things Scrivenist)
* 1 Proof Pad: Wind-proof, Water-proof & Whatever-proof (available at Boulliquiste's: All But Your Quills)

1 Kallegulous Key

The last item was handwritten. *How am I to afford all of this?* Ivy pondered, forgetting momentarily the sack of coins stuffed in the pouch now safely in her pocket.

Before Ivy could question Lionel, he shouted jubilantly and pointed out the window. In the foggy distance, peaks of odd structures poked through the mist. *That must be it. That must be Ravenshollow,* Ivy concluded. The center of Croswald. They were flying over town and the cabby storm had lessened, if only a little. Ancient Tudor-style row houses were tucked together tightly, their faded brown-and-white facades pitching skyward. Busy carriages made their way down streets; businesses bustled with customers. The storm and its passengers circled the town once, twice. Ivy saw a man tending a high hairie lantern, a woman hanging laundry on a line out her second story window, and the mountainside behind the town. There was a blue-roofed castle—formidable and cut from dark stone—partially built into the rock face behind it. A tall iron gate guarded the property.

On the third loop around the small, busy town, the cabby careened into a dark, wet alley, bumping and scraping the walls of the buildings. They abruptly came to a halt. The storm slowly dissipated and Woolem opened the door, standing drenched and dripping. Humboldt looked a little motion sick now.

"Your hand, Miss."

AN
UNEXPECTED VISITOR

ELSEWHERE in town, there was an unusual feeling in the gusty wind—something strange was afoot. The quiet had a strange, murky quality. Though the double moon hadn't risen in sixteen years, the current full moon was reminiscent. But if there were any creature that woke that morning with a flame of hope for a nice bright day, the blustery weather would have extinguished it.

That morning there was little sign of life on the usually busy street apart from a dark, somber carriage parked at the Crownerie's door. A carriage this dark—the kind of matte black that absorbs light, making all the trim and carvings difficult to see—could only belong to the Dark Queen. She rose to power in the terrible days after the death of Isabella and had lived longer than any other person ever known. Strangely, what with royals' penchant for sketches and the Dark Queen's seeming interminable rule, there was not one portrait to give away the slightest idea of her appearance. When she attended the annual Royal Coronation at the Halls of Ivy, she sat shrouded from view behind a black veil, speaking only through one of the Cloaked Brood. At a small gesture of her hand, a person might disappear forever. Some said she was a scrivenist. Others said she was a pure apparition of evil. The one thing everyone knew for certain was that she possessed mysterious and terrifying powers. All of Croswald was torn between wanting to know more about this terrifying figure and wanting to think of her not at all.

The Cloaked Brood had arisen with her. Never before did a Queen of Croswald need an armed guard, much less a terrifying one. This morning they stationed themselves directly in front of the Crownerie's imposing entry, stirring an atmosphere of terror that kept all residents indoors, quaking while the Dark Queen remained hidden inside her ebony carriage. Chosen for their size and brutality, the Cloaked Brood dressed in fur cloaks that swept the ground. Their faces were mostly covered by iron helmets and only shadows revealed their ghastly features. From what anyone could tell, the Cloaked Brood had descended from ogres.

Two blocks from the Crownerie, Ivy was getting her bearings on a backstreet. When they had touched ground, Ivy watched the cabby create an eye-of-the-storm as it pushed the clouds back to make a clearing just wide enough for Ivy to open her door. Ivy squeezed out and stepped behind a shingled two-story building. Lionel followed with his umbrella twirling, handing a second one to Ivy as they said their goodbyes. In such a tight space, the cabby occupying most of it, Ivy could barely unfurl her umbrella and was forced to choose what should stay dry. She chose her books, Rimbrick's gift— she felt as if they were part of her.

The door's heavy stone overhang was clammy from the storm and protected the bright purple door Ivy was to enter.

Two hairie lanterns hung on each side, lighting up the entrance, the damp dimming their glow. The hairies had the oddest color hair Ivy had ever seen—they matched the door exactly with the same deep shade of purple worn by traditional scrivenists.

"Good luck to you, Ivy Lovely," Lionel said before slamming the door with vigor she didn't think he could muster.

"Wait!" she called.

All at once the cabby was gone, leaving behind only dark clouds, full rain gutters, huge puddles, and a soaked teenager with a scaldron. Looking down the way, she noticed wryly that it seemed pretty dry down the street. The stones paving the alley behind Mr. Munson's were polished to almost a river rock quality. Clearly, he saw more weather than his neighbors.

The wind whipped water into the air, stinging her exposed arms and face. She squinted to read the ochre letters in a tiny window, written in a winding hand. They read: *Come In, Lots to See.* The handle just below the sign was an ancient cast iron feather. She reached out tentatively to touch it, but then pulled her hand back.

"What kind of place is this anyway?" Ivy wondered out loud, not expecting any sort of reply.

Much to her surprise, a cheerful voice replied from behind her, "All Things Scrivenist, the shop for all kinds of budding scrivenists, of course."

Ivy turned to greet a boy fast approaching manhood. He was a head taller than she was, and she was considerably tall. The young fellow had just enough scruff along the sides of his face to show that he had better things to do than shave. He reached to shake Ivy's hand.

"Hello. I'm Fyn Greeley, the class facilitator for the entering class of sqwinches, here to help assist you with any and all of your needs. You have that first year stunned look. I'm a third year. But if you'll excuse me, I have a few things to take care of myself. Mr. Munson's is a great place for you to start your shopping. Though the majority of what he sells is a bit above your grade level, I'm certain you'll make out just fine. If you'll excuse me, please. There are certain matters to which I must attend."

Before she could say a word, Fyn entered Mr. Munson's and the door closed quickly behind him. *Not really the gentleman type,* Ivy thought. She lingered outside, somewhat stunned. She could see from the sole window on this side of the building that whoever stocked the store had a penchant for odd items. A *lot* of odd items.

In fact, Solly "The Self-Proclaimed Scrivenist" Munson hoarded and repaired things, the most obscure knickknacks, tools, and charms he could find. As a jack of all magical trades, he knew nearly everything about the objects he collected. He repaired and sold just enough magical accoutrements to pay for his own habit of exploration and collection. He had traveled more than most scrivenists, and had done business with more species than anyone in Croswald.

All Things Scrivenist, hmm? Not a bad place to start, Ivy thought, though she did hope to exit out the front door and not in the middle of a cabby storm. Taking a deep breath, she pushed the feather-shaped handle and opened the door, hobbling along with her belongings still tucked under her skirt and Humboldt's cage. She could feel the door move heavily, as if it were pushing something behind it. And it was—a large basket of Loshes Washes cleaning supplies. *Cleans and cures most magic mishaps* was emblazoned on the label. A small hand-tinkered chime above the door made a jingling noise.

"You wait here," she whispered to Humboldt. "Be good! No smoky stuff."

The dim room was full of towering shelves that held boxes and bottles and jars and cans and stacks of things. Some items she was familiar with—even at the magic-less Castle Plum the scrivenist had carried a quill. But most objects appeared mysterious and dangerous: alluring to Ivy. The windows were blacked out by all the stuff piled high, preventing anyone from seeing in. Later Ivy would learn that this also helped keep out the sun, as All Things Scrivenist held many magical compounds that were sensitive to light. Looking up in awe, Ivy tripped over the hem of her own dress and went flying into a box full of spoken word spells, creating quite a ruckus. The spells, only identifiable by their invisible heaviness and small sparkles when shaken, grumbled loudly: "Ouch!" "Mindless girl!" "Foolish child. Stupid!" Their complaining, first directed at Ivy, soon turned to the typical discontent spoken word spells express when left unused.

Despite the clamor, Mr. Munson didn't rush to see who had entered his shop.

"Hello? Mr. Munson? Fyn Greeley? Are you, are you... AaaahCHOOOO!" A cloud of dust rising from the boxes had hit her face. Ivy muttered quietly to Humboldt, "The dust is so thick in here, it seems like no one has ever opened a window."

"Did someone mention dust?" a voice called out crossly

from the darkest corner in the cluttered workshop. "I certainly don't busy myself with cleaning what ought to clean itself! Come in, young lady. After you've locked the door! Lock it first!" Ivy followed his instructions, unsure as to why, and watched a small man unfurl from his crouched position in the corner, nimbly jumping up to flip a second sign from *Come In, Lots to See* to *Go Home, Would You?* Mr. Munson was a man who spoke (and wrote) whatever was on his mind. He changed the matching sign at the front door and drew heavy burgundy curtains across the glass display area at the front of the shop.

"What can I do for you?" he asked, somewhat settled. Mr. Munson's lank, gray hair was receding, leaving his forehead bare and adorned only by a pair of rusty green goggles with circular lenses. Below his goggles, which were askew, was a pair of the sharpest sapphire-blue eyes Ivy had ever seen. These eyes had exploring to do. His stiff leather tunic was held together by a belt that clearly wasn't meant for this diminutive man's frame, with the end looped twice and dangling down to his dusty boots. He smoothed his clothing with his hands to no avail; his tunic remained wrinkled and his buttons terribly mismatched.

"Um, I was told I might find some school supplies in your shop. That is, if you are Mr. Munson?"

His workshop's slanted shelves were as crooked as his goggles and full of his finds. Five hairie lanterns, mismatched like his ensemble lit the dim room. Below his hairies was a ten-foot-long cluttered table, full of tools, opened books, and detailed notes. For anyone brave enough to explore it, his workshop was actually quite fascinating.

"How did you get in here?" Mr. Munson's brow wrinkled.

"The cab—" Ivy stopped short as she remembered Lionel's rule to never mention the cabby. She wasn't going to ruin any chance of beginning her studies at the mythical Halls of Ivy. "I—I was dropped off back there. A boy let me in. He must have passed through this way. You must have seen him."

"Oh yes, yes…he came and went. Thought I locked the door, though." He carried on with a worried discussion to himself, "Oh dear, dear, dear…what are *they* doing here?"

"Is everything all right?" she asked him, looking around and spotting no one else.

Mr. Munson returned to his corner, quivering. He stretched to peer out the window and the curtains briefly veiled his head. He began pacing, seemingly unsure of what to do with himself and fearful—but of what?

"Is something wrong?"

Mr. Munson continued to tumble around his workshop, knocking over anything in his way. "I haven't a clue as to what she's doing here. She should take her Brood and leave!"

"Pardon?"

Mr. Munson disappeared into a back room, tripping over the same spoken word spells and setting them to grumbling again. When he returned, he answered her in a tight, strained voice, as if his fear could barely be contained in a whisper. "The Dark Queen, of course, outside of the Crownerie."

Mr. Munson's shop was located at the very end of Old Still Lane—the older part of a very old street—in a corner store. The east end faced New Hollow, where all the royals shopped and the south side overlooked Pairies of Hairies, a premier Hairie Rehousing Agency. The Crownerie, which Ivy had only the slightest awareness of, was Ravenshollow's most powerful spot: it was a store of sorts, but not the kind one could just walk into.

"Has she never visited before?" Ivy wondered.

"She has never visited town. *Any* town. My goodness, girl. Have you been locked in a cave like a troll? She never shows herself. Any normal person would know that. She hides herself well, that's for sure. And she hides herself well for a reason."

"Well, what do you suppose she's doing here then?"

"I don't know, nor do I intend to find out. No good can come from the Dark Queen being on *my* street, let alone so close to all those stones and crowns! My priorities are within these walls, in my treasured shop, and I intend to keep it that way. If you ask me, she should stay hidden inside her castle. The very idea of her is bad for the magic in here. And her Brood! The thought of them! Twice as tall as they should be." He shuddered. "The very idea that she could come in here, take my books, this magic, these precious things. Why, if she only knew what power was hidden here! What she could find!"

"Could she really be that bad? She is our Queen after all."

"Yes, that's just it. She is our Queen and a very powerful one. She hides herself well for a reason; she hides herself well."

"Yes, you've just said that. But why?"

She watched him run his quick fingers over his precious books, baffling devices, and ancient tools. She could tell that the rare objects he collected were his treasures, the sort he thought a Queen would steal. *Why would a Queen be interested in some dusty old books?* Ivy wondered.

"So you said you were here for some school supplies. How about it then? Your list, please?"

"Sorry." Ivy paged through her Compass Startus to her list. "Here you are."

"Ah. A first year, are you? Let's see here. All right, *A Guide to Identifying the Lesser-Known Magical Creatures*. You think your professors will settle for a copy of *Even-Lesser-Known Magical Creatures*? Same author?" Mr. Munson pulled a thin book from the depths of his cupboard that leaned against the corner of his cracked wall; the edition was practically falling apart.

"I don't think so."

He shoved it back in and pulled out another while reviewing the list.

"I see you've got Professor Royal. What wouldn't she give her students to read...no accounting for taste. *Perfectly Imperfect Potions* by Lois Squibb. Is she serious? How can they be perfectly imperfect? Especially when you can read a copy of Padomo's *Potions Perfected*. That way you'll be able to bypass all the do's and don'ts in Professor Royal's class."

"Is that cheating?"

"Of course not. It's called being prepared."

He shuffled through enormous stacks of books, looking for those on the list. "Well, this is no good for today's shopper," he exclaimed as he held up a mysterious book entitled *The Words of the Wandering* by The Wandering. He handed it over to Ivy and continued his search.

"The writing in this book is barely legible!" Even as she said it, the shaky words faded in the candlelight.

Mr. Munson shot her a strange look, "The words are off wandering with The Wandering. Not a single written word is visible to any but the roving group. Why do you think the boy who was just in returned it?"

Ivy looked at the now blank page in befuddlement.

"These books. Can't ever remember where I last placed them. So many!" He shrugged and began opening various drawers, shoveling through them.

"Ah. Here we go," Mr. Munson said as he pulled several other books from shelves and put them on top of the potions textbook.

"Now I know I've got one of those for you," he pointed at an item on the list. "One Compass Collectis."

"What exactly is a Compass Collectis? Don't I already have one?"

"*That* is the Compass Startus," he said jabbing his finger at the book in her hand. "The Compass Collectis is a glossary and thesaurus to the unique scrivenist language, giving meaning to all terms described and used by that very respected profession. This here is it."

The book was larger than large. Its exterior was of heavy, vintage leather and had a thick, worn binding that held many hundreds of gossamer-thin pages together. Across the front, written in bold italicized lettering, was the following inscription: *The Compass Collectis: A Collection for Collaboration and Comprehension.*

"A requirement for all scrivenist studies. Sold only, of course, in the All Things Scrivenist store. Fortunately you're not the last to pass through here: I don't have many left. This one here seems in the best condition."

At the top right corner of the book there was a compass, although rather than the traditional coordinates it was marked according to the alphabet, inscribed in tiny letters around the compass.

"You turn this dial here to reveal the range of terms beginning with the selected letter. As collective discoveries are made, the book grows. Shall I show you how to look something up?"

Mr. Munson turned the dial to N and the Collectis trembled and opened. N words were listed in alphabetical order starting on the first page. Mr. Munson flipped through a few pages and then read, "'Nixbean, n. A bean that resists cultivation. Found in random spots, blooming whenever it pleases. Typically used in mixing drinks and brews. Contraindicated (to the extreme) for mixing with boysenberry: the effected bean will cast a permanent heavy accent of unknown origin upon its consumer's speech.'" Mr. Munson forced the book closed with his hands and a cloud of golden dust puffed out around its edges.

"How much is it?"

"Four ketzels."

"Hmm. Pricey."

"Well, I can give you this potions starter kit for a deal." He held up a worn leather valise the size of a small, thick book. Inside were tempting looking vials and powders. "Has an extra vial of nevermore sorcslurry in it—a tincture of the plant slurry. It counters any effect of magic. Not much fun really. Have you heard of slurry?"

Ivy could barely keep from rolling her eyes. "Yes, I have. And no, it's not much fun, I'd agree."

"Well, let's see what else is on your list. Schooling inks you can get at Boulliquiste's: All But Your Quills. Not many options for inks. For porcupels, I can tell you that the best quality porcupines are sold at Pines and Spines. But if you are looking to save a bit and don't need top quality, I do have a few here. 'Course, you'll have to settle for a creature with a less-than-tranquil attitude. The ones I have can be quite temperamental. Best wait till the end of your visit before you pick one up." He gestured to a little cage from which a low growl emanated. It was stuffed so full of lettuce Ivy couldn't see the inhabitants.

"Very well." After skimming the last of the list, Mr. Munson set his eyes on something that clearly interested him: the very last item. His eyes grew wide like a toad's. "This…oh, this is interesting. Highly unusual, yes. Seems like someone wrote it in here a little less than 'officially.' Where did you get this?"

"Where did I get the list?"

"Yes."

"Lionel, the scrivenist. The Hall's admissions office, of course."

"Listen, I wouldn't show anyone this list if I were you. Not yet. Not until you understand why it's there."

"Why what's there?"

"The last item on your list—it's never sold. Not here anyway. '1 Kallegulous Key.' I'd say you'd have better luck becoming Queen than getting yourself one of those."

Suddenly, as if the very mention of a Kallegulous Key caused the hairies to flicker with worry, the whole room blacked out, leaving only a smidgen of light peeking around the curtains' edges. Mr. Munson lit a match and handed a burning candle off to Ivy. He pressed his nose against a corner window and, once he was satisfied there was no incoming threat, spun the dial on her Collectis. "'Kallegulous Key, n. A small key made of soldered metal, designed to fit any lock and imbued with the power of forgetfulness. Specifically created to imprison persons or beings or objects. Whatever door is locked by a Kallegulous Key—and whatever or whomever is locked within—shall remain so until the very same key unlocks the effected door. During the term of arrest under such a key, the prisoner shall be entirely removed from the memories of those who remain outside.'"

"That doesn't make much sense. Why would I need one of those?"

"Well, that's what's curious. Only a few Kallegulous Keys are known to exist in Croswald. Whoever is locked away by a Kallegulous Key is bound to bear a secret. Like I said before the lights went out," he continued, pointing a wiggling finger. "I would keep this list private. Especially away from her. It could bring you a lot of trouble. Four forty-three is your total, Miss."

"Away from who?" Ivy asked nervously, forgetting about the street's unexpected visitor. She counted her coins distractedly, preoccupied by Mr. Munson's warning.

"The Dark Queen! Something has her visiting town today, something has her suspicious. Can't be sure what it is, or who, but we must be careful. Her interest almost always has a fatal conclusion."

"Is she gone?" Ivy asked. His head was already at the window again.

"Thank the moon! Yes! Town is beginning to fill itself again. You won't be alone if you carry on your way. Here's your porcupine—careful!"

"I'd better go then. Thank you, Mr. Munson. You've been most helpful." Her satchel was much heavier now. She was grateful Humboldt was so well behaved—perhaps his motion sickness from the cabby wasn't a bad thing after all.

"Just don't forget what I told you."

She nodded her head, acknowledging his repeated warning.

"Strange day already," he muttered under his breath, watching the girl leave.

OLD STILL LANE

o   o   o   o   o   o   o   o

IVY was certain that she had never experienced a stranger two hours than the ones she had just lived. She closed Mr. Munson's door behind her, pulling tightly on its rusted knob; it was giving her some trouble. After fiddling, she finally got the stubborn thing to close. Just as she turned around, Ivy was nearly knocked over by a horse and carriage that flew recklessly by.

"Move out of the way," yelled the hasty driver.

Her nerves on edge, she jumped back as the magnificent carriage with polished wheels made its way up the street. The drapery inside the windows made it impossible to see who nearly ran her over.

Such an inconsiderate royal, she thought to herself. *Don't they watch where they're going? Of course not. They can't even steer their own horses.* Only royals plunged through town that way. The carriage parked outside the Crownerie, right where the Dark Queen's now-vanished carriage had been. This carriage most likely held a princess celebrating her birthday and receiving her crown before starting at the Halls. No wonder the hurry. According to today's *Scriven This* headline, three crowns were leaving the Crownerie today—an event sure to cause a traffic jam on New Hollow Road.

Mr. Munson was right: town was beginning to fill itself again and rather quickly. The old wood and stone buildings of the merchant area stretched for about a mile. Handmade signs by craft store owners anxious to make a brum or two hung as high as the owners' ladders could reach. Small dwellings were scattered above most shops in town and others clung to the walls between them. Normally it was a hard day's work for most that lived here and Old Still Lane didn't have much to be excited about. But today was unlike any other day. Not only was it Moonsday and the start of the school year at the Halls, but the Dark Queen's unexpected visit had everyone on edge. The delay set townspeople hurrying to wherever they needed to be. Curtains were now drawn back and windows throughout town swung wide open again. The town's collective chatter grew deafening.

Ivy nervously felt the small pouch that Rimbrick had given her: it was considerably lighter than when she set out from the cabby. Spotting Boulliquiste's across the way, Ivy took three short steps down the street when she heard a strange whistle from above.

"Hello, girl! Are you the one delivering Moonsday pies? I declare I've never seen someone so disheveled! Your bag does look heavy—we'll take five. Rather, we'll take ten. Whatever you have. Moonsday pies are his favorite. The cream! The meringue!"

Ivy looked up and saw a broad woman with all her hair stuffed in a nightcap, hanging out her dwelling window. She lived above and to the right of Mr. Munson's shop. However, her size would suggest she lived beside the town baker instead.

"Sorry, but I think you've mistaken me for someone else."

"Oh! I just saw the bag and the uniform, dearie. Ordered for delivery because, well," she nodded nervously in the direction of the Crownerie. "What have you got in that bag if it's not pastries?"

"Books. For school." Ivy herself could hardly believe that it was the truth.

"Well then, isn't that nice. You'll be in class with my Woodley! I can tell that you'll be a sqwinch—no crown!" She winked. "I'm Mrs. Butterlove, of course," she batted her lashes and pursed her lips as if Ivy should have known of her fame.

"Well, good morning to you, Mrs. Butterlove!"

"Is it?"

"I beg your pardon?"

"Is it a good morning?" Even though Mrs. Butterlove was clearly anxious, she also loved to talk.

"Are you worried about our Dark Queen's visit?" Ivy asked, craning her neck.

"Oh! There you are, Woodley," she intentionally interrupted Ivy. "You've finally woken I see. This girl—I'm sorry, what did you say your name was?"

"Ivy. Ivy Lovely."

"Pleasure."

Woodley's shaggy head popped out of the window, and the two of them stared down at her. He held a fistful of buttered bread halfway to his mouth. Woodley was a round boy who usually introduced himself this way: *Hello. My name's Woodley Butterlove and yes, I do love butter.* When shaking his hand, greeters were inevitably left with a sheen of grease on their palm. It was fortunate his name wasn't Woodley Toadlove.

"Nice to meet you. Well then, I'll leave you two to your, er, breakfast."

Mrs. Butterlove nodded then closed the upstairs window—though her voice could still be heard quite clearly. "Really, Woodley! How could you possibly still be hungry?"

As Ivy walked on, it became clear that the Dark Queen's visit was the talk of town. Everyone on Old Still Lane seemed ill at ease. Gossip pulsed through the air. Ivy overheard different snippets of conversations with each step toward Boulliquiste's she took. She listened closely, eager to hear what everyone was discussing.

"What do you suppose she's doing here?" a frazzled woman asked two others beside her while laying her shaking hand against her chest. "And at the Crownerie, no less! The Selector can't be too happy about that."

The three women stood close together, heads inclined to hear each other's whispers.

"Perhaps the Selector no longer cares," the tallest drawled.

The third interjected, "You two would just die to hear what I know..."

"Tell us. Tell us!"

"Well, one of the royals missed her appointment to receive her crown! And you know they are nearly always collected early. First chance at magic."

"What kind of royal wouldn't pick up a crown?" The tall woman nearly had to bend over double to hear the other two's chatter.

"It's the first time it's happened. And the first time the Queen's been here. Don't you think it's a bit odd? And right before school starts?"

"Hundreds of moons, thousands of sixteenth birthdays, and never a crown forgotten!"

"Perhaps she decided to pick up a crown from Munson's but then was scared off by those spoken word spells!"

The women cackled. Ivy giggled, too, and Humboldt squealed. At once all three women turned to see who was eavesdropping behind them.

"Sorry," Ivy apologized awkwardly. The three huffed and puffed before walking away in three different directions.

As the women cleared the way, an oversize iron inkwell came into view. It spilled the words of a sign that read: Boulliquiste's: All But Your Quills. The inkwell dripped of real ink—usually from the day's specials—which colored the hair of a patron or two. Unlike Munson's, the windows had no heavy curtains and the late morning light shone into the shop.

Boulliquiste's was perfectly symmetrical, with rows of varnished wood all chest high, inviting shoppers to sample the vials of inks that filled the store. Every counter had several writing stations, each equipped with a small stack of neat parchment sheets, an inkwell (in varied colors and sizes, but all made of hand-blown glass and etched with the initials BB), and a well-worn quill. Just looking at them Ivy could sense that these old quills had been retired—they were simply writing instruments, rather than magical instruments that happened to write. Many of these quills had come to call Boulliquiste's home after their first owners were revoked of the scrivenist title for any manner of infraction.

Bouvier Boulliquiste—who was himself shaped like an

old quill, tall and curved forward after an entire lifetime wrapped over a desk—guided Ivy through dozens of inks, each one serving a different purpose. She sampled a few. The ones that stood out were the ones she didn't want: Stink Ink, specifically, which had an awful odor, worse than rotten cabbage or cheese left in the sun. Then there was Visiblink, a school requirement, only visible from straight on, which made cheating in class impossible. Ivy determined that this was the most wonderful store imaginable. She was dying to sketch.

With a cheerful goodbye—and even fewer brums—Ivy was out the door. As she decided where to go next a hand on her shoulder startled her. It was Fyn again, this time with boxes stacked in his arms. "Ivy! There you are! Been looking for you! Forgot to tell you, it's best to drop off your supplies at Chidding's. You don't want to be carrying all that nonsense with you at midnight orienta—" Three barely closed boxes nearly tumbled out of Fyn's arms. "I've actually just come from there, picking up packages, but I wish I could have Warwick do the heavy lifting on these," he continued, gesturing to his three unevenly stacked boxes. "Looks like you don't have a hairie yet. Pick a bright one for the night's celebration! Have you ever been to a Moonsday celebration in Ravenshollow? The lantern walk is especially fantastic here."

"Um, no." Every Moonsday she could remember was spent laboring in the Plum scaldron cellar. "Who's Warwick?"

"The Cursus Publicus and Concierge. Delivers your belongings directly to your dormitory. You'll need to set up your account first—at the front desk. Not to worry, packages almost always get to their proper destination."

"Almost always?"

Fyn smiled: he had a wide grin that lit up his face and made his green eyes sparkle. Ivy blushed and thanked him. The top box jiggled and rattled.

"Well, got to go," he said somewhat urgently and rushed off. Chidding's awning was entirely made from wire mesh mailboxes bursting with correspondence. Ivy stood in the line that snaked inside, which, though long, moved forward at a reasonable rate. She took the opportunity to absorb the scene. One wall was completely covered by a large bank of tiny post boxes. These were lotts, which received mendlotts, short for Mail Ending in Your Own Lott, and used by scrivenists all over to send packages, potions, creatures, correspondence, and anything else they could think of, to colleagues near and far. Experienced mailers ran in and out, receiving and sending mail with ease. Ivy was amazed to see the tiny copper boxes swallow packages as big as Humboldt.

The overwhelming smell was of warm parchment, hot iron, and drying ink. At the head of the line, Ivy could see a man of middling height with a fedora atop his head, and a ripped leather jacket sorting mail with efficiency.

A wide range of students, probably first years, waited in line with their hands full, some fuller than Ivy thought advisable. She felt a little self-conscious with only her books, scaldron, timid porcupine, and inks in tow. Moving along, Ivy watched as the gangly young boy in front of her almost buckled under the weight of his items. A cart rolled up and down the line, distributing Chidding's complimentary bottomless knapsacks. The boy struggled to untie one with his chewed fingernails. As Ivy watched he shoved in odd objects in no particular order, including a feathered hat and a periwinkle wool suit. His polka-dotted underpants came next—"Oops! So sorry about that!" She noted with interest that his schoolbooks had different titles than her own:

Jousting, Wrangling, and Cajoling: Beast Management Strategies by Maurice Wrigley

The Beasts of Northern Croswald: An Illustrated Field Guide by Flume Field

Ivy noticed that he was also loading small jars of preserved paws and fur pelts: clearly he had an obsession with all things beastly. This was confirmed by a cage full of fascinatingly tiny critters squabbling and squeaking.

When they reached the front of the line, Warwick greeted the boy with a brusque, "Those all yours?"

"Bit of an animal lover, you could say." The gangly boy shot Warwick a sheepish grin, peeking over his shoulder as though embarrassed of what the other students might think.

"So you are. And where will you sleep with this riffraff? I imagine you'll have a fine time with your roommate. The one you have yet to meet, of course."

Warwick jiggled cage after cage to be sure each was latched tight, then running several laps of bright yellow tape around the exterior metal that read, *CAUTION: MAY BITE!*

Seeing the creatures ahead of her on their way to the school dorms gave Ivy comfort in shipping off Humboldt.

"This one here is of an extra delicate nature," the boy said, lifting an already wrapped package.

"Would you like to send it Priority?"

"No other way! Not with what I have in there."

"And your name?"

"Hayword Nesselton."

Once the box was stamped, two furry arms popped out of each end. The box's critter crawled with its hands along the conveyor belt, climbing the cages above and throwing packages out of its way, including those holding its fellow critters.

The girl behind Ivy muttered impatiently, "Someone should tell him it's not a zoo where he's headed! We don't have all day!"

Ivy turned around to see a girl with honey-blonde hair. She had not one but two bottomless stuffed sacks, each bursting with tulle and lace and taffeta of every imaginable color—more dresses than Ivy had seen in all her sixteen years. In her hand she held her crown; there was something irreverent about her not wearing it.

"Oh. Are you going to do royal studies?" Ivy asked, looking at the girl's crown with curiosity. She had never spoken to any royal, only prepared their meals.

"My mother thinks so anyway. Her daughter wouldn't dare study scrivenry," she replied in a mocking tone, rocking on her heels, looking back as if she expected someone to walk through the iron doors at any moment. "Come on," she muttered edgily.

"So, you're interested in sqwinch studies, are you?" Ivy ventured.

"Shhhh! Mother's preoccupied at Miraged, looking for a mirror that will disguise her aging. But I can't have her hearing you say that. She could walk in at any moment." Miraged was on New Hollow Road, a store much finer than Ivy would visit today, boasting a wide selection of ornamented mirrors, crystals, and a host of snooty clerks.

Ivy heard Warwick clear his throat.

"Here to drop off the goods, are you? Let's get on with it! Busy day today!"

Ivy hustled toward Warwick, kicking her bag of books forward and lifting Humboldt's and her porcupine's cages to the counter side by side. Warwick pushed paperwork and a quill toward Ivy.

"I'll see you soon, okay?" she reassured Humboldt who rattled in his cage, troubled. "You too, little one. Humboldt's good company." Ivy patted the cage in goodbye and felt something poke her hand. Her porcupine was spreading his quills and growing pricklier by the moment. Warwick wrapped her cages with the same yellow tape—*CAUTION: MAY BITE!* The porcupine's cage rattled with nervous energy. Warwick placed the knapsack with her books and dress on the moving conveyor belt.

"That's all?"

"For now at least."

Warwick handed Ivy a tattered ivory ticket with the number SCR72706 printed and lettered several times, front and back. She turned to say goodbye to her new acquaintance but much to Ivy's dismay she had gone, dresses and all.

At Pairies of Hairies, the only set of hairies Ivy could afford were the most dimly lit ones she had ever seen. The shop was packed with all kinds of people preparing for the lantern walk that night, jostling for the best and brightest of all the hairie families. Ivy elbowed her way out the door, holding the rusty lantern her hairies came in, the least ornate in the shop. She briefly wondered if it was true, what the salesman said, that their lighting pattern was backward: "They light when it's day, dark at night. I'll give you another discount for their constant chatter. Not much we can do about it." So far, he was right about the trio's non-stop chatter.

"Back to Chidding's with you, little friends. You'll be no use on the lantern walk."

The hairies' chatter grew louder and more anxious.

"What is it? Don't want to be mailed?" They tittered. "Well, all right then. You do seem a little too social to send in a box. I was only kidding. Honestly, I'm grateful to not wait in line at Chidding's a second time!"

But before long, Chidding's would be the least of Ivy's worries.

THE HALLS
OF IVY

I VY maneuvered through the growing crowd. It was early evening by then and everyone was eating Moonsday pies and preparing for the feast in town that night. Once the townspeople were stuffed to the gills, they would follow a midnight procession up to the Halls to watch students be inducted into the school.

On the other side of town was the Silver Tankard, a place known for its bottles of Luckluster, bubbling Oxtail's Frost, and Spinner's Foam. Scrivenists generally preferred the latter, as it caused heads to spin with the most creative ideas—a great way to devise a new spell or break writers' block, as long as they could remember their ideas the next morning. It was run by the Boones, a lovely and most peculiar couple. Mr. Boone had the strange habit of compulsively painting doors—the Tankard's door, as well as the door to their dwelling above, was constantly changing color.

That evening a group of professors—every one an acclaimed scrivenist—had gathered at the Tankard as was their tradition to celebrate the start of a new school year. Their animated, impassioned conversation punctuated with emphatic gestures was visible to passersby. At their favorite booth by a window they carried on: which parents of which students were off their rockers, what lessons they were looking forward to teaching, and how last year's graduates were faring at their castles.

Mid-discussion, each of the professors felt a tickle in their pockets. Then in a flurry of feathers, quills of every color flew up from the scrivenists' table. After a swirl and a whirl, a veritable cloud of quills blasted through the Tankard's door and sailed after each other, up the lane and off toward the school. Never before had anything like this happened.

Scrivenists on duty in castles nearby were not exempt from this oddity either—every quill within a crow's flight from the Halls abandoned its owner to fly toward the south end of New Hollow Road and down Old Still Lane. The rustled whooshing of the quills brought young and old to windows for miles around. Moonsday pies dropped to the ground and mouths hung open. The mad dash of quills slowed and swirled around a corner between Lessie's Enchantments and The Batty Tincture where a solitary figure sat on a small bench looking at her claim ticket. Hearing the whizzing, Ivy looked up and was transfixed by the darting, diving quills surrounding her.

As Ivy stood slowly, the quills reversed direction just a smidgen in reaction to her movement. There was a literal wall of feathers around her—quills had boxed her in, forbidding her return to the center of town. Ivy darted the only direction she could, to the Halls, holding nothing but her three hairies. Really, being surrounded by flying quills was the only thing that had quieted the hairies' din of chatter since she had first picked up their lantern.

As Ivy picked up speed so did the quills. The chaos seemed to focus itself into a more direct energy. They flew down towards Ivy, feathers back, pointy nubs forward. She felt a sharp prick on her rear and she yelped.

"What do you want?" she cried out to the feathered cloud.

Ivy sprinted up the hill, her hairie lantern hitting her legs as she fled the quills and toward the looming Halls. She had no idea what was transpiring but kept running, barely keeping ahead of the army of writing tools. The cobblestone way, lined with oranstra trees in bloom, lead straight to a high wrought iron gate that was closed tightly. The Halls would only open once the new school year began, that much she had picked up in town. She veered right and cut into the forest that surrounded the castle. There had to be another way in!

Then she saw a little dirt path that led to what looked to be a gardener's gate. There was a heavy latch keeping it closed. Still the quills pressed her on, herding her up the path, and she knew she couldn't hide if she tried. Out of breath and desperate Ivy held a hand up in front of her, toward the small gate as she sprinted, gasping for breath. A wavery glimmer of light went from her hands to the gate. There was definite magnetism in between her palms and the entrance. The gate jiggled, rattling the latch. Ivy slowed in surprise only to be poked by half a dozen quills. The tentative light from her hands grew stronger and she forced the gate open with every fiber in her body, stretching from her fingertips down to her pounding feet.

The gate swung open and Ivy rushed past it, feeling it swing back decisively behind her. She spun and saw the quills come to a dead stop. Rather than fly straight through the curli-cues of the gate or up and over, one by one they twirled and de-parted, each back to their owners. If it were possible for a quill to be proud of itself, it seemed that each of them was.

Ivy panted, slumped against an oranstra tree. She set the hairie lantern down and stared at her palms. What had just happened? Had the quills opened the gate for her?

It was now completely dark, which made the Moonsday lights downtown stand out more brightly and cheerfully in stark contrast to the dark castle. Ivy tried to tickle her little hairies to light. Typically, the more interesting the situation a hairie watched, the brighter its light. Hers seemed dull as ever, as if nervousness only dampened their glow.

"Figures," Ivy sighed. She didn't blame the hairies—she felt uneasy, too. This wasn't how she expected to make her first impression. Was she trespassing? The Halls were closed for the season until midnight orientation. Ivy was eerily alone. She steeled her nerves, biting her lip. A raw spot had formed after the day's excitement.

Ivy turned toward the castle, ready to behold her new school for the first time. She couldn't believe what rose before her eyes. She held her blinking hairies out before her, grateful for the faint light. She knew this place! Walking tentatively down the path toward the Halls, Ivy felt a rush of emotions. This was the castle from her nightly dream! The exact castle she had spent the last sixteen years on a hill sketching in the moonlight.

As if in a trance, she walked to the front entrance, the grand doors parting for her as she entered. The silence echoed in the cavernous entryway. The hairies in the chandeliers perked up, filling the intimidating room with a warm glow.

Ivy laughed. "Good thing I'm not relying on you three," she teased her flickering friends. Unlike the ones above, one of Ivy's hairies had fallen into a catatonic darkness post-quill chase, and the other two didn't look far behind.

Ivy walked up to a balustrade overlooking an impressive ballroom below. The walkway that wrapped around the ballroom's left would lead to the library. Had she come all this way—by cabby and foot, chased by quills and spurred on by hope—to finally meet the person that she dreamt of nightly? She tentatively walked down the grand staircase and across the ballroom floor.

As Ivy pressed on she heard footsteps echoing across the ballroom, quick and light. She stopped. The silence was so thick she could cut it. Backing up cautiously toward the wall, she bumped into a painting and squeaked in surprise. The painting was titled "Wanda Wetzel, 1679" as if it were a portrait, but in truth it looked more like a landscape that happened to have a small figure in it. The scene was of a wooded glen ensconced in fog. A statuesque woman stood in the back of the painting, posing for a portrait, but almost hidden by the encroaching, misty landscape. *Odd*, she thought. Ivy heard the footsteps again and spun around. No one was there. Turning back to the painting she was surprised to see the woman looked closer and the landscape slightly clearer. *Even odder. Maybe a little creepy.*

Behind her, a rapid-fire voice punctured her thoughts.

"Canitbecanitbecanitbe? Can. It. Be?"

A tiny, ancient man popped up in front of her, as if he'd materialized from shadows. He flailed his arms above his head like the air was buzzing with bees.

"You are here! It is you!" Then with a triumphant laugh, he dashed off again, circling the ballroom at top speed. Top speed for an old man, that is.

"Hope the little quills didn't poke too terribly!" he shouted over his shoulder from the far corner.

"What?" Ivy yelled back. "You did that? Well, that was terribly rude. But wait! Where are you rushing off to?"

"Lots to do; lots to do!" His white hair trailed behind him and he waved his hands in the air somewhat frantically.

"Wait! Please! Who are you?" But Ivy could spot the man no more. She heard a door slam and he disappeared as quickly as he had appeared.

Before she could rouse her strange hairies, the ancient chime in the ballroom—almost identical to Lionel's timepiece but perhaps ten times as large—rang out as it struck midnight. The candelabras and chandeliers went from dark to shining with flames, illuminating the grand room. In an instant the whole place was transformed, like it had suddenly awakened, from an abandoned castle to a majestic school. Grand staircases marked each end of the open ballroom, and a magnificent stained glass ceiling and dazzling crystal chandeliers soared overhead. It was breathtaking. For a moment, Ivy imagined how a glorious gala might fill the space with dazzling flowers and elegantly dressed princes and princesses. She shook her head to bring herself back to reality.

She ran to the outdoor balcony that overlooked the illuminated town. But before she could look out over the festivities, the grand doors burst open to reveal a crowd of students, each holding their Moonsday lanterns. At the front a woman dressed in an imperial, steel-blue dress and adorned with a long, elaborate fishtail braid walked the students down the stairs, her back to the ballroom. *The Selector*, Ivy thought, her breath catching in her throat.

"Before you is the Grand Ballroom. Here, we have our annual Masquerade, as well as fencing tournaments, commencement, and other gatherings." Her voice rang clearly through the entryway.

Ivy was frozen. Then she locked eyes with Fyn. He held a pole attached to one corner of a broad lantern canopy, several dozen brightly lit lanterns dangling from it. The canopy had obviously led the procession up the hill. Fyn's jaw dropped nearly as far as Ivy's when he saw her standing below in the ballroom. He beckoned her over, moving his eyes and nodding his head as if to say, *C'mon! Hurry and get over here before she sees you!*

"Let's continue this way, towards the left." The Selector directed the group as they walked along the edge of the open ballroom, looking out toward the columned railings on the open balcony. Ivy silently sped up the steps and ducked in behind the group as they rounded the balustrade. Once next to Fyn, she nervously held out her sleeping hairies, as if she had been there all along. She stuck out among the glorious forever-fitting dresses and tuxedos of the royals, and even among the sqwinches who wore their finest attire as well. She smoothed out her scaldrony uniform as best she could.

"You call that a proper Moonsday light?" A haughty princess sniffed in the direction of Ivy's sleeping hairies.

Ivy focused all her attention on the Selector, who had paused to give Ivy a strange look.

"As I was saying, there are many wings in this school, places you are welcome to explore during your Hour of Discovery should you choose." She turned and led them on. "Of course, on floors appropriate to your grade level."

Looking down at Ivy, Fyn whispered, "Breaking in, are we? How did you get in? School doors are locked to everyone except the Locksmith. You're lucky she didn't catch you."

Ivy looked at him in gratitude and signaled him to be quiet with her eyes. As the tour continued, Ivy relaxed and marveled at the Halls—it was exactly the castle of her dreams, only the library held books with words and no strange, silent man waiting for her. As they toured the Den, for that is what the Selector and everyone else called the library, Ivy heard a bold voice brag, "I can set things on fire."

She turned to catch a glimpse of a prince standing behind her, and couldn't help but smile thinking about how his fiery personality matched his power.

"Now, you'll find that your room assignments and roommates have appeared in your Compass Startus. Ivy flipped hers open: there was her room assignment, but no roommate. "This is the southeast bridge that leads to the dormitories, which were added when the Halls of Ivy was converted into a school so many years ago."

The air was chilly as they stepped out onto the bridge and the moon shone brightly on the limestone. Several stories below the Bitter Forest grew dark and thick. Directly across from them, dormitories were cut into the stone cliff's face, four rows of brightly lit windows shining back at them, warm and inviting.

Ivy followed the other students to the dormitories and

located her assigned room. She was relieved to see that her belongings had made it there before her. In fact, they had already unpacked themselves. She bounced on the bed—a real bed!—and felt the linens. Divine. Ivy opened the wardrobe to find her neatly pressed uniforms hung along with a cozy nightgown. She squealed with delight.

Turning to the books that Rimbrick had given her, she fingered their titles. *Wait a second.* There were no titles. Ivy pulled the books down from the shelf—her most precious possessions—and each one of them opened to blank page after blank page. She had last read part of them right before she crossed out of the slurry, but how could words walk off a page? Yet in her hands she held nothing but burgundy, crimson, and royal blue hardbacks with aged creases on the covers.

Without meaning to, Ivy yawned hugely. Try as she might she couldn't shake the bone-deep fatigue that was settling over her. *Maybe just a little nap, then I'll figure out the book thing,* she thought before slipping into sleep.

MINOR MAGIC

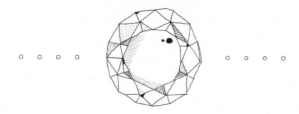

AFTER throwing on her uniform—a pleated skirt, a blouse with an embroidered quill on the breast pocket, and a thigh-length hooded cape made of the softest wool imaginable—Ivy followed the rush of students out of the dorm that morning. She was still in disbelief that she was here in the Halls of Ivy, not waking up to make griddlecakes she'd never get to eat. She found her first classroom and observed the room from the back, not wanting to take a seat too quickly.

The walls were decorated with bits of enchantment that helped light an otherwise dim classroom. There were floral arrangements with the fragrance of an entire field of fresh flowers and exotic blossoms like those that grew on the exterior walls of the Halls. These arrangements separated the rows of desks from a secondary space enclosed by long draped windows. While the rest of the class gathered, Ivy took a seat next to a petite, lightly freckled, brown-eyed brunette. In contrast with her prim appearance, the girl's books lay carelessly strewn on the floor beneath her desk.

As class filled, the girl began digging through her

bag faster than a troll on the scent of a pickled horned frog. She pulled everything out of her bedazzled satchel—a hair comb, her Compass Startus, a very thin book titled *How to Convince a Sqwinch to Do Your Work,* and enough feathered porcupels to fully plume a bird. After removing a mirror elegantly framed in a whitewashed wood, she neatly filed everything else as quickly as if she had fifteen hands. Ivy felt slightly embarrassed, as her satchel was significantly plainer and emptier.

"So, er, what sort of stone are you sporting in your crown?" she asked the girl. "You're so quick."

"The Jessel Stone." She shrugged her shoulders nonchalantly. "It's one of the swifter stones: it effects the speed of my hands and feet."

"So was it your hands or feet that knocked your books to the floor?" Ivy teased. Much to her surprise, the girl let out a little laugh. "My name's Ivy, by the way."

"Hannelore. Hannelore Lawler."

"Nice to meet you," Ivy grinned shyly. After pausing a moment she ventured, "Excuse me, but are you going to read those?"

"Probably not. Why? Are you interested in doing the work for me?" She smiled.

There was a clear distinction between the royals and the sqwinches: the former were bejeweled and becrowned and the latter seemed to carry their own weight in books. At the back of the classroom antique writing desks were outfitted with enormous storage underneath—sqwinches had a propensity to over-read, over-prepare, and over-collect. The desks near the front were light and airy in comparison, some inlaid with ivory and tiny non-precious stones.

Ivy smiled and nodded goodbye to Hannelore and then made her way to an antique desk in the back, hoping not to be too conspicuous. She felt a deep chill as she passed a boy and looked down, shivering. The poor prince's name was Quincy Fryer and he sat frozen to his ice-covered seat, his nerves having caused the magic of his Hoarfrost Stone to misbehave.

Ivy began to unload her things, all the while smiling at the difference between her satchel and Hannelore's. First, she placed her caged porcupine on her desk. The poor thing was trembling, a barrel of nerves—a little too like Quincy for Ivy's liking. Ivy patted the top of its crate and made a little shushing sound to calm him. Next, she opened her Compass Startus to the only blank page, thinking excitedly of adding pages as she went. In her eagerness to finish unpacking, Ivy knocked over her ink and a cloud of blue fluffed out around her desk, drawing other students' attention.

"Is everything all right over there?" the girl next to her asked.

"Yeah. Yeah, er, everything, everything is just, just fine," Ivy whispered back.

She was sweating in embarrassment—how could this happen on her first day at the Halls of Ivy? Her first class, for goodness' sake! Her shivering porcupine sneezed, jolting her from her thoughts. The hazy blue ink cloud had tickled its way into the creature's nostrils, and soon the single sneeze turned into a sneezing hysteria. *Of all the porcupines*, Ivy thought in a panic, *he's allergic to ink!* The creature's sneezes were so forceful that his quills, Ivy's unused porcupels, were jettisoned off his now nearly bald back; an entire coat of spines impaled the walls. Students ducked out of the way of the flying writing implements as Ivy hid below her desk.

A haughty girl shouted, "Whose sad excuse for a porcupine nicked my dress?" Silence. The girl repeated, "Well! Who did it?"

"I'm so sorry, my porcupine, he seems to have an unexpected allergy," Ivy stammered. The girl had shining black hair, tan skin, and cheeks that were a deep shade of red to reflect her annoyance. Her dress uniform was perfect, aside from the nick near her right knee that exposed her leg.

"An allergy to what? You? Look at your desk! All out of sorts. It's as if everything in this room is averse to you. Who are you?"

"My name is Ivy."

"Well, Ivy, you owe me a dress. Look what you did!"

"I'm sorry. Really I am. It was an accident."

Hannelore piped up, "Oh Damaris, you know the uniform mends and launders itself."

Thankfully Professor Royal had arrived, and just in time. "Welcome, class! Please take your seats so we can begin." The professor took in the cloud of ink, the porcupels, and Ivy's desk. Her patient smile made Ivy like her instantly. She had a trim figure and her good humor was effortless and genuine. Her ash-blonde hair hung long and beautifully curled.

Professor Royal paused, observing the new faces in her classroom. "This is the very minute you will begin mastering your special, unique gifts. And you sqwinches, it's your job to transcribe and illustrate all that you see! What fun! Each of you will develop an understanding throughout this year's class of your individual abilities as future scrivenists and also the power of stones as worn by your royal counterparts. Royals, you'll come to respect the sqwinches. They do, after all, carry a shadow of magic in their blood—the same magic that permeates your crowns. Some of you may take more time to learn while others are likely to take less. Regardless, you will leave here knowing much more than you do now. Practice makes perfect, I always say, and practice is what my class is all about."

Ivy pulled a porcupel from the wall behind her as there was no chance of getting one from her bald porcupine now. She held the brown-and-cream implement, thin as it was, snug between her thumb and pointer finger and readied herself for the day's discoveries. She picked up her Compass Startus from the floor, opened it, and pressed it firmly to the desk.

"There are five key elements in your journey of discovery, the components of my lessons: your *mastery*, your *application*, your *gifts*, your *intellect*, and finally, each of your individual *capabilities*!"

Professor Royal flicked her wrist and had her bright white quill with brown spots write the first letter of each element on the blackboard behind her. The class read aloud in unison, "MAGIC." A hushed wave of excitement swept the room.

"That's correct, magic! It's what your stones or your natural abilities have given you access to, isn't it? You won't believe the kinds of things that happen within these walls. I've seen it all! An angry whirlwind once shattered eight hairie lanterns hanging above us. The room sparkled with all the pixie dust. And once, a giant snake slithered its way across this room and tried to make its home beneath your desks. Why, new students have even sprouted a second nose! Just out of fear!"

The entire class laughed.

"One time, in an attempt to levitate a book off her desk, a student managed to lift every desk to the ceiling. She sat just there," she continued, pointing at a girl in the second row. "It was her first day. Students ran to all edges of the classroom afraid that the desks would fall on their heads. Fortunately, no one was hurt and it made for a good laugh and an even greater story! Mind you, that young lady is still studying here, and now she can levitate a book whenever she chooses."

The classroom was large and beautifully appointed. From the ceiling hung numerous lanterns like those referred to in Professors Royal's story, lit by dozens of hairies. The angled rooftop above the students' heads seemed to be filled with fairy air, dark yet sparkling with magic. A little creature flew from one lantern to the next, causing them to sway.

"What's that?" a princess asked.

"Oh, that's Restoro. He's my expeller. I bought him from Wheeler's Habbitry out in Ravenshollow a few years back. Has anyone visited that shop? Professor Wheeler teaches here."

Not a single royal had. Six seats down from Ivy sat Hayword Nesselton, who Ivy recognized as the zookeeper from Chidding's. Of course, Hayword raised his hand instantly.

"I suggest you pay it a visit sometime. It's an interesting place. Professor Wheeler sells creatures of all kinds there—dwindles, fledglings, no-names! But don't worry, you'll get to meet the colorful man himself, as he is your Creatures of the Night professor."

A student asked, "What's a no-name?"

"Creatures so rare they haven't a name. If you didn't already know, an expeller is an extinguisher of small magic.

They come in handy! This one attends all my classes with me. He puts out small fires, thaws bits of ice, changes ghastly creatures like snakes into toadstools, and calms students' moods. That's why I called him Restoro. He restores what's been broken, which is the main reason why my room looks peaceful and not utterly destroyed by burgeoning magic." Ivy noticed that, whether by Restoro's magic or by finally relaxing a bit, Quincy's chair had returned to room temperature.

Professor Royal explained that the space enclosed by the draped windows was their training room. Even with Restoro around, based on the stories she had shared the students understood that an empty room was preferable: it contained fewer objects to break, catch on fire, or disappear. It also reduced the likelihood that they'd hear from the Selector—or worse, the Dark Queen. Once such reprimand from the Selector had inspired Professor Royal to purchase the costly expeller and create the practice room in the first place.

"I think it's best if we start by introducing ourselves," Professor Royal suggested. "Any volunteers?"

She leaned against the edge of her desk facing the students while the expeller looked down from one of the many lanterns. No one was quick to volunteer. Ivy noticed that every seat was filled except one—a desk near the front. She glanced at the classroom door, curious as to who might occupy the last seat.

"I see we have a bit of a shy class this year. How about I'll go first and then hopefully others will follow. My name is Laverna Royal. I know, I know...yes, Royal is, in fact, my real name, and I am as royal as my name suggests. To make myself more than just a name to you, let me tell you that I began my studies here many years ago as you are doing now, and I was once as shy as you are today. I live in Ravenshollow with my husband, who teaches a class for princes in their final year, called Feather a Dreather. I'll let Professor Wheeler in your Creatures of the Night class tell you about the dreaded Dreather—a fiery beast only my husband has affection for, it seems!

"As a royal, my crown is fitted with a Stone of Abrise, and so I can lift and influence objects with my mind. One thing I learned in school, which I will pass on to you, is to not let fear stop you from doing what you want most. When I was new to the Halls my mind was clouded with fears of humiliation and I thought I would never be able to control my sometimes snagging magic. Once you learn to push your fears aside, your powers will shine as brightly as mine do now!"

At that moment, Professor Royal waved her arm in the air and opened every drape that covered the training room's tall windows, which had the appearance of a two-story greenhouse with an exquisite view of Croswald's north side. The room was flooded with natural light and the hairies dimmed accordingly. The entire class stood from their seats and gasped at the view of the Dark Queen's castle far beyond. The scenery was breathtaking, as was the bright classroom.

"Now, enough about me. Who would like to be second to introduce themselves?" There was silence in the room as Professor Royal prompted, "Come on now, don't be shy! What's the worst that could happen? Are you afraid that someone with a Hellexor Stone will end up looking like a dwarf with elongated ears and a prickly chin? It's already happened twice, you know."

As the rest of the class hesitated, the stunning girl with the ripped dress stood imperiously from her seat and said, "My name is Damaris Dodley and I wear a Lingward Stone in my crown that can make things disappear and appear—just as if reflected in a mirror. Would you like to see? I've been practicing on my own a bit."

"Oh yes, I'd love that, but that does remind me—one moment, Damaris—I must reiterate that all magic practiced outside of classroom walls is strictly prohibited until your fourth year in order to limit unfortunate accidents. That is, unless you invest in an expeller for a pet. We will, of course, practice plenty within the classroom until then. You do understand. Damaris, please continue."

Damaris checked to make sure her hair was in place and then turned toward Ivy, who shrank in her seat. Damaris held out a perfectly manicured hand and sent a beam of magic toward Ivy's shivering porcupine. In an instant, the poor creature and the cloud of ink were gone. The class gasped and then there was a small smattering of clapping from a few of the royals. Hayword mumbled something about *critter hater* under his breath.

But with a sudden sneezing sound the porcupine reappeared. Rather than bringing the blue haze with it, there was a swirling cloud of toads above the porcupine's cage. The look of shock in the young royal's eyes showed that this wasn't part of Damaris's plan. The appearance of toads scared the porcupine even further, if that was possible, and his sneezing became a bout of nervous gas. Damaris's stunt had quite literally scared the poop out of the poor thing. It was as if a stink bomb had detonated inside the room—even the large windows looking over Croswald fogged at the corners. Ivy was torn between concern for her porcupine, the safety of her books, and wanting to hide under her desk.

Restoro wasted no time. He jumped from his perch on the lanterns above and set about sucking in the fumes. His furry form flew around the classroom, inhaling and sending each toad back from whence it came. His flurry of work was so intense that the students' desks took to rumbling and jiggling. Ivy had the sense to spread her arms over her belongings. There was no need to find out if her porcupine was also allergic to red ink.

By the time Restoro reached the other side of the room, he had slowed and become quite green. With one last breath he inhaled deeply, taking in the last of the stench and also Damaris's crown, its Lingward Stone still shining bright with magic. Damaris let out a yelp, clutching at her head. Clearly full and exhausted, the expeller sunk to the ground and hobbled on his two hind legs, whip-like tail dragging behind him, toward a tiny door at the far corner of the room.

"Well, *that* was a first!" said Professor Royal with a surprised laugh. "Damaris, thank you for that little show but from now on, let's leave your schoolmates' supplies alone, shall we? Your crown can be found in the expeller's haz-bag, a veritable quagmire of toxic magical waste. Don't fret—you'll get it back and it should clean up fine."

Ivy's porcupine seemed slightly more at ease. Damaris sat back in her seat, livid.

"Did you get that sorry creature at Munson's?" Professor Royal smiled at Ivy. "That's where my first porcupine was from as well. Make sure to collect your porcupels—they'll keep well in a tincture that Professor Wheeler can make you."

Ivy was grateful for her kind words, even if she was still crimson with mortification. Professor Royal continued, "Would anyone else like to share? Come on now, Damaris would like a good laugh, too."

A toffee-skinned princess raised her hand next, but before Professor Royal could call her name, the princess sneezed and flew backward into the wall, knocking to the floor every book, potion bottle, and decorative piece that had been perfectly situated on the shelf behind her. Again, the class was in stitches. Ivy jumped from her seat, but Professor Royal rushed to help the student, asking if she was okay.

"Yes, I'm fine," she replied, rubbing her backside with both of her hands.

"Are you sure?" Professor Royal asked again.

"Yes, I'm sure." The girl's head was down.

"What's your name?"

"Colleen Holly," she answered.

"You must wear an Olerium Stone. Very similar to a Jessel Stone; however, their speed can be quite forceful."

As Colleen tidied up, Professor Royal said, "I suppose the silver lining is that you can clean up at least as fast as you make a mess!" She smiled warmly. "Tell us a little about yourself."

"Well, I enjoy reading and now read books four times as fast as I did before I acquired my crown. Although I'm afraid to admit, I sometimes tear the pages." She smiled sheepishly.

"Well, isn't that fascinating! And won't that be great for you during homework assignments? Fortunately for you, the Den has many copies of each title for that reason."

Professor Royal called on Ivy next. "When did you feel the 'sqwinch tickle' as we call it in the Halls? When did you or your parents know that you had a magical mind?"

"A tickle? Um, actually, a dwarf told me."

The class giggled aloud.

"Don't be rude, class. Dwarves are fine readers of magic, after all."

"And, and I've been sketching for as long as I can remember. Practically before I could speak."

"Like I have!" shouted a sqwinch in the third row. "Mom says I drew all over the drapes. You could imagine the day she bought me a proof pad! Good day for me, good day for the drapes!"

The classed chuckled and Professor Royal nodded. "Photographic memories and the impulse to capture what you see. The first clue for any sqwinch."

The student in the third row continued talking, "It's not always a good thing. I caught the town baker, Mr. Gruber, leaning over to pull baked goods out of his scaldron on my way to the festival. Unpleasant, but even worse when his britches split in two! Afraid I'll never get that image out of my mind!"

The class laughed uproariously and it took Professor Royal a full minute to get them into order.

"Ivy, please, continue."

"I love to capture castles in the moonlight—the sun makes them glow like rose quartz, but the moonlight is ethereal and mysterious. It makes them even more difficult to sketch. But I, I haven't practiced much magic—I grew up at the Castle Plum with its slurry fields."

"A slurry girl," Damaris sniggered. "No wonder your magic is so off! I doubt you'll ever master it."

"That's enough, Damaris and thank you, Ivy. Perhaps one day you'll share your sketches with us."

Soon half the class had introduced themselves. Restoro had another opportunity to make himself useful when a sqwinch lit his Compass Startus on fire and the creature returned to gobble up the flames. Time flew in Professor Royal's class and soon the end of the period was near. A brightly colored bird flew into the practice space, passing through the wall as if it was nonexistent. It squawked loudly through an oversized beak.

"For those of you who haven't met Didley yet, he's the school's feathered fledgling," called Professor Royal over the noise. "He will let you know when it is time for your classes to end. He's loud and obnoxious, but who wouldn't be with hundreds of students to keep on schedule? He's not the friendliest of birds, so do not expect a personal introduction. See you all tomorrow! You all did wonderfully."

GHOSTLY
HOSTS

THE rest of the morning passed in a blur. As Ivy walked past the Den's entry, she turned to find a room as cavernous as the library. It was sectioned into three separate dining halls, each outfitted with a horseshoe-shaped table. At the table, the similarities stopped: the three dining halls were wildly different spaces. Ivy's stomach grumbled as the voices of a pair of princesses drifted toward her.

"Did you hear?" asked one princess, clad head-to-toe in champagne chiffon.

Her companion, while checking her reflection in the glass of a picture window that overlooked the gardens below, replied in a lazy voice, "Hear what?"

"There's a ghostly trio inside one of the dining halls where we have lunch and dinner. One of them is the cook!"

"So?" The other princess didn't seem amused.

"So? What kind of dining experience is that? Eating a specter's food? I heard the food they serve tastes worse than those beehive biscuits served in the Uncommon Flicker dining hall. No wonder. How can the ghosts even taste the food they are serving? It'd fall right through their vaporous stomachs!"

Her voice was now shrill enough to carry past Ivy's ears and to wherever those ghosts were hosting. Cuisine from the afterlife or not, Ivy's stomach continued to growl. She'd found out too late that breakfast had been served in the first year's dormitory alcove.

"I heard the chef has been cooking dead for longer than he was alive," the second princess was saying. "Anyway, I heard no matter which of the three rooms you choose, the food is absolutely delicious and never runs out."

"Well, we'll just see, won't we? I'll have my servants deliver me a lunch if it's not."

"Excuse me," Ivy interrupted.

"Yes?" The two turned to see what bothersome thing had interrupted them.

"Did I hear you mention the dining halls?"

"What about them?"

"I was wondering if you could tell me which room is preferred? I'm starving and I...um, I can't seem to make up my mind."

The princess with the increasingly loud voice trilled, "Hopefully you won't be so unfortunate to dine with a ghastly trio—or rather, ghostly—at the Longbard! The doors to the Lolly Room may still be open. That Lolly Jester is a real amateur, nothing like what my father would have at his table, but at least he has a decent chef and functional, living taste buds to approve what his chef is serving! It's that way, right there. Off to the right."

"Thanks," Ivy said to the royals, who didn't bother to reply to her, already re-engaged in their discussion.

By the time Ivy found the proper doors, seating in both

the Lolly Room and the Uncommon Flicker were full. Ivy had no choice but to dine with the ghostly trio. The last entrance at the left end of the hall was marked by a pair of pale doors that stretched to the ceiling. They were still open. As Ivy walked in, the chilly breath of the Longbard Room greeted her. The room was decorated to be as white as its ghostly hosts. The ceiling, the floors, the candelabras across the tables, and the hair of numerous hairies—each hairie family contained in ornate, Gothic canisters—were stark white. Mirrors were stacked slanted against the walls and the oversized, pallid dining chairs looked like they came from another world, heavy and yet ephemeral at the same time. Ivy took a seat, reveling at their transparency. White petals lay gently in a thick covering over the dining ware and linens, creating the illusion of freshly fallen snow.

Suddenly, the doors to the Longbard closed. Ivy glanced around: every seat was filled and the anxious anticipation was palpable. A single ghost holding a long dangling scroll appeared in the center of the room. In a nasally voice he read, "Welcome to the Longbard, where our tables are long and everything you eat comes with a well-prepared song!"

A second ghost, an elderly man dressed in a chef's ensemble from a bygone era topped with a rakishly slanted hat materialized in a slanted mirror toward the back of the room. Fortunately, he spared the students the bad poetry and made an attempt at humor instead. "These wrinkles are evidence of my many years of masterly dining experience— my hand to a cooking pot is like your head to a crown or, for you budding scrivenists here, like your hand to a quill. Magic happens!"

Then a rotund third ghost appeared with a white platter of food upon one hand. The other hand he held close to his mouth, licking the residue of a delicious meal from his fat fingers. He had a tuft of hair, a thick mustache, and a tiny waiter's jacket stretched across his bulging belly. "And my name is Hungry Jule!"

Countless other invisible server ghosts flew through the room—at least, that's what Ivy thought they must be, because individual platters moved through the air seeming to float on their own.

"I haven't yet introduced myself. Duel will do," said the poetic first ghost. His most defining attribute was his hair: dusty and gray, it was slicked back and shaped into two horns. He then launched into another poem: "We ghostly trio will serve all of you, Clyde, Duel, and Hungry Jule. We craft your food by hand, not a crumb we waste; your leftovers will become our most delicious taste. Today's meal is a delectable stew; a blend of toads, cobwebs, and spices, too."

Duel paused and looked around the room before finishing with a devilish grin, "We live, rather *don't* live, to feed all of you."

Ivy looked around: everyone was lifting the lids of their strange meal. No one else seemed perturbed by what the ghostly trio considered delicious, despite the questionable ingredients. Ivy, on the other hand, was unsure of what sat steaming in front of her.

"How do we know what's really in here? Toads? Do they really expect us to eat toads?" Ivy asked the sqwinch beside her, who appeared as hungry as Jule.

"Sure looks like it," she said nonchalantly.

"Are you going to try it?"

"Of course. I've heard all meals are delicious, no matter which room," she said before taking a spoonful of stew. "Mmmm...and it is! Though it could use a bit of pepper."

Then the girl dropped her spoon and drank straight from the white porcelain bowl.

"Yeah, but...toads," Ivy mumbled. She sat staring at the bowl full of stew in front of her when suddenly Hungry Jule appeared through the table and above her plate.

"A certain gentleman asked that I deliver you a letter, Miss Lovely."

"A letter? What letter?"

"I see you haven't tried your stew yet. A shame, it was specially prepared for you."

"I'm not that hungry. What letter?"

"Not hungry? Don't be silly! You mean to say you won't be eating Clyde's most prized creation? He simmered that scaldron all morning. Is it the idea of toads that has you bothered?"

"Sort of. Especially after a certain incident in class. I might wonder where those toads have really come from."

"How about I trade you a letter for your leftovers?"

"Who is it from?" She couldn't imagine.

"If only you'd take a spoonful, you'd see!"

Ivy slowly picked up her silver spoon to scoop what looked like a chunky, rotten, gray stew. As she dipped her spoon in reluctantly she felt something spongy. She lifted it and, much to her surprise, fished out a drenched letter clinging to her spoon. Even as she reached for it the letter began to dry until it looked like it had never touched liquid.

"Your stew? May I have what's left of it?" Hungry Jule

asked. Ivy handed him her bowl and he slurped it down in one gulp. The meal passed straight through him and splattered all over the floor. The sqwinches on each side took little note. Ivy tried hard not to gag, guarding her unread letter close to her chest.

"Hmmm. That's his best stew yet! How unfortunate you didn't try it."

Suddenly, Duel appeared and began to sing loudly, "A bowl of stew sits here not dry. But the young lady, Ivy, she's afraid to try. Won't you try a spoonful? It's deliciousness you won't deny! Such a delicious meal prepared by Clyde, Hungry Jule, and I!"

Endless numbers of bowls full of toad stew floated through the air, dancing while waiting for Ivy. She was mortified for the second time that day. Clyde flew towards her next and said, "I'm certain after a single spoonful, you'll want to gobble up this bowl and many more!"

"Actually, I'm not feeling well. Perhaps tomorrow instead. If you'll please excuse me."

Ivy stood from her seat and left the Longbard, hiding the letter behind her back, as everyone in the room watched her abrupt departure.

She heard Clyde behind her ask sadly, "Was my stew that awful?"

Hurrying around the corner, Ivy hid down the hallway, opening the letter and wondering whom it could be from.

We no longer wander and I thank you, Ivy Lovely. Welcome home. Welcome home, at last.
W.M.

Ivy was bewildered. She walked back into the dining hall to take a quick peek to see if the mysterious author was somewhere inside, possibly hiding. She hadn't a clue who to look for. Duel noticed Ivy and began reciting immediately, "The girl has returned for another taste, a setting for her stew must be placed—"

Ivy quickly shut the door, hoping not to be forced into eating that disgusting toad concoction. Though the room Ivy left was quite chilly, she felt her temperature rising, leaving her without any sort of appetite. *Who is W.M.? What is "welcome home" supposed to mean?*

o   o   o   o

After classes Ivy made her way to her dormitory. She was again struck by how familiar the Halls seemed. How strange— and wonderful—that her recurring, frustrating dream had prepared her to be here, this magical place that she had yearned for all her life. She passed the Den and made her way down the grand hallway. Out of curiosity, she went down into the ballroom like she had that first night. She stopped in front of a spot where she had first noticed Wanda Wetzel's portrait but in its place hung a painting of a cottage imbued with friendly light. The cottage was hung with lanterns from every gutter and corner. She was sure this had been the spot of Wanda's portrait. *More strangeness,* she mused. She was getting used to everything being odd, all the time.

She passed from the Halls to the stone bridge that connected the main castle with the cliff of dormitories. The twilight was dimming and she could see the little portholes of warm light in the dark face of the cliff, each one a window into a sqwinch or royal's room. The wind whipped around her and she shuddered thinking about how high she was in the air, though it couldn't have been more than fifty feet. Any distance over her own height made Ivy nervous.

The guarding spell propelled her to the first years' level. The quill design on her uniform's breast pocket—lavender for first years—was a nod to where their quills would reside once they were scrivenists. Ivy realized with a start that it was probably a good thing to keep the years separated. With the photographic memories sqwinches were developing, one look at a fourth year's homework and they'd be able to shortcut the whole process!

Her room was the last at the end of the first years' hall. Most had rooms near the bridge. She looked in at rooms that were open, hearing snippets of conversations between laughing and arguing roommates. Every room had more belongings in it than did hers. One room was draped entirely in pink—that is, until it met the other side, which was decorated yellow down to the bed skirt the royal must have brought from her castle.

"Oh, look at this!" said the princess on the pink side. "*Scriven This* is saying that yesterday every quill in the area abandoned its scrivenist!"

"That's ridiculous! Dozens of quills just walking off?"

"No! Hundreds! And they flew!"

"That's nothing compared to the crown left at the Crownerie. Can you even imagine?!"

Ivy quickened her steps away from the room.

As she neared hers she felt the same excitement build that she had felt the first time she had walked in—it was her own room! Her own space, and a real room at that. Ivy practically skipped to down the hall to push her door open, half expecting to meet someone. But still no roommate. This was odd. *Doesn't everyone else have a roommate?* She checked her Startus, which was considerably thicker even with just one day's worth of notes. Still no name listed for her roommate.

There was a snuffing sound from under the bed.

"I do have you, don't I, Humboldt?" Ivy smiled at the little fire breather. The Halls of Ivy seemed to be agreeing with him: he was the picture of health. He shuffled over to the hearth to start the fire as Ivy put away her books and changed out of her uniform into her old sweater. The uniforms took on more and more of the plum color as the students got closer to becoming full-fledged scrivenists. Ivy had noticed that most of the first years chose to wear the oversized periwinkle sweater and riding pants. She fingered the jacket and scalloped skirt—they were lovely.

Before bed, Ivy pulled down what had been *The Whiz and The Weasel*, according to the book's crimson cover, fingering its blank pages.

"Humboldt, did you eat my book's words?"

He puffed out a stream of smoke in denial.

Ivy smiled at him, though she was flummoxed. Nestling in the down comforter as thick as a drift of snow, she found sleep.

FENIX'S FINEST GLANAGERIES

○ ○ ○ ○   ○ ○ ○ ○

BEHIND a heavy, thick door that was meant to prevent any light from entering (or leaving) was Fenix's Finest Glanageries class. The door was dungeon-like and framed with heavy nail heads. Students queued up behind the door, waiting for their individual admittance and their first glimpse into the room. Yesterday's class was held in the ballroom. Professor Fenix felt it necessary to prep the students before allowing them access to his sacred classroom. As her classmates filed in one by one, Ivy caught glimpses of a blindingly light interior. Something had the room shining bright and it wasn't the windows. In fact, she would soon find out that there were none.

When Ivy was finally admitted she found that the door opened first to a hall that curved and twisted like an underground tunnel. It was lined with small cubbyholes outfitted with iron cages, each weathered gray and constructed in a braided pattern. Inside each was a mysterious iridescent bottle, all wildly luminous, shaped differently, and of vivid colors. One slot below eye level was propped open and empty. Ivy, along with most of the other students that passed, peered inside the dark hole that seemed to have no end.

The corridor opened up into a round, cool chamber. Six rows of circular amphitheater seating lined the chamber. Down toward the front and center was a short man, the much-discussed Professor Fenix. He stood still behind a wooden lectern with posters plastered to its sides emblazoned with inspiring quotes about limitless imagination. To see over the lectern, the professor was perched not only on a chair, but on a stack of books on top of a chair. Even so, Ivy could barely see his nose but she saw enough to know it did quite live up to its legend as the largest nose at the Halls.

Ah. There it is. Ivy saw the missing bottle, not lost, but rather centered on a pedestal to Professor Fenix's right. The glowing vessel captivated everyone in the room.

"Perhaps it can…" whispered one student.

"Maybe," came a hushed reply. "I've heard these are incredibly powerful."

The students' speculation grew in enthusiasm and volume, the commotion of everyone rushing to his or her round back chair evidence of their excitement.

"Good afternoon, everyone!" Professor Fenix called in a croaky tone.

Ivy scooted her way around the room toward an empty chair.

The students listened closely, anxious. "I'm sure you're all wondering what I have here in front of me. Well, I am Professor Filbert Fenix and this here is one of my very special glass glanageries. They are incredibly valuable and volatile: bottles like these are not ones to take home. You're likely to get yourself in a bit of trouble if not used properly and under supervision. They are mostly used for magical instruction and practice, occasionally for sport. You need a Certificate of Glanagerie to operate one of these. I, of course, am an expert in the matter. Though there have been certain incidents..." he drifted off and then cleared his throat. "Well! Never mind that!

"For those of you not familiar, glanageries portray what the bottle operator has plotted, bringing to life the events and characters that heretofore had only existed in their mind. It's a sort of real life, mini stage. Rather than making a mess of practicing things out here, on a scale too large for an expeller to extinguish, I can create big scenarios within the bottle for you to conquer together using your own bits of magic."

The students trilled with excitement, eager to get started. Unlike the rest of the class, Ivy was a bit hesitant and wanted to hear more of what Professor Fenix had planned.

"Is this really happening? I mean...are things in the bottle real?" Colleen Holly asked.

"No. They are products of my prodigious imagination. There will only be scenarios I have created strictly as teaching tools. That's the magic of a glanagerie: anything can happen. Anything you want, but only within the bottle. You have the same powers inside the glass as you do outside it. The glanagerie is not harmful *per se*, but it does feel terribly real at times and brings out fears and weaknesses. To be sure, it's not even entirely safe, but that is its true teaching strength: only in a most fearful situation will you know what magic you are truly capable of. It can be quite challenging, yet very fun. Some of you may resent the scenarios, but I assure you, it's all for the best. I believe most of you will play the part well. Now come and gather around."

"How do we get in there?" Hannelore called out.

"Great question. It only takes a tug on the bottle's stopper to get you there. Once a bottle like this is opened, those selected will enter the owner's imaginary world. For today's exercise, I have imagined a character called Gale Tempest—a grumpy old man who's stored his violent temper away in the clouds, a violent storm we call a Bearded Cloud. I have a list here of those who will be visiting today. After the bottle is opened, I'll stuff the list inside, a veritable message in a bottle. Only those with their name listed will be swept inside. The rest of you will wait here while your classmates assist one another through a storm that can only be tamed by magic. The names are: Spinna Jolly; Hannelore Lawler; Gregory Gershwin; and Bobby Willcock. Let's see here," he read from an already-prepared list. "Nina Rose; Caroline Blunder; and Reenie Wallow."

A few were excited and fidgeted in their seats. Others, like Caroline Blunder, appeared anxious. "Why me? I hate lightning."

Reenie Wallow stamped her well-heeled foot and protested, "I'm not dampening my dress. A Bearded Cloud sounds wet."

"Dresses do not exist in such a world, you'll find yourself in britches and such so as not to effect your performance."

"You won't find me in a pair of any foul-looking trousers."

"Don't be silly! It's only for an hour." Professor Fenix added, "And you'll all be dressed alike. Breck Bronxton."

The last thing Ivy wanted to entertain right now were imaginary games, yet her name was called next. "Ivy Lovely. You, too, will be joining. Lila Reeves; Elaina Portal; Woodley Butterlove; and, lastly, Olive Haggerty. The rest of class will have their turn tomorrow in another setting of my choosing."

The thirteen lined up in front of the bottle where Professor Fenix directed the group to stand. He held onto the bottle's neck tightly and paused before removing the stopper. When he did, a whirlwind of gold sand swept around them like a windstorm.

When the magic of the glanagerie bottle had finally settled, Ivy slowly opened her eyes and found herself completely alone in a strange place. She stood on the deck of an old, ethereal vessel. The huge schooner sighed back and forth, back and forth, with a gentleness that Ivy didn't expect. The moon shone bright over the water, its light broken into a million sparkles across the vast ocean somehow contained in this strange glass bottle.

Ivy took a moment to breathe in the cool night air as she stood on the main deck. It took a moment for her to realize that she was just as surprised by the solitude as she was by the calmness of the sea. *Where did everyone disappear to? Where is this terrible tempest? Professor Fenix never mentioned any ship. I thought we were supposed to calm a storm together. Things seem pretty calm here.*

Not wanting to break the spell of quiet, she walked to the ship's railing with her characteristic curiosity. It was a good thing the moon was so bright, as not a single candle was lit aboard. *Where is everybody? Who is steering this ship?* She suddenly realized she was seeing the sea for the first time, but only in a bottle that she could fit in her satchel.

Her hand trailed on the well-oiled handrail as she walked along the deck, looking up to the vast sails. Ivy didn't know anything about ships, but the rigging and sails seemed impossible to figure out. *How many were there? Seven?* The well-worn but sturdy sails hung slack and the ropes gently hit the two masts in an easy, soothing rhythm.

Her eye caught a platform about halfway up one of the masts. She shivered, but not from the temperature—her flight on the cabby had done nothing to accustom her to heights. The only thing that could make being up high more unnerving was being up high over inky-black water. She made her way to the quarterdeck above what Ivy suspected was the captain's cabin, given its large door. From the upper deck she would be able to see better. Still not a person—not a sailor nor a classmate—in sight. *Maybe everyone is asleep.* It was the middle of the night, after all.

From the corner of her eye, she noticed a sliver of light coming from inside a cracked door. The same arched door that she suspected to be the captain's was now propped open. Pressing her hands to the door, it opened to the most gilded room she had ever seen. The edges of the room were sloped with treasure, gold piled halfway up the walls. There were delicate soffits in the ceiling and a blocky desk loaded with gadgets Ivy couldn't pretend to understand. Oddly, the desk jiggled as she walked by. She backed up.

On the desk among the extinguished candles lay a journal with a name all too familiar to her. "Derwin Edgar Night?" she muttered. She hadn't seen that name since Rimbrick's books contained words. She couldn't help but touch the journal, drawing her hand softly across its rough exterior. She fanned through the pages, stopping at a curious collection of detailed sketches, almost scientific in nature. The sketches, dozens, were of a single stone from different angles. Like it was some kind of obsession. *A Kindred Stone,* she read in a messy script. It was a mystery embedded within a mystery.

Ivy didn't have much time to dwell on the journal—she had heard something tinkling. She trailed the sound, leaving the room and taking the journal with her, looking all around and overboard for the source of the noise. The tinkling grew louder and more musical. But the sea was dark and still. *Was that music coming from the quarters below?* She spun on her heel to follow the noise below deck.

She called lightly, "Hannelore? Professor Fenix? Anyone?"

As she got closer the sound of a little fiddle, badly out of tune, reached her ears. It was an old sea chantey. After a bit of trial and error, Ivy found herself in the bulkhead, which was set up as a living space. Huddled in the center of the room was a crew. The twenty rough-hewn men smelled like they had been at sea for quite some time. Sunburned and weather-beaten, Ivy could tell that they had each lived a hard life. The captain caroused at the center of the group, his frock coat and buccaneer shirt open to reveal two thick gold chains around his neck. He stroked his pointy goatee, flecked with gray, as he told a story to raucous laughter. All the crew had some version of the same sun-bleached leather boots, but apart from that, their getups were quite varied. From waist-coats in bright hues to earrings to knee britches to jerkins, this crew was dressed in the style of many far-flung places.

Ivy hung back in the shadows on the outskirts of the room clutching the journal to her chest. Hidden by barrels of wine and treasure, the men hadn't noticed her. The fiddle launched into another song. Half the crew sang along and the other half seemed to be enjoying themselves telling stories. Then a short, wiry sailor's eye landed on Ivy. His gaze, at first disbelieving, turned to panic and he tugged at the captain's sleeve without blinking or turning from her.

Ivy felt fear squeeze the air out of her lungs. She may as well have been overboard for all she could breathe. The captain's face reddened into an indecipherable expression and he leapt across the room toward her. Ivy let out a cry and felt behind for the door. She whirled around and ran up the stairs, the captain and half his crew on her tail.

Above the deck a storm was building and the ship lurched, scattering pirates across the ship. Ivy grabbed the railing and looked out over the water. Raging clouds circled overhead.

"Is that Gale Tempest?" she shouted, but the captain and his crew looked at her as if she spoke a strange language. She locked eyes with the captain and he gave her a strange look. Was it pleading? Inquisitive? But before she could decide, a giant wave from out of nowhere shook the ship, throwing everyone on board back and forth like ragdolls. Ivy heard the cries of men tossed overboard. There was a thunderous clap, a flash of light, and with a giant groan from the creaking ship, Ivy was back in the classroom.

Rather than gazing at the captain, her eyes were now locked on that of Professor Fenix's expeller. These eyes were full of surprise rather than beseeching, a welcome change from the captain's. The expeller was twice the size of Restoro and not the flying type. Ivy shivered, grateful for its warm breath blowing her dry.

Most of Ivy's classmates hadn't returned yet, but Ivy was glad to be one of the first. She still felt like her lungs were opening up, catching breath. As they returned, one at a time, other students were chatty about their first experience. Ivy realized something heavy was wedged between her hands—the journal, soaked and soggy. In complete disbelief, Ivy opened it carefully to see that it was the same one she held in her hands before disappearing off the ship, and out flooded a school of silver fish and seaweed, their slippery bodies flopping on the floor.

The miniature flood, impossible to miss, brought the journal to the professor's attention. "My goodness child, what in all of Croswald did you do? It's not possible! It can't be!"

"I didn't do anything."

He removed his quill from his tweed jacket, which was begging to be released from his pocket. He swished his wrist slightly and cast a frosted spell, freezing his entire classroom, the glanagerie bottle, all the students, and time itself. Even the expeller's breath was frozen in the air. Nothing moved except Ivy.

"Come with me," he demanded. "And give me that book!"

Still half-soaked in salt water, Ivy followed. *The expeller will have to finish the job when I get back. If I come back.*

THINGS
DISREMEMBERED

ROFESSOR Fenix pushed back a heavy door and ushered Ivy into the presence of the Selector, the statuesque guardian of the Crownerie and headmistress to the Halls of Ivy. She stood quietly on the opposite side of the iridescent room, silent, as the diminutive professor and Ivy entered in a huff. The left side of the room was flanked with delicate, luminous glass shelving that held row after row of crowns. On the right the shelving was open and packed full of books. Each side curved toward the domed ceiling. The office's overall impression was of the inside of an opalescent pear.

Clearly ruffled by the surprise of the journal, Professor Fenix pulled at his hair; it looked as if he had a wild case of bed head. In contrast, the Selector's beautiful braid hung long; each loop represented a year of her esteemed guardianship and not a strand was out of place. It coiled at her feet like a snake guarding treasure. Ivy had never seen hair so long, even with her own heavy mane weighing down her head. There was a glow around the Selector. Ivy thought that she was as beautiful as legend had it.

Professor Fenix cleared his throat, "Selector. Forgive me, but you must look at what this child has done. Strange what she's done and she's a bit strange herself."

"Says the man with a room full of nothing but strange things."

"By far, this girl is the strangest." His words hit a raw spot with Ivy. This was something she'd always felt deep down, especially after sixteen years of Helga's disdain. "Never in all my years have I experienced an incident such as this. Well, not in many years. It's unacceptable. It's dangerous. It's fortunate she brought back only a book. And not even a book that was in the glanagerie scene I concocted! She went to an entirely different place unknown to me! I request she be removed from my class until such matters are handled. Others could get hurt. I can't risk her bringing back some monster. Or worse!"

"I don't know how it happened! I swear it!" Ivy shook, lost in confusion.

"Don't be silly, Professor," the Selector replied without so much a smile. She was, at the same time, very serious yet unperturbed.

Exasperated and even a little frightened, Professor Fenix lobbed the book on top of the Selector's pristine desk. "See it there. It's a blank journal! Now, what would that be doing in a scene I've concocted?"

He continued to yammer, but Ivy was frozen. A blank journal? No, this one had had a very specific author!

"Derwin Edgar Night," she blurted. "It said Derwin Edgar Night only minutes ago, and—and there were sketches and notes. Right there!"

The Selector shot Ivy a sharp look that made her blood turn cold.

"Did it?" the Selector asked calmly.

Ivy then noticed that the wall behind the Selector was a façade much different than the rest of her office, dark in comparison to the sheen of the crowns encased on her cut-glass shelves. The opening was enclosed by a wide and sturdy iron gate. Behind that, black brick encased a large steel door. It appeared to be more secure than even the Crownerie. The brick wall stretched to the domed ceiling. The iron bars were too narrow for even a mouse to squeeze past—a mosquito, maybe. Gargoyle-like dragons sat on high columns flanking the opening. Each dragon sizzled, emitting small tendrils of smoke from their nostrils.

"Don't mind them. The dragons are quite comfortable up there. It's when they fear intrusion that they blow fire. Best not to mess with them, not that anyone ever does." The Selector's voice was powerful yet soft and soothing.

"What are they guarding? I mean, what's behind the door?" Ivy wondered aloud.

"Nosy girl, aren't you? That is the Forgotten Room. Things disremembered and incidents immediately revoked from the collective memory. I can't tell you what's in there for that very reason. Clearly, it's the only place for a book like this." She took the journal into her hands. "You certainly can't keep it. Once it's tucked away inside, no one—not you, not your classmates, not your Professor Fenix there, not I, not even the Locksmith—shall remember."

"But why? It's just a journal! And an empty one at that."

The Selector looked stern. "This isn't just a journal, Ivy.

It's something that has crossed from the imaginary to the real, something that could bear power unknowable to us at this time. Best-case scenario, it's just a hiccup in magic. Worst-case, the very purpose of the Halls, the magic we seek to protect and grow, could be under threat. And the name you mentioned—please don't use it again. With any luck, it will be forgotten along with this. Let this be a warning to you."

"But—" Ivy protested.

"We have to lock it away for safekeeping. Forgotten doesn't mean destroyed. Not yet at least. This is something that should have never existed in the first place. Filbert, please, call upon Ivory Lucky."

"It's Ivy Lovely. And I'm right here."

"You have misunderstood," said the Selector as Professor Fenix bowed and left the room. "I was referring to the school's Lucksmith and Locksmith. The only one with access to each and every door here in the Halls."

"The only one? You just named two people."

"Well, there are two sides to her."

"And how did she become so fortunate to acquire such a position? Positions, I mean? More than one?"

"I wouldn't consider her fortunate, not at all. In fact, her luck is quite split."

The Selector spun gracefully toward the book side of the room. The books varied in size and age, though they were all variations of a deep shade of raisin. Each Compass Individualis represented one student and his or her body of work. The volumes were ordered according to year, getting thicker as they moved from first years up to the fourth years on top, with a few scattered geniuses among them. The

Selector made a small gesture with her polished finger, almost a curl, and a book from the packed bookcase floated across the room even though she hadn't spoken. As the book landed in her hand, the pages opened.

"'An orphan found near the slurry fields,'" the Selector read. "Interesting."

"I beg your pardon?"

"Just trying to get a glimpse into who you might be. Says here you arrived at school hours early, chased rather aggressively by some quills on your way up the hill? And, let's see here, your traveling companion is a, well, is a scaldron." The book grew in her hands, "And now it says, 'Brought a book from a glanagerie world to Croswald.' Tsk tsk. All of which is of note. Also notable is that your record is quite spotty, even your birth year. Such a curious year, that one. All those strange incidents…"

"How do you know all of this?"

"This is a Compass Individualis, my dear. Only one per student, documenting all your deeds and mishaps. Basic registrant information from Lionel, your class records, your habits as reported to me by the Halls themselves, as well as older biographical information through a spell of my own design. You agreed to allow the spell, right here." She produced a letter initialed by Ivy. Ivy recollected not having time to read it in Lionel's cabby.

"You all really should start coming up with new names for things," she told the Selector. "It's all very confusing."

"Not at all. A Compass Collectis is shared among all of you thriving scrivenists for the purpose of learning and referencing the language. Your Compass Startus is both your

workbook for school and a source of new information for the
Collectis. Anything you discover that is worth knowing is
transferred to each and every Compass Collectis at the end of
the school term and is part of your school final. The Compass
Individualis is for my records and handled only by me, so you
won't need to worry yourself about it, dear. Just know it's best
to stay out of trouble."

"I don't know how it happened," Ivy repeated. Then she
added, "So my Compass Individualis won't remember this
last incident, with the book then? Right?"

"I assure you there will be no trace of anything, anywhere."

"Why just shove it away? Aren't you at all curious where
that volume came from and why?"

"We've discussed this as much as we can."

An awkward silence descended on the room, the kind
that only occurs when someone is hiding something.

But the silence didn't last long. The two were startled by
a knock at the door, two heavy pounds followed by several
light, fluttery knocks. Then, with a jingle, in walked Professor
Fenix followed by the strangest woman Ivy had ever seen. She
suddenly understood how Ivory Lucky had two jobs. The
woman was composed of two persons, two faces, evenly split
down the middle. The left side of her was dressed like a
librarian: she wore a mint-green, freshly pressed blouse,
primly tucked into a sensible skirt, and a double strand of
pearls around half her neck. Her mouse brown hair was in a
limp bob with bangs on that side. She wore half a pair of eye-
glasses that nearly tripled the size of her left eye, which was a
lovely olive shade. Her right side had bright red lips to complement the large garland she wore tucked in her elaborate

coif, shaped like a feathered wave. A plunging red polka-dotted dress exposed an intricate tattoo on her right arm, a riot of red roses. Her lips lifted into a small snarl—that side didn't seem the type to do anyone any favors.

"Ah. Yes, Ms. Lucky. Just in time. If you could unlock the door, please. Something to be forgotten."

"Certainly," the timid woman on the left side replied in a low and gentle voice. She fidgeted with dozens of keys on a large brass ring, before the right side of her yanked the keys from her hand impatiently, stopping on one elaborate and large enough to fit the keyhole. She turned the key with a grunt. As the door opened, a strong wind spiraled out and towards the ceiling. Ivy had the sensation that the wind was made of memories, things that she had once known but couldn't put her finger on, now swirling about her. From the looks on the others' faces, they felt it too. Ivy's Compass Individualis flew back to the shelf, jolting Ivy from her reverie. *Is this whole incident actually disappearing from my Compass Individualis?* She watched the Selector solemnly hold out the glanagerie journal toward the door where it was swept into the blackness. Strong winds circled the group, disappearing as Ivory Lucky forced the door to close.

"Is there something I can do for you, Professor Fenix?" The Selector looked fresh and even less troubled than before.

"Hmmm…I can't seem to remem—perhaps just to say hello, Madame Selector. And you?" He turned towards Ivy. "What are you doing skipping class?"

With a little surprise, Ivy realized that she remembered it all. She could even summon the feeling of holding the journal in her arms, the terrifying glanagerie ship—all of it. She needed some space to think about what happened, so she played along. "I can't remember. Am I in trouble? Who are you?" Ivy asked the Lucksmith. Or was it the Locksmith?

"Ivory Lucky. Good day to you." As she retreated Ivy almost laughed as the poor woman's distinctive walk almost had a limp: the right side of her body undulated and swayed provocatively, while the left drew a straight line without so much as a wiggle.

"You may be excused," said the Selector. She met Ivy's eyes and Ivy felt a little shiver. Something about the Selector's stare made it seem as if she suspected Ivy of something. Casting her gaze to the Selector's timepiece, Ivy realized she was probably terribly late to her next class. *How am I going to explain this one?* Ivy thought a little ruefully. She excused herself politely then ran from the room.

She pulled her schedule from her pocket and groaned. She had Professor Petty—the one thing she remembered best about the first Art of Ink & Memory class was how her instructor was incredibly persnickety about punctuality. All of her fellow students had already dashed into the room rather than incur the professor's wrath. She hurried toward the classroom but was shortly stopped in her tracks by a deafening noise. The surprise nearly sent Ivy off the edge of the school's interior balcony and right into the middle of a class of fencing princes. It sounded as if a horse and carriage had careened off the road over onto a helpless pile of screeching cats.

Ivy was eager to know where the sound was coming from and what its source was. Considering all that had happened recently, it occurred to her that it might be yet another odd event intended only for her. She stood still for an instant, waiting to confirm whether or not the noise was simply in her overactive imagination, which cooked up things quicker than scaldron's breath, but then she heard it again.

Clack! "Meeeooooww!"

The racket came from behind a door directly across from the balcony. Perhaps there were members of Professor Wrigley's Brave a Beast class on the other side, actually braving a beast. Or was it an empty room full of random things—just some errant spell bouncing off the walls? The door was half her height and rusty and looked like it hadn't been opened in years. She hesitated. She didn't know of anyone who could walk through doors but with halls full of magic, you never knew.

The riot grew louder. Not only was Ivy dying of curiosity, but she would feel terrible if someone (or something) needed help and she walked away. Taking a deep breath, she shoved her shoulder into the door and barged right into a tiny closet with a very surprising inmate.

"Oh my! Are you okay?" Ivy had stumbled on a young girl locked inside a small crate. Her arms and legs were hanging out in odd directions. Her face was pushed up against the side facing Ivy and her lips were mashed against the crate's metal mesh, making it difficult for her to speak.

"Can...you...get me out of...h-here, please?" She would have been better off in one of Wheeler's habbitries: at least his sort of cage resized to fit whatever creature Hamel Wheeler caught for the market.

Ivy yanked the crate open and pulled the girl out.

"Thanks," she said while taking Ivy's hand to steady herself. "I was wondering how long it would take for someone to find me in there."

"Of course," Ivy said. "That looks like it's going to leave a mark."

"No kidding," she said, taking her first deep breath.

"You." Ivy smiled, realizing the girl was the very same one who had been in line behind her at Chidding's with all the dresses. "I wondered where you disappeared to—haven't seen you in class. How long were you in there for?"

"I was afraid it would be forever. School has barely begun and I was almost a dropout."

"Are you okay?"

"Yeah, I'm fine," she replied, while dusting off and pressing out her dress's newly formed wrinkles. "How long have I been in there for? I got caught at the tail-end of the Selector's tour."

"Almost two days then. Aren't you hungry?"

"That Beast Keeper kept feeding me nasty stuff. I won't even tell you what I ate for breakfast today."

"Well, how did you manage to squeeze yourself inside there?" Ivy asked as she pushed a flask of water from her book bag to the girl.

"Thanks. Do you really think this is a place I'd choose to be? The Beast Keepers are always locking up stray creatures walking these halls."

"Creatures?" Ivy asked.

"Yes. In this instance a mink. This crown here—wait. Where is it, anyway?" She felt for the crown on her head, circling on the spot. "Not that I care."

"There it is!" Ivy pointed to where it lay upside down on the floor.

The girl grabbed it, blew off the dust, and shoved it back in her bag roughly. "This crown has me changing into a mink every five seconds. One of the Beast Keepers caught me at the wrong time. Anyway, I don't know why the Beast Keeper is so opposed to minks. It's not like I turned into a warthog for goodness' sake! I'm only a first year. I barely know where my classes are let alone how to use my Hellexor Stone properly. Of course, if I put any effort into learning I may have broken out on my own. It wouldn't have been my first choice of crowns, that's for sure," she said with a gloomy expression on her clammy face. "I didn't want a crown at all."

"I bet you're the first royal to say that."

"Well, it's true!" The girl glared. "I want to be a scrivenist! Not some princess who can do a party trick. But my mother won't hear of my being a sqwinch. I was hoping the Selector would allow me to switch studies. And not tell my mother!"

"Are you sure you're all right?" Ivy asked again.

"Yeah, I'm fine now, thanks to you," she said as she stood. "I don't mean to seem ungrateful—I do appreciate your help—but I really must be going. I've already missed so much, if I'm late to class my nerves will have me changing back into a mink! Before I go, who can I properly thank for freeing me?"

"My name's Ivy. What's yours?"

"Ivy, is it? Well, I'm Rebecca. If you see any stray minks around here, do me a favor and leave them alone! I really appreciate and empathize with the little creatures more than ever before, you know. Knowing I can so easily transform made standing in line at Chidding's terrible! I half thought I would get boxed up and shipped with the rest of that boy's zoo."

The two laughed. Then Rebecca rushed off, leaving Ivy alone inside the closet. She climbed over the battered cage feeling the dread of certain tardiness.

At Professor Petty's door, Ivy peeked through the glass window in the center. All the students were already in their assigned seats. Ivy's empty spot was all the way up front—perfectly situated for Professor Petty to notice an absence in her classroom.

When Ivy opened the door, the entire class looked back at her. Even Professor Petty, who was a hefty woman and not easily deterred from droning on, fell silent. The class watched every timid step Ivy took, eager to see if the rumors were true. The quiet rustle of Ivy's uniform was the only thing that broke the silence.

"Sorry I'm late," she said timidly.

"Not as sorry as we are!" the professor glowered, breaking her silence once Ivy was seated.

Ivy noticed Rebecca already seated near the edge of her row and out of the professor's direct eyeshot. Rebecca shrank with guilt and kept quiet, but Ivy didn't mind that she did. Being caught by a Beast Keeper in her animal state was simply bad timing. It seemed she had suffered enough. She only hoped that Rebecca could return the favor one day.

"Please stand, young lady, and remind us all of your name."

"Ivy," she said in a voice barely above a whisper, standing from her seat. Her cheeks turned scarlet.

"Tell us something about yourself, Ivy."

"What would you like to know?" She wasn't sure what she was expected to say.

"Perhaps why you were so late. We are most curious to know."

Could she blame it on her visit with the Selector? Finding a mink in a cage? Neither seemed plausible.

"I was lost." This was not entirely a lie; first, she was lost and over her head in the Selector's office, then she was lost in thought dwelling on the journal, then she was lost in a closet with a caged girl. Even now her thoughts returned to the journal. Why could Ivy still remember?

"A familiar excuse. I feel like being a bit easy on you today, Ivy, fortunately for you!" Ivy breathed a huge sigh of relief. She was too distracted looking around at her classmates to notice that Professor Petty had marched toward Ivy's desk with a stack of thick books, each of which appeared to be four hundred pages long. She dropped five of them at once on Ivy's desk with a startling boom.

"You are to read each page in these books and next week you shall be quizzed. Should you fail, well...we can discuss then what should happen," Professor Petty said sternly, as if failing wasn't an option at all. Ivy's face turned from one of relief to one of despair. She looked over at Rebecca who appeared even more dismayed than Ivy. It was she who should have received this assignment.

"All of them?" Ivy clarified.

"Is there a problem? You're the first of any sqwinch who doesn't enjoy a good read."

"No problem at all." If only the forgotten journal were in this stack. That was the only thing Ivy was interested in reading at the moment.

"That should teach all of you never to be tardy again, or you may as well not show up for my class at all! You will find that I'm very strict with rule abiding in my class. It may at times come off as being unkind, but I assure you that is not my intention. If you follow my rules and are both punctual and attentive in my class, we'll get along just fine. Class will be as pleasant as you make it.

"As you know, we will discuss in-depth the history of sketching before you are allowed to wield a porcupel in this class. My tableaus will not be wasted upon those who don't appreciate the evolution of the art over the ages. Nor those who can't be bothered to show up on time. Today's discussion will begin with the history of scrivenists' picture-perfect memory…" Professor Petty droned on. Ivy couldn't wait until they actually started sketching.

By the time Didley's squawks rang out, Ivy was ready to leave and begin Professor Petty's assignment. The stack of books was piled so high she could barely see over them. She knocked into the wall on her way out the door and almost fell down.

Rebecca was waiting for Ivy right outside the door. "Can I help you carry those?"

"No thanks, I'm fine," Ivy replied.

"I'm really sorry I got you in trouble today." Rebecca's apology was sincere. She walked beside Ivy while she struggled to carry the stack of books.

"I got myself in trouble," Ivy sighed. "As usual."

"Are you sure you don't need any help carrying those?" Rebecca asked again.

"No thanks. I've dealt with far worse."

"Is that so?"

"Unfortunately," Ivy said, thinking of flue flem.

"Okay. I don't know if it'll be of any use but you could rent yourself a notical inside the Den."

"What's a notical?" Ivy stopped in her tracks, books swaying precariously.

"Little itty-bitty creatures that love to read: they squeeze through the pages in your book, read ahead of you, and highlight the key passages—they make the letters larger and blacker with the residue on their tongues. Some are better than others and ordinarily you'd have to reserve them ahead of time, but you could see if there are any available."

"Thanks," Ivy smiled at her.

"You're welcome. And thank you."

"I actually do have a favor to ask." Ivy smiled slyly. Rebecca's head tilted, wondering what she had to say. "No more crates tomorrow? Not even one of Wheeler's!"

"Hopefully not even that kind," Rebecca smiled back as she walked off.

The books were heavy and Ivy regretted that she had been too stubborn to accept Rebecca's help. The books weighed a whopping ten pounds each, leaving vicious red imprints on her forearms. As Ivy wished that she had help, the books floated toward the ceiling like bubbles, as if paper-thin and weightless. It looked like they were on little clouds made of light. She leapt and tried to catch them, though they didn't wander far. She didn't mind not having to carry them but Professor Royal's voice rang in her head, warning students not to practice magic in the halls. *This has to be magic. But I'm not really trying to make it happen. Bewitched books, maybe?* Unfortunately, the books didn't keep in line and they floated carelessly in opposite directions, knocking into anything in their way, students included.

"Sorry," she apologized to a prince who was bumped in the shoulder.

"Oh, be careful!" Ivy yelled again. While looking back at

the prince who had been bumped, Ivy accidently knocked into the next person in front of her. Every book fell to the floor at that same instant—some open, pages bent, and others upside down.

"Oh my!" Ivy heard the voice of the student who caught her fall.

When Ivy turned around she was pleased and more than a little embarrassed to see Fyn again. "It's you!"

"Aren't we meeting in the oddest of ways?" he smiled.

"I'm so sorry."

"Here, let me help you." They exchanged smiles and bent down to pick up the books together, accidentally bumping heads. Ivy awkwardly rubbed hers while he rubbed his.

"Bending the rules, are we? Pretty sure these aren't self-flying books."

"Well, it's either bending the rules or my back."

"You shouldn't be doing magic in the school halls. Fortunately for you, I'm not much of a stickler for the rules—even though I suppose I'm supposed to be."

"I wasn't. Wait, what?"

"Can I help you carry them?"

"I can manage."

"I see that. Are you as good at making friends as you are making books fly?" he teased.

"I guess I could use the help," Ivy grinned. "Thank you."

"Where are you headed with this mountain of books anyway?"

"The Den. I'm skipping lunch."

"With all those," he gestured to her books, "I thought perhaps you were leaving the library. We have a real scrivenist on our hands. Well, you've almost made it."

"I have Professor Petty to thank for these particular books."

"You were that late," he said understandingly.

"Not by choice. I—I was helping a friend."

At the end of the hall was a large door that looked as if it had been cut out from the enormous page of an open book. It was entirely paned with beautiful leaded glass so Ivy could see most of what was inside before even stepping in. Beyond the door was the most enormous collection of books she had ever seen. The room looked busy and inviting. The lettering atop the giant page door read, *Welcome All to the Den.*

Before Ivy could step through the threshold, time went slack. The air became thick and slow and the students, whether jostling or studying, faded away. The light went dim, as if she were underwater. The library, the Den, appeared just as it had in her recurring dream from her days at the Castle Plum. And then she saw him. He was wearing a scrivenist ensemble but she still couldn't make out his face, just as it had been a thousand times before in her dream. He walked to her, holding out his hand and beckoning.

Then time snapped back into place.

"Pretty great isn't it?" By Fyn's posture and tilt of his head, Ivy could tell he was repeating himself. She couldn't say a word.

The room held more books than Ivy had ever dreamed possible. Ivy spun slowly, taking it all in. It was strange to see this familiar place full of people. Full of sqwinches, that is.

In addition to more books than Ivy could have imagined, there were dozens of ladders that extended would-be readers' reach. Some ladders swayed in the direction that hopeful readers pushed them. Ivy watched a student pull a book from the shelf. Immediately the same book reappeared in its place like it was never removed.

"Did you see that?" Ivy asked Fyn.

"See what?"

"The book…the girl just removed it from the shelf and another appeared."

"How else do you think an entire class could read the same book? That way a scrivenist doesn't have to waste time rewriting his or her work."

"And I suppose extras for those with an Olerium Stone who tend to tear out pages," Ivy muttered, remembering Colleen Holly's speed-reading confession.

"Where would you like me to put these books down? How about in back? Most of us like to study in the quiet rooms, each dedicated to a different genre or author."

"Sounds great."

Fyn walked Ivy down a quiet passage to the private study quarters. As he claimed an unoccupied study room Ivy hurried to find the librarian. She spotted a cart full of books with an ancient dwarf sitting on top of the messy pile.

"Oh, hello. I'm looking for a notical. Are you the librarian?"

"Actually, I'm the librarian." An eccentric-looking woman introduced herself as she climbed down a ladder from where she was reshelving books. "I'm Mistis. And that there is Tinsel," she added, pointing to the dwarf who was industriously checking in returned books. Tinsel swept her hands over each book, sprinkling the volume with a fine mist of sparkles. Every book she handed to Mistis was squeaky clean—brand new, really.

"Oh. Hello."

Mistis had short, curly hair and a frumpy dress. She wore spectacles on top of spectacles, so Ivy was hardly able to tell the color of her eyes.

"What did you say you were looking for?"

"I was told you might know if a notical was available."

"Rented the last one to her over there." She pointed to a sqwinch fast asleep with her nose buried in her books.

Mistis smiled and magically put the next book away, where it teetered atop one of three precarious piles. One stack was all about scrivenists of note; another was about magical management (a class in the second year); a third stack was unified only by the smell of boiled cabbage.

"Well, is there anything else like a notical? I'm kind of pressed for time."

"Hmmm…I have a turnpager right here in my cart that might assist you."

"Am I correct to assume it only turns pages?"

"You would assume correctly."

Why would someone need that? And then Ivy realized, *Of course. Colleen Holly would be first in line.*

"Well, I can turn my own pages, thanks, but if anyone returns a notical, could you let me know? I'll be in a study room all the way in the back."

"Of course, dear. No problem at all. Enjoy your reading."

"I'll try."

Fyn was waiting for Ivy inside the last room on the left, which had a distressed brass sign labeled *A.B.C.R.O.O.M.* In small letters underneath it read, "All Bugs, Critters, Rodents, Or Odd Monsters." *No wonder the room is empty*, Ivy thought. There was just enough room for one desk and a loveseat stuffed in between an entire wall covered with an unbelievable variety of books on the topics. The carpet in the room had an elaborate pattern of intersecting exoskeletons.

"This is perfect. It's so cozy and quiet, if a little creepy-crawly."

"Maybe I'll see you at the Quality Quills Club? Consider this my formal invitation. We get to ditch the porcupels and practice with retired quills. But don't tell anyone; it's a secret club with secret meetings. It's what you caught me picking up from Chidding's," Fyn said sheepishly. "Not illegal, *per se*, but not on the up-and-up either. Even though it's mostly fourth years, with your ability to fly books already, you'll fit right in."

"Like, real quills?" Ivy was intrigued.

"More or less. I imagine the real thing works better, your own quill, I mean. Great fun, though!"

"I'll think about it," Ivy smiled. "And thanks."

As soon as he left, Ivy dove into the seemingly endless pages of her first book, *Sketching Scrivenry: A Primer.*

PIES, PIES, AND MORE PIES

IVY was still marveling at the novelty of a warm room, a soft bed, a window, and privacy as she drifted off to sleep that night. Since she had been at the Halls, the setting of her recurring dream with the mysterious man had changed. Her nightly adventure narrowed to a single unfamiliar door. The only clear detail of the entry was a lock the size of a clobber coffee mug. In the dream, Ivy knew that she needed to see what was in the room behind the door, but had no way of getting in. She stood before the door feeling stumped and powerless. Then, as soon as she recognized that it was a dream, the door disappeared as if it were never there. The dreamscape went blank and Ivy woke in a state of confusion.

Where am I? she wondered anxiously, short of breath.

Her glassy eyes reflected a rainbow of color in the morning light. *Wait. Am I still dreaming?* Dozens—hundreds?—of pies were stacked precariously all around her room. Ivy closed and opened her eyes. And again. And again. *Okay, so they aren't going away.* Pecan, raspberry, mincemeat, mushroom, and lemon cream pies loomed like a mountain peak frosted in white powdery snow. How an absurd collection of pies got into her room overnight was a mystery, and already they were making her tummy grumble. The piles of pies were just a touch away from tumbling down and splattering the room with their filling.

The timepiece on the wall now read 6:55—only about a half hour to get to class. Ivy sat up, careful not to disturb the pie stacks. Thinking of the cleanup job that lay ahead of her, she mumbled, "This is going to be a long day, isn't it?" Then she smiled. "I suppose it brings some color to the room." No family portraits or art hung on the walls, so all she had were her now-empty books, her uniforms, her dress, her hairies, her porcupine, and her scaldron. *I'm becoming a bit like Hayword Nesselton.* Even though the view was stunning, looking out over the castle and to Ravenshollow beyond, it was gray that misty morning—an extreme contrast with the colorful confections that now decorated her room.

Setting her jaw, she stepped out of bed and straight into a mushy, warm dish. Judging by the color it was salmonberry pie. She rolled her eyes, wishing for a different kind of slipper. Then she felt a rough tongue lapping sloppily at her ankle. It was Humboldt, licking with all the energy of a freed scaldron, finally able to eat the delights he cooked for so long.

"At least one of us is liking the early morning surprise." Ivy blew a heavy breath, puffing out her cheeks.

Just then her door burst open. It was Damaris. But just as Ivy opened her mouth to say something, the topmost pie teetered and fell, splatting on Ivy's head. Instinctively, Ivy licked her lips—a delectable buttercream.

Damaris's laugh pealed out. "Ha! When I heard you were a scaldrony maid, of all things, I thought you'd like a reminder of home. And look!" she pointed at Humboldt, who by this point was on the bed, gobbling away. "You've brought an actual scaldron with you! How quaint."

By this time a large group of sqwinches and royals had gathered, sketching the scene and tittering. Ivy's face and hair were practically hidden by the whipped cream and speckled nuts—she was a sight. She recognized one familiar face in the group, Woodley Butterlove, who was only excited for a taste of pie and not the daily gossip like the others. What one could see of Ivy's face was bright red, and she stumbled and slipped over to shut the door. Closing out their laughter, she slumped down against the door, holding back her tears.

She whispered to herself, "I should have remained at Castle Plum. I have no business being here at the Halls!"

The hilarity outside dulled and there came a polite knock at the door.

Hesitant, Ivy opened the door just a smidgen, and a crack of light shone through.

"Yes?" she called softly.

"I heard there's a herd of pies in here? Can I come in?"

Ivy waited.

"It smells delicious from out here. Are you going to open up?"

She finally opened the door and let Fyn in. The green feather—sign of a third year—matched his eyes almost perfectly.

"Is all this pie a creative way to introduce yourself to the neighbors?"

"It was that awful Damaris."

"Why don't you let me help you clean up? We're not

supposed to perform magic in the residences, but neither was Damaris, so here we go." Fyn produced a bucket of Loshes Washes scrubbers, which set about swooping up all the pies in a flurry of bubbles.

"Don't worry! We'll leave a few pies for you and your critter to snack on. What's your favorite?"

"Blueberry. At least I think so, by the smell. I've actually never had one. Baked about a million, but never was allowed to eat a slice." Ivy ineffectually brushed her now gloopy nightgown. "Look at me. I'm a mess. I'll be the talk of the Halls today, won't I?"

"That's not always a bad thing, you know. As long as it's not trouble you're in. Sorry about Damaris, though. She has a bit of a reputation for being, er, snobbish." He looked around at the now clean room, save for a few pies. "Has your roommate not shown up yet?"

Ivy shook her head, disappointed. "No. And I doubt anyone's going to show up at this point."

"More room for you then, right?"

"I suppose. Might be nice to have someone to talk to. Well, thank you for helping me. I don't know what I'd have done."

"Throw them out the window? Force feed your scaldron?" He grinned playfully. "Really though, you might try a pop-of-gold."

"A what?"

"Pop-of-gold, a nice hot cup of it. It brings out the best in you, sort of helps you see the brilliance in yourself." With that he opened a panel at the end of Ivy's oak bed to reveal a little hidden bar, much like a tiny kitchenette, stocked with half a dozen steaming hot cups of tea in simple white china cups of the finest make. Each sat in a little cup-sized compartment labeled left to right: pop-of-gold, studysesh, dormdaze, and others.

"How wonderful!"

"Legend has it they are an old Halls of Ivy recipe, I mean before it was a school. They're brewed fresh every morning."

Ivy took a sip of the pop-of-gold—lightly sweet and herbal, it was the perfect temperature. Almost too hot to drink, but not quite. She could feel it warming her belly and a strange sense of ease came over her.

"I don't know how to thank you, Fyn."

"Well…you wouldn't mind if I took a pie or two, would you?" he asked sheepishly.

"Of course not!"

As Fyn reached for a mint meringue, Humboldt grumbled possessively.

Ivy and Fyn laughed together.

"Cheeky little dragon. I'm off! I'll let you get ready, then." His cheeks pinked slightly. And then he was gone.

As quickly as she could, Ivy readied herself and hurried through the dormitory—down the long hall cut into the rock, through the great cavernous room, and across the ancient bridge to Professor Royal's class.

o o o o

Now that they were through the introduction phase, the class Ivy was most looking forward to was Art of Ink & Memory, despite the uptight professor. It probably helped that she knew more about sketching thanks to Professor Petty's terrible as-signment. The class, now that they were getting to actually *do* something, was an enchanting mix of art, theater, and magic. Art because students practiced their sketching techniques, theater because the classroom's dramatic tableaus, and mag-ic because it exercised the photographic sqwinch memory (able to capture an image instantly) and the magical speed of their hands (able to perfectly replicate a setting in seconds).

She arrived at class just in time and out of breath.

"Well, would you look who it is?" Damaris strolled by Ivy's desk with an overly cheerful grin. "It's the pie girl."

Damaris presented her with a sketch—a close up of Ivy's pie-smeared face, clearly made in the middle of the morn-ing's humiliation.

"You should have been the tableau! Nothing behind those curtains could possibly be this funny."

Ivy was taken back by Damaris's boldness. "Do you take pleasure in humiliating people? Why would you do that?"

"I tried to arrange for something you're more accustomed to, like rats." At this, the three girls behind Damaris laughed out loud.

"Damaris, leave the poor girl alone," said Hannelore.

"Poor girl is right," Damaris smirked.

Professor Petty had entered the room. "Welcome class. Today we start the real work, honing your most basic scriven-ist skill—your ability to translate your captured memories to sketches. As we discussed yesterday, this helps you become better observers, better rememberers, and better artists. After a brief introduction, I will draw back these curtains," she gestured toward the gold and purple velvet drapes behind her, "to reveal the day's tableau. You will have 500 seconds to record it, and we'll be reducing that time over the year. After you've drawn your best effort, we will critique."

She continued speaking as she passed out small rust-colored inkwells. "Please put away whatever ink you brought. This morning's ink of choice is ruddy ink. It is the preferred ink of scrivenists for memory sketching. Royals, as usual, you won't be sketching unless you'd like to try your hand at it. But be warned: if you think this class is going to be an easy one because you won't be doing much work within it, please review the suggested reading list." Professor Petty's reading list was two or three times longer than any other professor's.

One brave sqwinch raised her hand, "Why do we use ruddy ink?"

"Of all the inks, it most fluidly links with your thoughts. It's an embossing ink; its script appears to float above the parchment. Now, ruddy ink is a combination of many things, including two portions of night mushroom, a single petal of rose-red mallow, and a sprinkle of unicorn blood.

"Ready?" She waited until each sqwinch was ready, spine in hand. Then with a swish of the professor's vibrant green quill, the curtains drew back. The tableau was an elaborate, gold vintage chandelier casting dim light over a vitrine that held an enormous brown spider. The quartz table was covered with a warm layer of white wax from the candles that still burned. There was a tangerine teapot resting on the edge of the table, which was the last detail Ivy could sketch before her professor announced time was up.

Ivy was only half satisfied with her work as she handed it over to Professor Petty.

"Not the first time you've sketched, is it?"

Ivy shook her head with a small smile.

The compliment lingered in Ivy's mind as she dawdled her way out of Professor Petty's class.

o o o o

The rest of the day passed in a blur, Ivy's mind bouncing from pie to sketching to the Selector. Mostly the Selector. That evening, Ivy sat cross-legged on her bed eating a thin slice of pie. She could see a sliver of the sun setting and thought that this day was ending a lot better than it had started. She was just thinking of getting herself a cup of dormdaze when Ivy heard someone outside fidgeting with the keyhole. She froze. Could it be Damaris trying to pull another prank on her? The rattle grew louder until the lock opened with a *thunk*.

When the door swung forward, however, it didn't reveal a person but rather a huge rack of forever-fitting dresses—all gorgeous and sparkling. The rack was forcibly shoved through the arched doorway from behind, a veritable library of dresses filling the room.

"Well, look what the cat dragged in. Rather, the mink." Ivy recognized the sarcastic, confident voice. It was Rebecca!

"You?" Ivy blurted, thrilled. "Are you my roommate?"

"Yes! Sorry it took so long. You know why, I suppose," she said, throwing her bag onto the empty bed.

Ivy's mind flashed to Rebecca locked in the cage.

"So it's true what they are saying in the Halls. Before me, you only shared your room with pie," Rebecca teased.

"Actually, I have Humboldt here," Ivy smiled. "Am I going to have a mink as a roommate now, too?"

"Ack! A dragon? Is he safe?"

Humboldt seemed to take offense and he hissed and scurried under Ivy's bed.

"You two will get used to each other. Here, give him a slice. Can I offer you any?"

"Can you?! I'm starving! First, I'll say hello to your little friend there."

Rebecca took the pie from Ivy and held it under the bed, making peace with the scaldron.

"I've known I wanted to be a scrivenist—and I have the gift—for as long as I can remember. And then that Crownerie invitation showed up at our door and all chance of turning scrivenist went out the window. But now, I can study what I want, no matter how much my mother dislikes it."

"Well, I'm glad you're here."

After Rebecca finished setting her bed with pillows that matched her sparkling bedspread, the two sat cross-legged across from one another. Ivy's hairies were, of course, asleep, so she was grateful for Rebecca's brighter ones.

"So where did you get all these dresses?" Ivy asked in awe.

"You should see my closet at home! It's a hobby of mine."

"You made all of this?" Ivy stared at the assortment of challis, lush velveteen, brocade, sheer chiffon, leather, and lace.

"Every bit of it," said Rebecca proudly. "I just hope I can fit these ones I've just brought in. I prefer the company of my sewing machine to that of the princesses nearest my castle. Speaking of which, you've met Damaris, I hear. Awful girl. To think I shared a room with her!"

"How terrible! I'd rather live in a cave than share a room with her."

"It really was, for all of the miserable days I roomed with her. What kind of pie is this anyway?"

Before Ivy could reply, Rebecca already had a mouth full. As Ivy said, "Berryluck tartlet," Rebecca accidently discovered another pie by sitting on it. Goopy purple filling soaked through her bedding. Ivy gritted her teeth.

"That girl! I'd curse her if I could. Should be called a berrybadluck tartlet!"

The two laughed and talked late into the night.

THE
UPSTAIRS CLASSROOM

WITH all the excitement, Ivy had nearly forgotten Professor Petty's assignment. She spent all her free time over the next few days in the same dark, windowless study room decorated in bug art while reading the less-than-riveting *Sketching Through the Ages*. After perusing what felt like countless pages on the topic, Ivy was both restless and sleepy.

How does Professor Petty expect anyone to read all of this in just a week? I should have minded my own business! Ivy thought angrily. *No. I couldn't have just left Rebecca where she was. Not her fault that my desk is front and center.*

Suddenly a book from the packed bookcase above fell forcefully in front of Ivy, first hitting the opposite wall and then thudding on the floor. She nearly fell out of her seat in surprise at the crash. Even the third year sqwinch next door paid Ivy's study room an unexpected visit.

"Is everything all right in here?"

"Yes. I mean, I think so," Ivy said as she picked up the book.

"Try to keep it down in here, others are trying to study! Like actually *study*."

Ivy put the book back in its place, sat down and read another line:

"Sketching is one of the oldest arts associated with scrivenry. Often overshadowed by flashier spells, potions, and mega-magic, sketching is a foundational art that enables a well-practiced scrivenist to..."

CRASH! The book jumped off the shelf again, just as loudly. The same disgruntled third year returned for a second time. She was clearly irritated—her glasses were lifted, her cheeks were flushed, and she had one hand on her wide hip. The bookish girl looked like she spent most if not all of her time in a library. "Shall I put it back for you?"

She yanked the book from Ivy's hands and climbed to reach the book's spot. She wasn't tall enough to reach it, so she shoved it where she could.

"There!" She shook off her hands like she had accomplished a great feat.

"Thanks," Ivy said, feeling slightly embarrassed, but the third year had already gone.

Ivy skipped ahead in the book and resumed reading: "...enables a well-practiced scrivenist to observe new details in their environment, envision the future, memorize critical magical basics..." Ivy couldn't focus. She had a sinking feeling that book was going to fall a third time. She lay on the small couch with Professor Petty's book open against her chest, watching the shelf. After several minutes, something hidden from view struggled to push the very same book off the shelf again, only this time from where the petulant girl had placed it. Ivy propped herself up from where she lay on the couch, half-thrilled and half-frightened.

She hurried from the room to ask Mistis to summon the closest Beast Keeper. While waiting for the Beast Keeper to arrive, she stood in the corner of the room and held tight to the flying book. It wasn't long before an elderly man with a cart full of habbitries arrived. Most of the habbitries were already occupied by an assortment of strange creatures—owls and warthogs, as well as smaller types like stray hairies, squirrels, and mud rats. Others Ivy couldn't pretend to guess. She did, however, take care to ensure that there were no minks. The Beast Keeper was a brisk, sturdy little fellow, whose long pointed nose almost reached his chin and whose ears looked like they could take off flying at any moment. His cart was full of odd contraptions, including a magnifying glass that extended and twisted to see the tiniest of spaces behind and between the books on the shelf. The Beast Keeper searched the whole room thoroughly with detective-like skill.

"There's nothing inside here, Miss, nothing but cobwebs and books. I see you have your hands on quite a few of them already."

Other students, mostly sqwinches, were curious as to what the commotion was and even the same third year next door took another prying peek. Blushing, Ivy insisted there had to be a creature loose in the room somewhere. "I know I saw something up there."

"Only dust," he shrugged.

"Well, thanks for having a look, I guess."

"You're very welcome. If anything causes you any more trouble, don't hesitate to call upon me."

Ivy felt deflated. She thought that once she got to the Halls, she would finally be in the place where she belonged, but here she was, weird stuff happening only to her. *Strange girl.* She sighed and took a good look at the book that had leapt at her, turning it over: *Thinking Outside the Walls: Creative Strategies When You Feel Stuck* by Winsome Monocle. She was intrigued by the title and even more so by the name of the author. *Winsome Monocle? W.M.? Like my note? Hmm...* She looked up and stopped the Beast Keeper on his way out the door.

"Excuse me! Could I borrow one of your hairies? I could use some extra light inside here."

"Of course," he responded. "Help yourself to one of these errant ones in the cart. You can leave them with Mistis on your way out the door after you've finished."

"Thanks so much," she said as she grabbed a white-haired hairie in a lantern off the cart.

The Beast Keeper left and Ivy ran her fingers over the spines of the books along the shelves. *Thinking Outside the Walls: Creative Strategies When You Feel Stuck* was the only book in the room not about bugs, trolls, or other creatures. Looking over at Professor Petty's books she knew she wouldn't be able to even think about reading them until she figured out what was going on with this strange book. And the mysterious whatever that was pushing it.

Who is this Winsome Monocle and what is his book doing in here? Ivy walked quietly over to the door and latched it: she didn't want anyone walking in on her while she explored.

"Is it beyond the walls where you're hiding?" Ivy spoke softly, hoping not to disturb the irritable sqwinch next door. Shifting the books around, she found nothing to the left where the third year girl had re-shelved the book. Ivy went to the third shelf up on the right, where the book had been launched originally. Pulling the books off, she couldn't believe her eyes. There was no creature to be found, but instead a latch at the back of the shelf, corroded and well hidden. Ivy grabbed the hairie and peered close for a better look. She wondered how the Beast Keeper had missed it, even with all of his fancy tools up in these same shelves.

Ivy took a breath and reached to pull the latch. As soon as she did, the shelf gave way and gently swung open, dropping books onto the floor. Ivy had to cover her mouth to prevent a squeal from ringing out. A hidden door was cut into the shelf—perfectly proportioned but tiny. It was only about twice as wide as Ivy and half as tall. She held up the hairie lantern to reveal what appeared to be a short and narrow hall beyond the door. The walls were lined with shelves stacked with books leaving not an inch to spare amongst any of them. A decrepit spiral staircase was just visible at the end of the hall, even narrower than the hall itself. A shaft of light filtered down from above the stairs.

Ivy ducked through the door and stepped tentatively onto the checkered floor, clutching tight to the hairie's lantern. Nervous as she was, she was too curious about the light to not climb the stairs. She walked forward and gripped the iron railing, looking up before taking her first step. As soon as her foot hit the step, the door between the study room and the secret hall closed loudly. Ivy jolted backward and quickly turned, heart pounding in her chest. Now the only light was from the shivering hairie and a faint glow from the top of the stairs.

"Please, keep bright for us, will you?" She patted the lantern, whispering in the hairie's ear.

It was a tall staircase, and when Ivy finally did reach the top she found another closed door. She hesitated before knocking lightly, thinking perhaps it might be a door to the second floor of the library. There was no reply at all. Ivy pushed it open slowly and entered even more cautiously than she climbed the stairs. Unlike the downstairs room, this one was bright with a dozen or so hairie lanterns.

"Hello? Is anyone here? I don't mean to intrude but I found my way here accidentally. I'm not sure how to return to the Den."

Ivy's words echoed in the empty room as she waited at the threshold. No one responded.

"Hello?" she called timidly.

Ivy gave the door a push and it swung further open. Inside was a strangely decorated room. There were hundreds of scientific specimens in jars—fascinating and repulsive. Heavy burgundy drapes hung from the three arched windows that circled the rounded room, providing stunning views of a beautiful nighttime Croswald. There was a window above the desk with a striking view of the Dark Queen's imposing, gloomy castle.

Ivy walked over to the vials and bottles that were arranged in what looked like no particular order. She could make out some labels in a strange, old-fashioned script: *Weary-Eyed Weeper*, *Salamander Serum*, and some strange creatures floating in a bright preservative. There were countless volumes and rolls of vellum.

Ivy heard a scratching noise behind the large door, the one she had come through. Peeking behind, she discovered a mysterious man sitting at a tiny desk stacked high with piles of parchment and almost-dried-out bottles of ink. His quill was moving at a speedy rate, though its feathers were frayed quite badly. He hardly noticed Ivy over his shoulder, until she cleared her throat.

"Hello?" Ivy called quietly. Still the man wrote at a manic pace. "What is all this stuff?" Ivy wondered aloud, her eyes circling the room.

"Thought I was done with this concoction here, but then again I'm never done, am I? Takes moons of tending to," the man muttered. A pool of something in between a liquid and a solid jiggled around on his table next to a box festooned with a giant padlock. The blob shimmered like a pool of quicksilver. Then in the next moment it wiggled into a metallic glob with probing tentacles. Then back to a puddle of quicksilver.

"So, you can hear me?"

"I'm a bit hard of hearing but not totally deaf," he replied, first clearing his throat like he was out of practice. His voice was croaky and gruff. "I suppose you received my letter."

"You're W. M.," Ivy concluded.

"Why, yes, I do believe I am." He finally swiveled around with a grin from ear to ear.

A short, older fellow, he had a beard, curly white hair, and broken glasses that sat at the tip of his button nose. He had a raised purple scar that came down his forehead on an angle, stopping right before his left eye. He stood, still hunched over, and wiped his dirty hands on the sides of his torn trousers. Ivy grimaced at the awful smell; she wanted to clutch her nose while staring at him. He shook her hand roughly. The handshake was rough enough that Ivy held her hand close after.

"Winsome Monocle at your service. I've been waiting a long time for this day. If you'll allow me a few moments, I'm still cultivating this unlocker, little tot. Doesn't like the light much, only wants to stay in it's unlock box, but they are useless creatures unless well trained. Been working on it for moons now."

"Um, what do you train it to do?"

"Unlock things of course! This thing can slither its way into the darkest of holes and the deepest of crevices. They like extra care, like a child, really. Back into your box, you slippery thing."

"Are you a professor?" she asked. He looked familiar. Where had she seen him?

"I'm a retired scrivenist for a wonderful family—though they've run into hard times—and an alcheturist."

"A what?"

"My specialty is the study of dangerous potions—preferably explosive, as is evidenced by the smoke and burn marks on the ceiling—and the careful documenting of the results. A bit of literature and alchemy, danger and duty, combined."

"Wait a minute, I know you, don't I? I've seen you before."

He smiled mischievously. It was the smile that did it.

"Yes, that's it! You, you were the first person I saw in the Halls. In the ballroom that night. I guess I didn't recognize you without your nightclothes. You sent the quills after me. You ran off without so much as a goodbye."

"Did they hurt you? Sorry if they did. Just so anxious to get you into the Halls. Not safe out there!"

"Scared the life out of me, to say the least."

"There, there. I suppose I got carried away; too excited to

see you. For years I have waited! But you're finally home."

At that he took her hand tenderly: in contrast to the handshake, the touch felt warm and protective. Ivy's eyes filled with tears. Despite the curious circumstances, for the first time in her whole life she *did* feel at home. She was in a strange, potion-filled room with a peculiar old man, but home nonetheless.

o   o   o   o

Despite getting lost in conversation with Winsome (and likely thanks to his ancient notical, which she borrowed), Ivy managed to finish reading the art books and passed Professors Petty's intimidating quiz, only missing two questions. When she handed in the quiz, she summoned the courage to ask Professor Petty if she had ever heard of a Winsome Monocle.

"Of course, I have. One of the finest scrivenists ever to serve—very devoted. Unfortunate appointment, however. Long dead now."

"Dead? Surely he can't be dead."

With a look of annoyance, Professor Petty snorted, "Surely yes, dead. Turned tome about, well, no one knows when exactly—fifteen, twenty years?—but he is indeed dead."

Tome? Ivy pondered.

The weeks passed, and Ivy spent every possible moment with Winsome Monocle in his "classroom" exploring potions. Far from dead, he reminded Ivy of Rimbrick and they quickly grew quite fond of each other. Truly, most of their time was spent blowing stuff up. She learned more alongside him than she did in most classes. He taught her to make ridiculous things like unpoppable bubbles and terribly useful things like wellness remedies and how to occlude the appearance of light (critical to his laboratory being kept a secret up in its tower) and everything in between.

Mid-semester, Ivy climbed the steps to Winsome's laboratory and watched him from the doorway. He hauled a box the size of four Collecti up onto the table. The box looked like it had been salvaged from a shipwreck. The metal straps that held together the splintered wood were rusted. He shook the box, ensuring that it was locked. On the front was a giant keyhole.

As she watched, the unlocker he had been working with the day they met shimmied and wiggled. Then it seemed to get agitated, blowing bubbles and sputtering.

"Oh my, oh my," Winsome said worriedly. "Now let's see here...*Rest, rest, this storm shall pass; calm yourself, peace surpass.*" As he spoke the spell, he sprinkled a vial of dust over the unlocker. A tiny pale-pink cloud exploded and covered the agitated half-creature, half-substance. In the mellow drift of pink, the quicksilver calmed and then slid in through the box's keyhole.

"Hi, Winsome," Ivy called from the doorway. "What was that noise? Everything alright?"

"Just fine. You know, just a little louie pollen and a copper cocoon. My signature way of calming any agitation, natural or otherwise."

"You would like to calm things with a blast."

"Only a small one! And with ingredients the most basic sqwinch has access to. This unlocker is not quite ready, but we are making progress! Oops, there you go," he said as he jiggled the last tentacle through. "Now, let's get to it?"

They gathered around a square table made of wrought iron and steel. Winsome dropped a troll hair and dried herbs into an already simmering concoction. They had been working on what he referred to as a Celebratease potion, which granted celebrity status to its imbiber for one star-studded hour. Both Winsome and Ivy leaned their heads over the boiling blue liquid. While waiting for the potion to set, Ivy peppered him with questions:

"Um, so, I've asked around a bit and…um…people have a hard time believing that you're still alive. Are you a ghost like the kind we have in our dining hall?"

"Nothing like them."

"Well if you're not dead, what are you?"

"I'm cursed. Well, I was. Cursed—by a dwarf, no less."

"Interesting. We just had a dwarf scenario in a glanagerie bottle. Reminded me of an old friend…wait, cursed by a dwarf? That's not very common behavior is it?" Her thoughts raced. "My friend actually, wait, you can't mean that you are part of the wandering family?"

"Yes, I was their scrivenist."

"Weren't they cursed ages ago? How old are you, Winsome?"

"A coot but not entirely that old! They were cursed seven generations ago. With that, seven scrivenists have been sent to them and upon their assignment, each fell under the curse. Each cursed royal generation matched with a scrivenist."

"So you wandered? With them? You're the seventh scrivenist."

"Oh, what's the difference," he grumbled. "Sixth or

seventh?! Who's keeping track?"

"Well, what are you doing here?"

"When the double moon disappeared sixteen years ago, the generation I was assigned to passed on and I was released from service. Came here." He rubbed his scar. Then his eyes lit up. "The potion's ready! Let's try it on that flea, shall we?"

By this time, Ivy knew that once Winsome was on a magical tear there was no distracting him, even if she still had questions. She would have to wait for the rest of the story.

THE
FORGOTTEN ROOM

A mixture of warm, mouthwatering scents—roasted carrots, creamy potatoes, and the buttery crusts of hand pies—wafted down the Halls. Ivy determined to arrive at the dining halls for supper a bit early to get a seat at the Lolly Room. Her stomach had been rumbling loudly since the start of her last class. The lesson had run late—Professor Wheeler thought one of the tiny creatures from the demonstration might have escaped, which wouldn't have been the first time. The class was rescued by Didley, who fluffed his crimson crown and let out a second "you're going late" squawk.

The sweet smell was magnified at the entrance to the Lolly Room, whose doors were open wide. Ivy stood at the doors draped in black velvet taking it all in. The floor was an elaborate pattern of small gold-and-white squares and the walls were vertically striped black-and-white: the overall effect was quite dizzying. The ceiling was a mosaic of large, overlapping parasols intertwined with strings of round lights that gave off a warm glow. As she watched, several of the glittering umbrellas let down bubbles from their tips, which floated down toward the diners. One bubble, about the size of a hard candy, burst near Ivy and she was taken aback by a tiny explosion of glitter that fluttered over her hair. Another bubble by a table of rowdy princes burst and squirted them with water. Then a third burst and let loose a merry bit of music—or what would have been merry if it was half as loud.

Ivy scanned the room and noticed Rebecca wave at her from the far corner, behind a mountain of gooseberry pies that would have towered as high as her crown if she were actually to wear it. As she walked toward her roommate, she noticed the Lolly Room Jester was proving himself to be more prankster than jester, delighting in the parasol bubbles and sending around a few of his own. He clearly took more pleasure in the devious bubbles, setting a napkin on fire here and a honk in the ear there.

The Jester was like a strange man from a carnival—someone it's best to avoid, but who still draws stares from a distance. He loved his elaborate costume and makeup but not as much as he loved to torment students, whether teasing a girl about the dullness of her dress or pointing out a pimple on a prince's nose. He always dressed in some variation of head-to-toe bright colors, stripes, winter-white face paint, and a thick ruffled collar. Ivy snuck by at the edge of the room, careful to avoid eye contact.

"Can I offer you a playing card?" he asked any student who would listen. The Jester busied himself handing out—with one glove on and one glove gone—cards from a deck. The cards were old and yellowed, some with tattered edges. Ivy had learned in the last few moons that it was best not to play. Most of the cards were titled, "You Are What You Eat!" signifying that the diner would momentarily turn into whatever they ate first, such as a pork pie. Looking for a new player (or victim), the Jester adjusted his hat. Or was it hats? It seemed as if he had jammed twelve on his head, the top one a classic jester hat with bells on each of the many prongs.

After greeting Rebecca, Ivy sat and let her mind wander. Rebecca was talking to Woodley across the way. Ivy wondered if perhaps the match for the Jester's missing harlequin glove might have been lost or cast into the Forgotten Room—it was terribly ugly, after all.

"I have to get in there somehow," Ivy murmured to herself.

"Into where?" Rebecca asked.

"The Forgotten Room," Ivy turned to Rebecca as she spoke, and a wide, mischievous grin spread across her face. "And I need your help getting in there."

Rebecca choked on a bit of pie and then spat, "What? Are you out of your mind?" She knew better than Ivy that sneaking into the Forgotten Room was impossible; only the Selector could enter, and even then not without Ivory Lucky's key. "I can't even imagine what you are thinking but I can tell you, whatever it is, it's a bad idea. I couldn't possibly! I could be expelled! You could be expelled and then where would you go? Back to the slurry and Helga? Worse yet, we could be locked inside that room and never return. No one will even remember to look for us there. No way! I won't do it and I won't let you either."

But Ivy had been gaining courage, in part thanks to her sessions with Winsome. "It wouldn't be the first time you've been stuck in a cage."

Rebecca glared at Ivy. "I won't do it. It's so dangerous! You don't know what's in there. Isn't the Forgotten Room meant to protect us from terrible things?"

"Like a journal, Rebecca? That's what we need to find out."

"What journal? You think it's just a journal they have locked in there?"

"I need to figure out why I can still remember that it happened."

"Remember that what happened?"

"The journal. The glanagerie journal. Derwin Edgar Night."

Rebecca looked at Ivy blankly, as though the sweet smell of gooseberry pie was flushing her memories away. She looked away only to reach for a second piece, perfectly golden and crisp around the edges.

"You really don't remember? Do you?"

"Am I supposed to? What did you say you were looking for? And what was that name again?" Rebecca replied with a mouthful, crispy flakes flying as she spoke. Ivy raised an eyebrow. She had to muster patience—she knew it wasn't her best friend's fault her memory was like a sieve when it came to the journal, but she almost couldn't bring herself to explain it again.

"The journal—it came with me from the glanagerie world to Croswald. Earlier this year," Ivy sighed, exasperated at having to explain this again. "I've told you this a million times. Remember, Professor Fenix dragged me to the Selector's office where she locked the journal away in the Forgotten Room with a key that only Ivory Lucky has. The Selector was sure I would forget the journal the minute they locked the door, which is why she didn't mind that I watched it all happen." Then Ivy lowered her voice to a whisper, "But I didn't, obviously! We have to find that key. We have to sneak into the Forgotten Room. We have to see what's in there."

"Is that even possible?"

"I wouldn't think so if I hadn't witnessed it all myself."

"And if this journal does exist, why is some book worth the risk?"

"Something about this man, the author, Derwin…it's like there's this little wisp of a memory waving at the corner of my mind. He was the author of three books that Rimbrick brought me and now I feel like he's calling for me. I can't explain it."

"Are you in love?"

Ivy laughed, "No, nothing like that. It's like…like he needs my help. I can't explain it. Everything inside of me can feel it. Please, Rebecca. I need your help finding that journal. There was something written in there. A note—more than a note, obsessive notes. And I saw a sketch of a large, very large stone. Something worth keeping secret."

"Well, where is it? And who wrote it?"

"Are you not listening to anything I tell you? It's locked away in the Forgotten Room!"

"What's locked away?"

"Oh, for goodness' sake!" Ivy drew in a deep breath. "I suppose I can't get mad at you. That Forgotten Room really does its job. The mention of the journal doesn't even last a second."

They were interrupted by the Jester, who was jumping side-to-side nearby like he had ants in his pants. He was thrilling only himself by playing pranks on a redheaded boy eating carrot casserole on the other side of the table. He had convinced the young sqwinch that he had food on his face, though he had none, by making the young man look upon his reflection in a charmed mirror that showed carroty mush all over his mug. The poor chap commenced to scrubbing, embarrassed, while the Jester howled with laughter. Ivy suddenly felt less hungry. And she liked the Jester even less. Perhaps it was the right time to carry on with a plan she had been concocting.

"Anyway, we've got to get into that room. I can count on you, can't I? Don't forget that I know more about the history of sketching than I ever thought possible because of you." Ivy shot a meaningful look at Rebecca.

"Ugh. You know I can't say no, especially when you put it that way. I don't believe we can even do it, but I guess they can't really expel me from scrivenist studies when my mother thinks I'm here for royal studies. Can't we just enjoy this casserole though? What is it we need from that room again?"

Ivy could barely keep from rolling her eyes. "The journal! This is how we sneak into the Forgotten Room." From her satchel, she removed a small vial with bubbling blue liquid that looked identical to the one from Winsome Monocle's shelf. It looked identical because it was: Ivy's alcheture skills had improved greatly over the last moons and the volume of her Compass Startus surpassed that of her classmates.

"I didn't know a potion could open that enormous door. Besides, how will we even get into the Selector's office? We'd need a big distraction. A huge one!"

"This is our distraction. It's a Celebratease potion. Basically, it makes whoever drinks it fake-famous for a bit. Everyone follows the drinker around and can't take their eyes off them. I was thinking we sneak this into Damaris's drink. She'll love the attention. And while the students, our professors, and even that wretched Jester are all following her, we'll head to Ivory Lucky's nook. About time someone played a joke on the Jester for once. We'll watch for Ivory Lucky to catch wind of 'The Damaris Dodley' passing through the Halls and the minute she goes to find her favorite celebrity, we enter the key room."

"Damaris will probably love that." Rebecca rolled her eyes, reluctant to give her fellow royal the pleasure.

"Well yes, but won't it be funny when the magic wears off and she sees just how uninteresting she really is?"

"And what if Damaris walks a different way? Not past Ivory Lucky?"

"The smell of this stuff is too strong. It's more pungent than anything that Jester could bubble up." Ivy flashed back to creating this potion in the upstairs room. Even with the spelled-shut windows, one of the gardeners had sniffed a whiff and tried to scale the tower to Winsome's laboratory, begging for an autograph from the flea they practiced on. "We'll take our chances."

"And what about us? Won't we be effected? We're sitting so close to her. I would never forgive myself if Damaris thought for one second that I actually liked her."

Ivy scrunched her nose at that unpleasant thought then replied, "I never wanted to see the stuff again, but I have some sorcslurry. You know, the flower that ruled my life for the first sixteen years? No enchantment can effect us if we take this tincture. There was some in my potions kit. I suspect it won't last long, but long enough to get inside the Forgotten Room."

"You're obsessed, do you know that? Can't understand why you want to get in that room."

Ivy took a big breath, trying to not show her exasperation. "It's not the room, it's what's forgotten inside. We just need the key. I barely saw it that time in the Selector's office. I wonder if I could recognize it..." That's when a memory unlocked in Ivy. "A key! Of course! The Kallegulous Key! From my school list. It couldn't make any more sense! How could I be so blind?"

"What?"

Ivy removed her Compass Collectis from her bag and turned her dial in a hurry. She flipped through the pages and recited what Mr. Munson had shared with her inside his dusty old shop.

"'Kallegulous Key, n. A small key made of soldered metal, designed to fit any lock and imbued with the power of forgetfulness. Specifically created to imprison persons or beings or objects. Whatever door is locked by a Kallegulous Key—and whatever or whomever is locked within—shall remain so until the very same key unlocks the effected door. During the term of arrest under such a key, the prisoner shall be entirely removed from the memories of those who remain outside.'"

"Am I supposed to understand that?"

Ivy pointed to the quill and ink illustration that shimmered slightly above the page. The key looked to be longer than Ivy's hand and was made of tarnished silver. The head of the key was large and flat with an intricate symmetrical webbed pattern. There were two tines, heavy and thick with little, serrated teeth at their ends, that extended from the shaft just enough to suggest the letter K.

"Listen, Rebecca. On my school list, before school even started, someone handwrote that I was in need of a Kallegulous Key. It had Mr. Munson at a loss of words. He said I was more likely to be Queen than get my hands on one of them. The Kallegulous Key is what's causing everyone to forget what is behind that huge door in the Selector's office, don't you get it? It's the key that will allow us access to the door! Right here," Ivy turned her book around, now in Rebecca's direct eyeshot. "That's what it looks like. That's the key I'm after. So are you in? Or are you out?" Ivy closed her book confidently with a clunk.

"That all depends. Will that Kallag…"

"Kallegulous."

"Right. Will that, that key be keeping us in? Locking us in that creepy room?"

"Oh, come on!" Ivy pressed, her eyes sparkling with excitement. "We won't let the key out of our sight."

"Fine! I'm not happy about this, though. Except for the part about pranking Damaris."

"Well, we can't very well walk up to the soon-to-be-famous Damaris and serve her a drink, can we? Not looking like this, at least," Ivy said, giving Rebecca a pointed look.

"All right, all right, all right." Rebecca huffed off to the restroom, blue potion in hand. Shortly after, a petite waitress Ivy hadn't seen before swept through the room straight to the table where the loudest, most ornately adorned royals sat. This waitress lowered down a ridiculous-looking drink in an enormous flute shaped glass before the royal's queen bee.

Damaris received the drink politely then brushed the colorful waitress off. The waitress dashed to Ivy, where she and Ivy both took a quick sip of sorcslurry. Rebecca was immediately changed back into her original form. Damaris took a slow sip of her potion-spiked drink and then began guzzling in a way that was completely out of character, like a drunk thirsty for her third pint. Her eyes lit up as if not even molten chocolate from the Jester's fountain could taste better. A whirling vortex of blue and golden dust consumed her as bubbles circled and popped around her.

Ivy was growing nervous that maybe Winsome wasn't as skilled as he seemed, or that she'd administered the potion incorrectly, but she was quickly set straight as every single one of her classmates turned toward Damaris. They *oohed* and *ahhed* as the royal's dress spun itself into layers of bright, sparkling gold and a bevy of hairies floated around her, acting like high-beam spotlights circling the royal's head.

Damaris stood dramatically from her seat to capture the entire room's wide eyes. Even those in the adjoining dining halls flooded in to catch a glimpse of her. As she moved away from the table, the incessant blinking of the hairie's amber lights drew everyone—including the Jester—down the hall after her. The crowd trailed every glittering step she took.

"Oh, Damaris, I can't believe it's you!"

"She touched me! Did you see it? She touched me," cried one girl as Damaris shoved her out of the way. "I'll never wash my arm! Did you see it? She touched it!"

"Just look at her! She's eating a plum—it's so amazing! I could never eat so beautifully. I don't believe my eyes!"

"She's walking! Walking!" A second year royal trembled as she pointed to Damaris.

Another tearfully sniffed, "If only I could see her yawn,

my life would be complete. Her teeth! They're probably perfectly white!"

Rebecca rolled her eyes. Ivy kicked back her chair knowing they were on borrowed time. Rebecca followed closely as they dashed down a side hallway and tucked themselves into a doorway near the Latchkey Livery. As the crowd tumbled past Ivory Lucky's door, the Locksmith stumbled out with starry eyes.

"It's Damaris Dodley," shouted the left side of her, excited as no one had ever seen her before. Even Ivory's right side was overwhelmed. "Damaris, wait! Will you tattoo your name on my arm?" She ran to catch up, both legs working in synchronicity for a change. She left her door—typically locked with four padlocks, eight skeleton keys, and one deadbolt—ajar. Ivy and Rebecca popped in, Rebecca laughing a little in surprise.

"Well, that was easy! Where did you get that magical little potion anyway?"

"Um, Winsome."

"The dead guy?"

"He's not dead. He's just old. Very old."

Ivy shut the door behind them and then took in the room. She would never have believed that a workshop and livery so full of things could be so organized. Not a spec of dust lay on any of the richly painted teal tables. The keys, and there must have been thousands, hung from custom copper hooks arranged on the walls by size.

"My goodness, how big do you think this door is?" Rebecca asked while she picked up a key nearly the size of her hand. "It's so heavy!"

"Don't touch anything. Not unless it's what we need. That

woman, at least half of her, probably knows where she last put everything."

Plastered to the walls like wallpaper were handwritten sheets of spells in shorthand. The handwriting was tidy enough that Ivy knew it must be the left hand's work. Panels of deadbolts and locks hung in a similar orderly fashion. Along the edges of the wall were trunks, large and small. Ivy could guess what was in there. "Woah. So many keys!"

At the center of the round room was a workshop table. The chair was left askew, but other than that it was the opposite of Mr. Munson's cluttered workshop. To the right lay a host of one-of-a-kind soldered tools, some for hand keying, some for casting, and some for cutting keys and locks. Ivy walked up and leafed through a journal full of ideas, sketches, and key pipedreams.

"You see anything?"

"Not yet."

A nearby wall held the most elaborate keys in the workshop. Right at chest height hung an ornate key with a margin around it, as if the other keys were giving it room. The Kallegulous Key. Rebecca spotted it first and squealed, "I'll get it!" She reached for it but her hand hit an invisible wall.

"It's spelled! I can't touch it," cried Rebecca.

Ivy ran up to the wall, biting her lip. She took a breath and extended her hand toward the key. She could feel her hand passing through the spell's thick and cool air. She closed her hand around the heavy, cold metal. She shivered. Rebecca stared, her jaw slack.

"Let's get out of here!" Leaving everything as it was, with the notable exception of the Kallegulous Key now clutched in Ivy's hand, the pair dashed to the Selector's office. Along the way they saw Damaris waltzing along through the gardens, professors and students alike falling all over themselves. It was the Selector's day at the Crownerie—a shame, as Ivy would have liked to see the regal woman look foolish. But then again, she was happy to have the office all to herself.

They pressed into the Selector's office and rushed behind her desk. Bathed in the opalescent glow with the imposing—frightening even—door in front of them, it occurred to Ivy just how dangerous this idea was. The dragons were quietly watching them, dark smoke rising ominously to the ceiling.

"Ivy, what if it doesn't work?"

"Then we'll have lost nothing. Only forgotten something."

"Look at the dragons up there, Ivy. They don't look too happy."

"We'll be fine. Quiet down."

But Rebecca magnified her fear. "And what if we're not? What if we are forgotten? We could die in there with no food. No water. Maybe we should have brought that Jester with us. We could at least count on him for food and entertainment."

"The worst entertainment."

The dragons were now fully alert and tracking the girls' movements. The one on the left even sent off a warning flame, singeing Ivy's cape. Thinking quickly, Ivy ran to where she knew her Compass Individualis was kept. She couldn't resist peeking in. The last sentence read, "On the fifth day of the second moon, Ivy Lovely sneaked into the Selector's office with a purloined key of exceptional origin and..."

Ivy slammed the book shut and said, "Let's use this as a door jam. It's going to be tough if it's mine!"

With Rebecca holding the Individualis and the entry

dragons seeping smoke lazily, Ivy pushed the key in. The dragons roared. Flames licked all around the girls. Rebecca readied herself to jam the book between the door and the wall and Ivy cranked the key with a grunt. The door opened and a rush of memories born on a magical wind swept the two inside. Ivy could feel the key stuck in the lock, yanked from her hands. The door slammed against the book with such force that the book flew out of the door jam, back onto the floor of the Selector's office. The two landed in the room, Ivy on her back and Rebecca with her generous skirt thrown over her head. Ivy immediately looked at her empty hands— no key. And the door had shut behind them!

Ivy felt panic rising up in her throat. Rushing to the door, she banged on it. The door's metal bracing was still hot from the fire. Ivy turned and slumped down on the door, drawing in deep, slow breaths. Ivy rubbed a cut and what was sure to be a giant bruise now growing on her arm.

"Am I mistaken or has the door shut behind us? Don't say it did. Please don't say it did."

"It did."

"Now what are we going to do?!" Rebecca groaned. "They'll know something's amiss the minute they see your Individualis on the floor and out of place. Or, might I add, the key in the door! We are in so much trouble. Even worse, what if we are *forgotten*?! I told you we shouldn't have done this! I knew it wouldn't work! If by some stroke of luck we are remembered, we're as good as expelled tomorrow." She was on the verge of panicking.

"I—I didn't think that would happen."

"I did! But did you listen to me? No!"

"Rebecca! Enough. We're here so we may as well make the best of it. At least my Individualis will clue them into us being here! Or I think it will, anyway. Besides, you'd rather be here than worshipping Damaris."

"True," Rebecca groaned. "But please remind me again why I listened to you?"

"Because you're as curious as I am, but for some reason you don't care to admit it."

As their eyes adjusted, they picked their way over to a clouded window almost entirely covered with ivy. They could hear nothing from the other side though Ivy knew the Damaris fiasco was continuing noisily in the gardens. Beyond the wall hairies flashed, professors sketched, girls cried, and boys swooned.

The air was still now, but there was something electric and magic-imbued about the atmosphere. In addition to great heaping piles of objects, items were recklessly strewn about the room—probably the result of the overwhelming wind to which this forbidden room was subjected.

"It's amazing to know that at this very moment, while people are fawning over Damaris, they've completely forgotten about us," Rebecca murmured.

"You could convince people to worship a rat with that potion. Wait till the magic wears off and they realize it's just Damaris Dodley they're chasing."

They rounded a corner and came to a stack of portraits. Lifting one, Ivy recognized it as the one that had been replaced by the cottage painting.

"I know this painting." She stared into the eyes of scrivenist Wanda Wetzel. Gone were the forest and the fog. The image was beautifully rendered and the sharp details made the face leap to life. It gave quite a different impression than the clouded portrait Ivy had seen in the ballroom that first night. The scrivenist's quill virtually leapt out of its painted pocket.

"Well, now we know where the portraits have gone," Rebecca remarked. "Funny it's just these six that have ended up in here. Why not other paintings?"

Then she was distracted, picking up something with extreme care. "Look at this. It's a map."

Rebecca held an extremely dusty, marked-up map to the light. Dozens of arrows pointed in every direction, causing more confusion than clarity. Ivy was struck by a spot on the map marked as slurry and circled with a note: *We hide her here.*

Ivy felt herself shaking, and chills that had nothing to do with the room's temperature raced up and down her body.

"Rebecca, this," she touched the map with a quivering finger, "this is where I grew up. You don't suppose..." Ivy looked at her friend nervously. "You don't suppose this map, whoever its owner is, you don't suppose it was me they hid, do you?"

The pair stood in silence for a moment not quite meeting each other's eyes.

Ivy broke the silence. "Oh look!" She pointed to a faint green glow from around a pile of old swords. She couldn't bring herself to think about the map and what it might mean for another second.

"Ivy, slow down!" came Rebecca's worried whisper as she headed toward the glow. "It's probably some terrible creature or spell better left forgotten!"

Ivy climbed over the mountain of mess on the floor, taking in the view from the top of the pile. The green glow emanated gently from under an old copy of *Scriven This*. Bracing herself, she slid down the pile and approached slowly. Lifting the newsprint with a sword she'd found, Ivy saw that it was just a glanagerie bottle, glowing verdantly.

"Rebecca! What do you suppose it's doing in here?"

"Haven't you read *Glanageries Gone Wrong*? No? Well, I haven't read it either—that's the royal in me. But I heard terrible, terrible things can come from a glanagerie. Unthinkable things. Don't touch it whatever you do. We are in deep enough without being swept into that bottle!"

But Ivy had already started to look around. They were right next to the largest pile in the room; it sloped up almost to the ceiling. There were some clothes and magical devices, yes, but mostly it was books. Books and books and books. Ivy picked one up. "Derwin Edgar Night," she read in soft wonder. She picked another and another, picking up speed—all the same! Every book was written by Derwin Edgar Night.

"I—I don't believe it!" Ivy stuttered, a slight smile creeping across her face. "I knew it. I knew he had to be here somewhere! Derwin! Mr. Night?!" Ivy called out, hoping he was somewhere inside. "Derwin!"

"I don't understand…" Rebecca muttered, trying to catch up with Ivy's thoughts.

"Look at this stuff! So much of it is his. I've been seeing a scrivenist in my dreams for my entire life. My memories. It has to be him. Right? It's no wonder I can't picture him fully, even in my dreams. Someone wants me to forget him; all of Croswald—except me—has forgotten him. Even my books from Rimbrick. Look at this place. All his things, here…but why? Why would they try to hide the thought of him? Who is he to them? To me? The Selector hid his journal. It wasn't the glanagerie mishap she was hiding, it was him, it was Derwin."

"How is it possible that you remember someone in the Forgotten Room?" Rebecca asked.

"I don't know." Ivy moved the books aside, one by one, searching for the journal from the glanagerie.

"More importantly, why does the Selector want the very thought of him, all his belongings, forgotten?"

Next to them stood an old, beat-up desk—perhaps its flight into the room hadn't been as lucky as Ivy's and Rebecca's. Scattered around it were an ancient-looking pair of rounded spectacles, a silver, square inkwell filigreed on all sides with beautiful, swirling arabesques, and a dozen quills or so. Could this desk belong to Derwin?

Ivy approached—it looked familiar but she knew the desk hadn't appeared in her dreams. She lifted the book that rested on top and almost dropped it—it was the journal! Just like she had found it on the ship. She fanned through the pages, committing the sketches to memory.

"Hurry up!" Rebecca called. "That's the journal, right? Let's get out of here. You have the journal you came for, so why are we not leaving?"

"Because we're locked inside. Have you forgotten that, too? Besides, I can't take it."

Rebecca looked shocked. "All of this, sneaking in, stealing keys, using magic outside of classrooms, and a little book theft has you nervous? All this way, only to leave it here?"

"If I take it, then everyone will know what I know. I can't

let anyone, except of course you, Rebecca, know what I know. If I brought this journal out I'd get more unwanted attention than if I drank Celebratease! We're getting close to finding Derwin, I think." Ivy smiled ruefully. "But then again, once we're out of here, you'll forget all this, too!"

"Lucky I have you to remind—"

With that last word, a harsh wind spiraled into the room out of nowhere, a wind of a cyclone's strength swept the journal from Ivy's hands.

"The door must be open!" Ivy hollered over the gust's intense howl, gripping her sketches.

"What do we do?" Rebecca yelled.

"Hold on!" Ivy reached for Rebecca's hands.

"I can't! My dress, it's caught!" An ancient armchair had rolled over onto Rebecca's dress, nearly crushing her. The girls' hands slipped apart and just like that Ivy went flying through the corridor, banging into walls and swirling detritus. It was as if she had a fresh pair of wings and she didn't know how to use them. Rebecca was left behind as Ivy spiraled through the air. She caught a final glimpse of Rebecca's expression—sheer terror.

BALDING HAIRIES

SUCKED violently back through the Forgotten Room's door, Ivy tumbled across the floor of the Selector's office and rolled into the shelves holding the gorgeous crowns. They shook and rattled, but thankfully stayed in place. Ivy looked up to find Fyn standing over her. He held her Individualis and the Kallegulous Key and wore a stunned expression.

"Fyn! What are you doing here?" She rubbed her new bruises.

"Really? You're asking me what *I'm* doing? I didn't just come tumbling through the Forgotten Room's door. How did you get the key?"

"How did you know I'd be here?"

"I didn't. I just…I had a feeling. Not sure why it is but sometimes I think of you and…it's as though, I don't know."

"Wait, you think of me?"

"Never mind."

"And, you didn't forget me?"

"No. I guess that's strange, isn't it? Anyway, I came in here and saw your Compass Individualis on the floor and

I guessed what had happened. Didn't want you to be forgotten! Everything about you would have been gone in that whirlwind."

Ivy bit her lip. "I guess I should be happy it was you and not the Selector. It's just…" Ivy looked painfully back at the door.

She gasped, realizing that the Celebratease must be wearing thin if Fyn was here.

"We need to get that key back to where it belongs!"

"Wait! But my friend! Rebecca—"

Suddenly the dragons above the Forgotten Room's door roared to life again. The fire they breathed heated the whole iron gate, which quickly glowed red. As they backed away, Fyn said to Ivy, "I don't know anyone named Rebecca but we'll have to come back later!"

They dashed down the hall and replaced the Kallegulous Key where Ivy had found it. A moment after they exited her room, Ivory Lucky rounded the corner, rubbing her head as if she had a massive headache.

"Scram, kids!" snarled her right side. "You'll be late for class," sniffed the left condescendingly.

All that day Ivy fretted about Rebecca. She had the sensation that her friend was safe, but it was extremely disconcerting to see Rebecca's name erased from rosters. Even her prickly porcupine vanished. Worse, Ivory Lucky hadn't left her office since the Celebratease and the Kallegulous Key was further from Ivy than ever.

What am I supposed to do now? she wondered gloomily.

○ ○ ○ ○

Rebecca's desks had entirely disappeared from every class, as if there had never been a student there at all. Even in Professor Wheeler's class Ivy found herself craning her neck to see—but the desk was gone. Ivy's heart sank into her chest just looking at the empty space. She squeezed her eyes shut. Ivy couldn't get the idea of Rebecca being locked away out of her mind.

When she opened her eyes, Professor Wheeler had laid out twelve wire-wrapped vitrines, each with a dark, twisted figure inside. The figures were perhaps the ugliest creatures that Professor Wheeler had presented in class so far and certainly less notable than, say, the mythical shorehorse. Regardless, Ivy loved the beast class and was interested in every creature she'd seen yet. These ones were hairless and their little bodies slumped despondently against the glass. Ivy got the sense that they weren't very friendly, either.

"Please open to page seventy-seven in your copy of *A Guide to Identifying the Lesser-Known Magical Creatures*," Professor Wheeler called in his characteristic booming voice. The crisp whisper of rustled textbooks followed.

As usual, the page was packed full of writing with a tiny picture at the top left to match the creatures in front of them: pint-sized with gray, cracked skin and sporadic clumps of hair. *Balding Ha*—Ivy wasn't even able to finish reading the title before the lights went out with a pop.

"I can't see!" yelled a high-pitched voice.

"Don't be alarmed," Professor Wheeler spoke reassuringly. "These creatures are lesser-known both because of their extreme rarity and also for their ability to make their surroundings dark. Makes it more challenging to catch them, you see. My research indicates that the reason for this behavior is self-protective and also vindictive. These are balding hairies—one of their primary characteristics is their pervading grouchiness at having lost their hair. No hair, no light. No light, no purpose. No purpose, no cheer. Angry little fellows, they are! Don't stick your finger too close to their mouths—always hold them from behind. They are frisky little biters and highly, highly aggressive. I request that you stay seated until I have turned the lights back on. I'll use candles for the day's lesson, as the balding hairies have a harder time turning those off."

As Professor Wheeler spoke, the few remaining strands of hair on the balding hairies' bodies twitched with desperate light, but only for a brief second.

"They hide from the light because they resent it. They are envious of it. It reminds them of what they once were. See how they occasionally spark a bit? Just like static electricity. Their little lights flicker with desperation, with anger. Once bald, their mission in life is to pluck the existing hairs from other hairies. The cause of the hairlessness is the bite of a hairless, rabid rat from Norchburry. The virus sets about denuding the hairie, and after about a moon the creature has been transformed into a shadow of itself."

He walked around, lighting candles.

"Now tell me, class. What do you see that would help you identify this creature in the wild?"

Elaina Portal raised her hand tentatively. "Um, they are bald?"

"Most obviously! Thank you. And another?"

"How they force the lights off?"

"Yes!"

"What is that on their heads? A bump?"

"Wonderful observation, Ivy. As you can imagine, making their way around in the darkness they create can be quite challenging. Goose eggs upon their heads are a near permanent feature. Now, please group yourselves into pairs for the study portion."

Ivy looked around the room and back at the door, still with hope that Rebecca might show up. That hope was extinguished when Damaris sauntered over to Ivy.

"A sqwinch, just what I was looking for. And one who makes 'wonderful observations,' no less."

"What do you want from me, Damaris?" Ivy hissed.

"To do the work, of course. I'm not picking up my porcupel. My nails are still drying. You don't mind getting your hands dirty do you, pie girl?" Damaris sneered.

Ivy bit her tongue.

"And when you take our notes, make sure to make two copies."

Ivy gritted her teeth and decided to make the best of it. *I'm not going to let her get in the way of learning about these sad little creatures.* She set to writing.

Several minutes in Damaris announced, "I'm bored." She made a dramatic yawn and tapped her fingers annoyingly on the tabletop.

"Pie girl, what do you say we make this a little more interesting?"

Ivy stopped her work to look cautiously at her partner.

"Don't worry—I'm only trying to help. Give you something exciting to write about." Damaris smiled slyly. "Professor

Wheeler said they are sad about losing their light. What if I add a little bit of fire?"

"You wouldn't. You could hurt them!"

"What do you care? They're so ugly."

But Damaris already had lit a match that appeared in her hand. "*A hairie's light should be bright; Add a little fire and sparks ignite.* Isn't that what the book says?"

"Stop, Damaris!"

But before Damaris could apply the touch of her lit match, the vitrine shattered with a crack, setting the balding hairie free unharmed. It flew out, emitting an arc of faint sparks. The angry little creature made a beeline to attack the nearest hairie lantern and set to plucking with fury. Little sparks and cries echoed in the chamber. Both Damaris and Ivy dove under the table.

"Quick! Open the window!" Professor Wheeler hollered.

Screams filled the room, which had gone dark again. With his Weatheritall Stone, Gregory Gershwin directed a spiraling rush of wind toward the direction of the window causing it to burst open, practically flying off its hinges. Professor Wheeler produced a great swirl of pink light with his quill and sent it off, whirling out the open window like a comet. The balding hairie dashed out after it; the comet only made it to the edge of the forest before the dark little creature caught it and extinguished its light in a flash. The balding hairie's escape lasted less than a firework's flare.

Professor Wheeler hurried over to Ivy's desk.

"Why did you do that, Ivy?" exclaimed Damaris, feigning surprise.

While Damaris was busy trying to pin the blame on Ivy,

Ivy wondered if she had somehow shattered the glass. The timing was just too coincidental. Damaris's spell was supposed to incinerate the creature, not set it free. Did her protective cry make way for the creature's escape before a slip of fire even touched the jar?

"Are you all right?" Professor Wheeler helped them out from beneath the table. "That's the real concern here. We can find another balding hairie—a bit of trouble, but possible—as long as you are feeling well. Don't step on that glass."

"I'm okay. No thanks to her," Ivy replied with a snippet of attitude directed at Damaris.

"Of course she's all right. She shouldn't have done that! I told her, Professor!"

"I didn't do anything!" Ivy protested, watching Professor Wheeler's eyes rest on the charred matchstick that Damaris had set on Ivy's side of the table.

"I told her not to! That lighting a match so closely," Damaris went on, quoting the textbook almost perfectly, "will cause balding hairies to rocket themselves across the room like a lovely display of fireworks. You saw it, didn't you, Professor?"

"Interesting you would know so much about balding hairies, Damaris, and yet not be well educated on other creature matters. Matters that don't involve you, perhaps. To the Selector's office, now! Both of you. Go!" he pointed. "The nerve of you two, fooling around so carelessly. Treating helpless creatures no better than you treat each other."

The girls' bickering had distilled into a cold silence by the time they were in front of the Selector. Two volumes—one notably thicker than the other—lay open on the Selector's desk. Her quill jumped side to side, making notes.

Meanwhile, Ivy couldn't help but stare at the door to the Forgotten Room. She almost forgot the squabble with Damaris.

"So, what does my Individualis say?" ventured Damaris. "I've heard they aren't always accurate, when it comes to assigning blame, that is."

"They record all," the Selector shot Ivy a meaningful look. "And all shall be held accountable."

"I didn't do it, Selector," Ivy pleaded.

"She did everything! I watched her do it! I watched her. She lit the match and—"

"Watched me is right! You wouldn't lift a finger to help with the work, but then when it came to—"

"Honestly, the two of you. You are on record. As you can clearly see, your Individuali are recording the disturbance. Professor Wheeler and I have agreed upon a consequence for both of you. Because you display an eagerness to know more about balding hairies, you are each in charge of the care and study of one for the remainder of the week." She handed them each vitrines, each with an angry, ugly little hairless hairie in it.

"Mind you, these two are Professor Wheeler's personal pets—take extra care. Your performance will be on your permanent record. That and perfect behavior from here on out is what I expect of you. If you fail to deliver in those areas, you can excuse yourself from the end of the year Ball. The decision is up to you both."

As she and Damaris made their way back to the dorms, darkness followed them in a little cloud. Hairies dimmed and fizzled out when the grumbling bald ones were carried past. Ivy smiled a little to herself—it was fitting that the atmosphere matched her mood. When they got to the bridge, Damaris held her vitrine over the edge. Looking tauntingly at Ivy, she said, "We know which of us will be a better caretaker, pie girl. I'm just not cut out for dirty work. So what will it be? You taking both or..." Damaris cast her eyes meaningfully over the edge. "I'll make it look like you pushed me."

"You know, you could have just asked. I wouldn't feel comfortable about any creature in your care anyway. You don't have to be so terrible all of the time." Ivy grabbed the creature out of her hands.

Damaris called after Ivy's retreating figure, "Hope you don't mind the dark, slurry girl!"

Ivy slammed her bedroom door behind her and threw herself on the bed. Humboldt edged over to her, careful to avoid the hissing hairies in their vitrines. He nudged her, then blew a bit of smoke over to the tea hutch.

"That's a good idea, Hum."

Ivy made herself a cup of peppitup. "Well, the joke's on that terrible princess. Little did she know that my hairies rarely light at the right time anyway. No offense, little ones!"

She followed her first cup with a second. As she drank, she tucked the balding hairies under her bed—nice and dark for them down there, and they wouldn't snuff out the candles once night came.

"Hum, I need to get Rebecca out of there, but how? I could ask Winsome for help, but I won't be able to see him till the morning. I don't want her waiting another second in there."

Across the room, Rebecca's bed was perfectly made. It looked as if no one had ever slept in it. Her entire side of the room looked unoccupied: not a hairie, nor a painting, nor the smallest personal touch to be seen. Ivy walked over and inspected her roommate's closet. It was perfectly empty. The uniform dress, trousers, and sweater that were usually lumped at the bottom of Rebecca's closet were gone as well as the gorgeous custom-made dresses on hangers—another reminder that their owner was lost in oblivion. The only noise was the hissing from the room's newest occupants under the bed. Ivy sank into the soft bedclothes and let the yammering of her thoughts overwhelm her. After some time, the peppitup tea took effect.

Hearing the balding hairies gave Ivy the sliver of an idea. *If the Selector is going to punish me for what Damaris did, I may as well make use of it and pay her office a late night visit with my new little friends. I don't even have to wait for the lights to go out, thanks to them.*

She bent over to retrieve the balding hairies but then heard a tiny tapping noise. A bright red starling perched itself on the sill outside the glass. Its yellow beak reflected the fading light as it cocked its head at her. She found it strange that this bird was requesting to come in, and so politely, but stranger things had happened.

She opened the window. "Hello, birdie."

For some reason, the appearance of a bird in the room had Humboldt in spasms. At first, Ivy was worried he was going to scorch the starling, but it soon became clear that Humboldt was excited to see the bird, shaking with happiness as if it were an old friend.

"Down, Hum! Down. Let's see here; I'm not sure if this is where you belong, birdie."

With a whoosh and a swirl of red glitter, the starling

transformed itself into Rebecca. At first, Ivy couldn't breathe. She was thrilled. Her eyes filled with tears and she blurted, "I'm so sorry, Rebecca! I can't believe you're here. I'm so glad you are all right—you are all right, aren't you? Will you ever—"

Rebecca held up a hand. "Ivy! *Ivy!* Stop. Of course I'm okay. And forgive you? For what? Allowing a windstorm to sweep you away?"

"For that and for talking you into going! It was all my idea!"

"Oh, Ivy! You couldn't talk me into anything I don't want to do. Don't you know that yet? I'm the boss of me. Just ask my mother."

"I'm so sorry. I had no idea how to get you out of there but I was just leaving to try. I didn't want to tell anyone where you were—didn't want us both to get kicked out of school. Besides, no one would even believe me! Fyn, the one person I did tell, couldn't even remember you existed. It was the strangest thing. It's like you disappeared from life. Your desk wasn't in class, your dresses, your décor, everything, wait, it's back?" Ivy glanced around the room. "When did it all come back? It disappeared like you never existed. Like I never had a roommate. I was lonely and worried and scared. I thought I was losing my mind. Strange! Look, all your things are here again. I'm so exhausted." Ivy wrung her hands.

"Slow down, Ivy! It's good to be back. A bit behind in my work, I imagine...oh, and did that spell wear off of Damaris? I don't have to deal with Damaris the celebrity, do I?"

Ivy shook her head with relief then made a face. "No, she's back to her version of normal. She had me in trouble earlier today. How did you get out of there without getting caught? You're not in trouble, are you?"

"Well, I knew the door was bound to open again soon. I got the idea when the Selector threw in another portrait. A seventh. Strange! I thought they might come back with another and they did. Only this time I was ready." She made a fluttering motion with her arms. "When I flew out, I sailed over the Selector's, Ivory Lucky's, and Fyn Greeley's heads! Not even the dragons noticed."

"Fyn?" Ivy was shocked.

"Yeah. Well, the Selector was the one opening the door, of course, through the Locksmith. Or the Lucksmith? I'm never really sure. Looked like Fyn was the one charged with hauling around those paintings. Probably just because of those big muscles.

"You know, I got the idea from a book near that desk, a book about birds. I've never been so excited to have my crown!"

"What a relief! I'm so glad you are okay!" Ivy threw her arms around Rebecca.

Laughing, Rebecca pulled away. "Gee, you were really worried, weren't you? Anyway, I stayed a starling to come back over here. I didn't want anyone catching me walking around so late at night."

"What in all of Croswald would Fyn be doing with those paintings?"

"Surely it's just what the Selector commanded. He's at her disposal, being the advisor and all."

"But why?" Ivy sat back down at the edge of her bed, confused.

Rebecca had drifted off into thought. "The Forgotten Room is even stranger at night than in the day. Things come out of hiding. I stayed tucked under that desk for most of the night. Thought I might starve. Speaking of, do you have anything to eat??"

"Er, I have some drumnuts. A whole sack of them." Ivy threw open the tea cupboard. "Of course, there's always tea."

"Anything's better than nothing, thanks. If it's good enough for a shorehorse, it's good enough for me," Rebecca continued talking with her mouth full, chomping enthusiastically on the nuts.

"Shorehorses eat drumnuts?"

"Got to do a little reading in there—not just the bird book. Shorehorses are mythical creatures. Giant, horsey things that swim."

"Professor Wheeler doesn't spend enough time on the really fascinating creatures."

"Yeah, well, probably because he knows the chances of spotting one are as slim as escaping a Forgotten Room. Drumnuts are their favorite delicacy. About the only thing that can tempt them to leave the water."

Ivy smiled—her typically pristine friend had crumbs flying everywhere.

Rebecca stretched out on her bed. "Ah. You know, you don't appreciate a mattress so much until you've spent a night on the hard floor."

"I know," Ivy whispered as she watched her friend fall asleep, shoes and uniform still on.

YOU WINSOME, YOU LOSE SOME

IVY had spent nearly seven moons with Winsome, testing concoctions and learning more about scrivenry than she ever thought possible. Their time together was so full of experiments and wild concoctions that they had little time for anything else. While Ivy was more at ease in the Halls and at home in Winsome's quarters, the questions about why she was at the Halls and the story of who she was nagged at her.

Her Compass Startus was now so large it was like carrying a pile of bricks between classes, thanks to the Hours of Discovery she dedicated to Winsome Monocole in his upstairs room. This was exactly where Ivy shuffled now, having finished the day's classes. A torrential rain hammered the windows and most students were holed up in the library or socializing in the dorms.

Winsome stood over the blazing crockhot, a specialty scaldron shaped like a caldron, which hovered above the iron table. The windowpanes rattled and shook with the wind. Even the crockhot fizzed as if it could detect the rain showers.

"Almost done with this one here! Just a few more minutes." Winsome mixed the molten contents in a constant circular motion with ease. "It's like grits! If you stop stirring it goes all clumpy on you. Nasty stuff then."

"Aren't you warm wearing all that? Your face is as red as the crockhot! It's toasty in here. Let me help you out of your coat."

"You never know what the weather's going to be like in Croswald. You've always got to be prepared! The skin of an older man is not as resilient. Though it is a bit warm."

He asked Ivy to stir for a bit as he unbuckled dozens of awkwardly placed buttons and snaps before hanging up his oversized coat on his coat rack. The rack's brass hands grabbed it, gathered it, and hung it neatly. Ivy, amused by the process, was momentarily distracted from their concoction—one, two, three clumps. *Spoiled.*

"So sorry, Winsome. I'm having an off day, I suppose. I'm only half here. I'm afraid to say my mind is in, well, other places."

"I guess we'll have to try it again tomorrow. Or perhaps we'll practice the bubble potion you've been working on?"

"I don't feel like doing much today, and probably not tomorrow, either. A few absences never hurt anyone. I feel like I need a break."

"A break from what?"

"Life."

"No need to beat yourself down, young lady. Cheer up! You're right where you need to be."

As Winsome stretched to pat Ivy on her shoulder, she caught a whiff of something foul circulating in the air. "What is that smell? Can you smell it?"

"It's that Wandering Curse Repellent. Sorry, my dear!" Winsome smelled like rank body odor. He always blamed it on the repellent, though Ivy suspected otherwise: the wide stains beneath his armpits were key evidence to the contrary.

Changing the subject she asked, "So, now what should we do?"

"There's always time for sketching, isn't there? Your favorite."

"I'm not really in the mood to be honest. Never thought I'd say that." Ivy rested her cheek in her hand, looking out the windows.

"What is bothering you, child?"

"Winsome, what do you know of the Forgotten Room?"

"There are lots of things to be forgotten."

"No, really. I mean, what's the point of it?"

"Protection, I suppose."

Ivy hardly saw anything dangerous living in there. At least, nothing more dangerous than the gust of wind that forced her out.

"Protection? Or is it a sneaky place to hide things? Even the Crownerie opens its doors to people. That door only opens to one key at one person's demand."

"So you've seen it? You've seen the door in the Selector's office? Been in trouble have you?" Winsome looked at her out of the corner of his eye.

"You could say that. I mean, I didn't mean to get in trouble. At the beginning of the year I brought a book back from a glanagerie world in Professor Fenix's class. He sort of freaked out."

"Those professors. They're not fit for strange work." He rolled his eyes even as he was selecting ingredients for the next potion.

"The Selector tossed the book—a journal, actually—into the Forgotten Room. I haven't been able to get that room out of my mind ever since."

"So there you have it—your answer. I'd say the room exists to hide things."

Winsome had picked up a strand of slurry from his stock and he now tickled the blossom under his nose, repeating himself. As though speaking to the purple flower he pondered, "It does hide things, doesn't it?"

"What I want to know is, well, I think that I'm meant to know about someone. Someone who is related to these Halls, someone whose stuff might be in the Forgotten Room."

He peered over the edge of his glasses. "And how might you know what's in the Forgotten Room?"

"I—I mean I just think it might be there," Ivy stammered.

"Have you asked your professors about it? The Selector perhaps?"

"What could I ask them? Professor Petty would probably punish me for bringing up a topic not meant to be discussed. The Selector might boot me out. I mean, if this person's meant to be forgotten, it's not part of her plan to tell me anything."

"She wouldn't dare kick you out of school," Winsome scoffed. "Those professors of yours, silly folk. All that magic you have inside of you."

"What? What magic?"

Winsome's eyes lit up in disbelief. "You mean to tell me, seven moons of studying here and you still don't know? It can't be so. What *has* the Selector been teaching you?"

"Teaching me? The Selector? Well, how *not* to get in trouble."

"For heaven's sake. She hasn't spoken to you about this person whom you seek? I could curse that woman!" Winsome flushed—the first time Ivy had seen him upset. "Well, since it's up to me, let's start with the basics. You, Ivy Lovely, are magic."

"Well, every sqwinch has a little magic in their blood— that's how we are called to be scrivenists." But Ivy remembered the first-day quill shenanigans, how she'd opened the gate, how she made her books float, and how she could remember Rebecca when no one else could.

"The magic you have in your blood is far beyond what a run-of-the-mill sqwinch could dream of. Here, this one's just about done," he added, grabbing a ladle. The luminescent mint-green liquid oozed around the glass. Ivy took a sip, and a coughing spell overcame her.

"Drink up. And really take the time to see if you feel any different after sipping a Revealavue—my latest concoction! Quite a funny feeling it'll give you! Don't worry—it's supposed to make your tummy buzz. What you're feeling isn't actually the potion but the magic in you that momentarily reveals itself."

"Ack. It tastes terrible." After guzzling the last of it, Ivy wiped her mouth clean with her wrist.

A sudden and involuntary expulsion of magic came over her. First, she sneezed snow flurries. Next, she coughed fire. A warm knot in her heart started to pulse outward.

"Make it stop! Make it stop!"

"Only you can make it stop. Take control, Ivy."

She focused on drawing steady, even breaths. The pulse gradually synced to the pattern of her heart.

"The effects wear off in a minute or two. And look,"

Winsome held up a mirror, "you can see the magic all around you." A glow illuminated Ivy. "A sort of magical aura of action."

Cut from light, little figures flitted around Ivy's head, doing things that she had done or could imagine herself doing. Laughing with Rebecca. Reading in the library. Treating Humboldt to a tart. And other things, each growing a bit more bright. Throwing open the grand doors. Pulling the memory of Rebecca from the Forgotten Room. Setting a balding hairie free.

"There's a reason I opened my door to you, Ivy Lovely. The same reason you've been hidden away for sixteen years. You are special. Here. Does this place look familiar?" He removed several detailed sketches from the depths of his desk drawers.

Ivy looked in awe. The sketches—obviously drawn by a more experienced hand than her own—were hauntingly familiar, so like the ones that she made in the moonlight on the hill above the Castle Plum. It was the exact same castle.

"How is this possible?" Ivy pulled out and unfolded her own sketch, now worn and creased and soft, from what would one day be her quill pocket. Laying them side-by-side made Ivy's mouth drop and her heart pound.

"Do you dream of this castle, too? It's the Halls, isn't it? But it looks so different now," she said in wonder.

"In a way," he replied softly. He spread more sketches on the table, obvious companions to the first. Each one was a different room or angle of the castle, more in-depth than her knowledge allowed.

"So, the Halls of Ivy was the castle in my dreams. But,

but, it's a school. When I go in my dreams, it's still a castle. And empty! I feel like I'm dreaming now. Something about this place, I can't help but feel like I'm meant to be here, you know?"

"That is because you are."

"Winsome. I'm a scaldrony maid, for goodness' sake. Scaldrony maids don't go to magic school. The stay in the shadows, unnoticed."

"Yes, you *were* a scaldrony maid. And a good one! But that's not who you are. Magic," he said with a twinkle in his eye. "That's who you are. Tell me, what's the difference between your sketches and these ones?"

"Well, yours are really beautiful and your hand is steadier —your sketches have more detail."

"No, Ivy." He brushed away her modesty and pointed to the shadowy figure in Ivy's library sketch.

"Hmmm...this man," Ivy slowed down her question. "In my dream, I mean. He's always there at a distance like he's in hiding. I can't make out his features but something in me feels like...like he's connected to me in some way. Like he needs my help. Or I need his. I don't know. Like he's, let's say, forgotten. That man I keep seeing, is he you? Locked up here? Was I meant to meet you?"

"I am certain the man you seek is Derwin Edgar Night."

"Derwin? The author of the journal I found in the glanagerie?" *The author of Rimbrick's books.* "You know him? And you can remember him?"

Winsome nodded. "A prolific author. And the artist of these very sketches. You see what he sees because you are connected. To a lesser degree, you and I are. That is why you could see this place from miles away without so much as a memory of it. Those are visions, and a person of your heritage cannot help but have them. You are capable of visions of the future, places you are meant to visit, connections to be made. Like making memories for things that haven't even taken place yet. This can be meddlesome in your mind, but these forward memories are entirely helpful if you only open yourself up and listen."

"Helpful? Winsome, I don't even know what to say. I've got—what's that expression?—a bundle of nerves, or more like a bundle of questions."

"Let's start with one."

"Okay." Ivy took a deep breath. "Who was he?"

"Derwin was a scrivenist assigned to this castle long ago."

"And what does that have to do with me?"

"I need your help finding him, Ivy. It's very, very important. You're the only one that can help. He has the answers to your questions. He also has something just for you. Something no royal, no scrivenist, no professor—and especially not the Dark Queen—is meant to have. You, and only you must have it."

"What is it? You'll tell me, won't you?"

"I wish I could remember," he said mournfully, and took a swig of a potion that he kept in his pants pocket—it smelled like eggs and old sweat. *Maybe that anti-wandering potion is real,* Ivy thought in a flash. "I remember bits and pieces, enough to know that he's missing. My ability has been restored in part since you have come, but I'm on borrowed time. Have been for going on two decades. Overdue for the Hollow Shaft."

"I don't understand anything you're saying."

"Ah, I forget you've grown up behind the slurry fields. The Hollow Shaft is a highly sacred place, past the deceptively smooth waters of Lonefellow Loch. You have to be granted permission to visit. Unless, of course, you're a scrivenist crossing over. Then they send you an invite direct." At that, he made a gesture to the stack of unopened stationery on his desk.

"Crossing over?"

He nodded.

"Are you sure you can't tell me any more about who Derwin is?"

"Gone, gone and forgotten. With memories, especially those effected by a decades-long Wandering Curse...well, you win some, you lose some, right? Finding Derwin is the win that all of Croswald needs. To set the world right."

THE
LOQUATOR MAP

o   o   o   o   o   o   o   o

S TUDENTS were instructed to arrive specially
prepared for Professor Royal's class that morning.
They were to bring their entire uniform wardrobe:
something warm for the winter, something less cumbersome
for the summer, something light for the spring, and something moderate for the fall.

Damaris arrived in her spring uniform because she knew
she looked fantastic in it. When she saw Rebecca enter she
snarled, "What, is it snowing out? You look ridiculous in that."

"I'm trying to remember a day when I didn't look ridiculous to you, Damaris." Rebecca rolled her eyes.

Those with a Weatheritall Stone—granting the ability to
alter weather, a little rain there, a light wind over there—were
going to be the day's focus. Meanwhile, all sqwinches were to
collect the output of the changing climates for their portion
of the study session: potion making. Clouds were a great base
for the classic Light as Air potion, an entry-level levitation
potion. The creation had been in the Compass Collectis for
decades now, though Woodley Butterlove had discovered on
accident that an added bit of pollen could make the levitator

sneeze uncontrollably. By the end of the class's rainy season, Woodley had chipped his bucktooth in a fit of sneezes. Like a good sqwinch, he recorded that fact as well.

Then the class found themselves standing thigh deep in clusters of pumpkin-orange leaves. Ivy's desk, whose drawers she kept wide open because burrowing was the only thing that calmed her emotionally unstable porcupine, filled with the beautiful foliage. She collected specimens of each type and took special note of the rare silvered oak leaves in her Startus. Sqwinches were in heaven, recording all the unfamiliar leaves and testing their properties with the potion ingredients that Professor Royal kept stacked neatly on the classroom shelves.

"Look at this one here!" Hayword Nesselton shouted. His crockhot was simmering and the liquid inside was turning red, then green, then puckering pink as if it couldn't make up its mind.

"Ah! Another classic. You must have used a combination of elder tree leaves and liver oil?" Professor Royal asked, looking over the pot. "Class, Hayword has made the Elixir for a Mindless Whim. Come and take a look. Damaris, please read its definition from *Perfectly Imperfect Potions*."

Damaris was annoyed to be asked to do anything, but she read out, "'Elixir for a Mindless Whim: The perfect tincture when one is seeking a scattered mind not easily pleased. For a thought unplanned, all one needs is a well-worth-it squeeze.'" She broke off, "Why would anyone ever want that?"

"It was traditionally used to relax an overtaxed brain," Professor Royal smiled.

"Not that she'd ever need that," grumbled Rebecca as she glared at Damaris.

Hayword took a sip. "Such a beautiful potion—hey, have you guys heard of reversible rain? *Reversed and then cursed, but then curses reverse.* Heard that somewhere. Sounds like reversible rain suffers from impulsiveness."

He picked up his porcupel and wrote half a letter in his Compass Startus, which typically only grew in their Creatures of the Night class. Then he dropped his porcupel and began wandering around the room, still chatting to no one in particular.

"All right. But first, I'm off to clean my creature cages. They left me hot presents earlier this morning. The creplers, they love wallowing in bowls of their own filth—it's their hunting technique, you see. Oh look! More leaves. Have you ever wondered if leaves—on second thought, maybe I'll go for a climb! Find me some beasts to bring back. My roommate moved out. Got plenty of space."

"And what are you going to climb?" Ivy laughed.

"The Evernoughts. I hear that mountain range is quite cheery in the early spring," he said, brushing aside his tawny hair. Then he inexplicably sat down and asked, "Don't you think that the scrivenist purple should be orange?"

By now the class was full of riotous laughter. It wasn't until the end of a rather intense snowball fight that Hayword came around to his usual self. The snow led to a flurry of Stop Motion potion making (two parts freshly fallen snow, one pinch of lizard scale, and two asteroid pellets).

After Didley's cry, Professor Royal approached Ivy. "I can't help but notice you were fairly quiet today, Ivy. Usually you have so much to say and contribute. It seemed that all of your observations and concoctions were a little, shall we say, off. Something bothering you?"

"Nothing really. Just thinking. But, since I'm here, I was wondering, Professor, do you ever organize school trips to the Hollow Shaft?"

"The Hollow Shaft, dear? The Den doesn't have enough reading material for you?"

"I guess I'm just really interested in history."

"And it shows in your work," Professor Royal smiled.

"Thanks. It's just, well, I like to read up on ancient scrivenists. Random things. I like random facts."

"Random facts are fun facts," Professor grinned. "I'm sorry to say that it's not until your fourth year that you'll make an official trip. Your final paper will be a biography of a selected scrivenist turned tome. I'm sure you would be prepared for a visit, even today, but can you imagine taking an entire class of first years there?"

Ivy shared a laugh with Professor Royal, picturing the snowball fight, the chipped tooth, and the dazed Hayword. And all of that was just within the last hour.

"To say nothing of how many rules you'd be breaking going on your own, I don't think that it's possible to even find it without being sent an End Letter or joining an official visit. Certain hours and certain temperatures effect one's ability to locate the Hollow Shaft. Very dangerous. The loch it sits on is spelled cold and only official vessels can resist being frozen. Plus, the Hollow Shaft only reveals itself to people on the official visitation list. I don't believe even Mr. Bingle's maps could get you there."

"Mr. Bingle?"

"Bennett Bingle—the Hall's official map dwarf. A profound scrivenist and third year professor. Odd fellow, but very, very bright."

"Thank you, Professor," Ivy nodded and headed off toward glanagerie class, letting visions of maps and lakes fill her mind.

During her Hour of Discovery, she stopped by Mr. Bingle's little library nook. Though she had never been, she instinctively knew right where it would be. The dwarf was sitting at his short, stocky desk. Behind him was a wall of cubbyholes, each containing a rolled-up map. Many others leaned side-by-side against the wall. Still more maps were stored rolled and tied by ribbon in assorted wicker baskets on the floor inside his very tiny chamber. The maps ranged from enormous to the size of Ivy's palm. Upon his desk was a yellowed globe, an untouched apple in use as a paperweight, and a magnifying glass almost as large as the dwarf himself. He stood on a stool, barely high enough to peer over the map he was studying.

"Bennett Bingle?"

"Mr. Bingle to you. What can I do for you?"

"Mr. Bingle," Ivy paused. "I hear you're the guardian of the school's maps."

"I am. Are you here to rent one?"

"Could I?"

"Do you have a library card?"

"I'm afraid I don't. I haven't taken any books out yet. Always do my reading in here."

"One moment!" He summoned his apprentice, a young scrivenist who had been tracing topography at a tiny desk in the corner of his nook. It seemed that she and Mr. Bingle might be better off if they switched desks. In a flash, the apprentice began sketching Ivy on a miniature scrap of vellum. With a whirl of her quill, she made it into a card.

Mr. Bingle handed it to Ivy. "You've got to sign just there on that line."

The words in the fine print were not clearly visible, which made Ivy a little nervous—especially after learning the preliminary documents she signed with Lionel had assigned her an Individualis. She had come to see that book as the tattletale of all tattletales.

"What does all that say?" Ivy asked.

"You know…that you don't mind having a library card, good for maps and books!" He didn't explain further. After Ivy signed it, the apprentice stamped the back with all her might and then Ivy had a brand new library card. There was a sketch of her below the Den's swirly monogram, her signature, and a tiny little compass icon.

"What's that little compass for?"

"For that map there," Bennett pointed behind him, "so we know where you are taking our materials. What kind did you need?"

"I'm not sure. You have so many."

"This one here is a Master Map. It shows all rented books inside the Den. I've even got a map to keep track of Didley! We've got to be sure he's visiting classes and not just going for a jolly fly. I've got to have all kinds you see. I even have maps for my maps.

"Let's see here," he said, while throwing a handful of rolled-up maps across his desk and unrolling one at a time in the tiny available space that remained. "This one's a map of all the lavatories in school."

Ivy laughed. "And what do you have for those, bum prints? Well, I know where they are."

"All of them?" he asked seriously, his eyeballs round like a fat toads.

Ivy shook her head.

There were literally hundreds of maps in assorted colors. Most were old, with dull, sun-bleached colors and torn edges. Mr. Bingle even had to hold some of them open with heavy items from his desk drawers, as they had been rolled-up for far too long.

"The Beast Keeper mostly uses this one here. Keeps track of most loose creatures inside the Halls. You're not looking for any creatures are you?"

"No. Not today. What about that one?"

"This one here...oh, this one is special. It's called a Loquator Map. If you'd only tell it where you want to go, it'll show you the way!"

"Loquator? Did you mean a Locator?"

He attempted a closer look with squinty eyes.

"Is that what it reads? Goodness me, and by now an entire school refers to it as the Loquator Map!"

Ivy giggled. "That one sounds perfect."

"I'm certain the Loquator Map will be familiar with wherever it is you are going! It tells you your desired area within a twenty-foot radius of what's circled. It's most accurate on less humid days. Of course, I assume you'll have an official escort with you? Might I remind you it's against school policy to leave school grounds unattended."

The map he handed Ivy already knew where she was headed. A blue circle in the middle of the Lonefellow Loch darkened before her eyes.

"There you are," Ivy muttered.

"Pardon?" Mr. Bingle asked distractedly, cleaning up.

She ignored the question. Fortunately he only cared for his maps. "How long can I have it for?"

"Two days, just two days. Then you'll have to renew the rental."

"What if I'm late with it?"

"Then you'll have to find your own way home."

THE
OLD CARRIAGE HOUSE

A T dawn, thoughts of Derwin Edgar Night flooded Ivy's mind—she could see his pile of belongings in the Forgotten Room, she could picture his silhouette from her dreams. Winsome's words came to her at that thought: "Gone, gone and forgotten." She sipped on a warm cup of studysesh.

"Forgotten by all except me," she whispered to herself.

She splashed water from her basin on her face and watched the water make little waves. By instinct, she spread her hand and calmed the water so that it was as glassy as a lake. She focused on the water: a modest beam of light made the air shimmer ever so slightly and the water began to swirl, just as she had intended. She recognized that feeling. It was the same sensation as when she unlocked the school gate that first night. She was partly in disbelief, partly in awe, and partly relieved. Winsome was right. She smoothed the water again. It was as glassy as Lonefellow Loch. She lit a tiny candle, feeling grateful that the balding hairies were back with Professor Wheeler, and pulled down her Collectis, spinning the dial and opening to the entry for the Hollow Shaft, intrigued by the place.

The Hollow Shaft, n. A repository for the knowledge and wisdom of exceptional scrivenists. Each scrivenist's entire life story and lessons are bound into a manuscript custom built to reflect the individual's work and personality. The purpose of the Hollow Shaft is to protect scrivenists' knowledge in perpetuity, especially in the event that a force of evil threatens to destroy it. Located north of the Bitter Forest in the center of a spelled lake, the Hollow Shaft is an important destination for scholars and those wishing to harvest wisdom...

She scanned ahead:

Not open to the public, the waiting list for an invitation to study is currently seventeen moons long. Since its inception it has been guarded by the waters and creatures of Lonefellow Loch, which is in itself a spell (see Lonefellow Loch, always winter and always dark). When a scrivenist has reached completion in his or her life of service and is ready to turn tome, an invitation...

A thought dawned on her. Perhaps Derwin was so difficult to find because he had passed on. If she could get there, she could find Derwin's tome! He'd be certain to have something to say about the Forgotten Room, what with all his things in there. She had to find the Hollow Shaft.

Ivy opened her closet, threw aside her uniform, and quietly pulled on one of the few items of clothing that she still had with her from her Castle Plum days: her snuggly, oversized sweater that had kept her warm in her larder bedroom. She grabbed her satchel and snuck across the ancient, creaky herringbone floors, hoping not to disturb Rebecca. She peeked out from behind her bedroom door down the dark, silent hallway. She may have been quiet, but Humboldt's snores echoed, shaking the crystals on the sconces of the corridor. Just as her foot was out the door her hairies woke with sudden curiosity and uncharacteristic brightness.

"Of all the times to work properly! For once, I'd be grateful for the dark," Ivy whispered. The three flashed in weak protest for a brief second before their light fizzled away. Meanwhile, Humboldt's snore grew and Rebecca woke.

"Where are you going?"

"I'm, er, I have to use the restroom."

As Ivy reached the end of the hall, a light flared behind her. Ivy quickened her pace. The side entrance of the dormitories let out to a stone stairway cut into the rock and down to the frosted forest. Even though it was spring, the Bitter Forest remained, as it always did, winter-white. Only once she was in the deep shadows of the pines did she exhale the long breath she didn't know she'd been holding. It rose as steam into the cold air.

Ivy hadn't ventured off on her own since the very first day of school. She wished Rebecca could be there with her, though she wouldn't dare put her through an adventure like their last one. She swallowed her nervousness and pressed on, the lilac chiffon of her nightgown dragging along the sooty, frozen ground. The forest overhead made the morning even darker, the pine needles above her head a thick canopy. It was too dark to spot even her own shadow. Dozens of dilly owls perched on branches, their white wings little bright spots against the trees. Ivy inhaled the forest's strong earthy smell, a combination of frigid underbrush and frozen pine needles. Snow floated from branches through the blustery air and Ivy began running: she didn't want to miss her Minor Magic class and she needed to stay warm. She didn't know how long she ran—she was surprised that the morning remained so dark. She stopped once or twice to check her map.

Finally, Ivy slowed as the trees parted to reveal a clearing, which led to a rough sand and snow beach that eased its way into beautiful blue water. The Loquator told her this was the edge of Lonefellow Loch. *The Hollow Shaft is near!* Ivy thought with glee. Then with some dismay, she realized that she had no way of traversing the almost-freezing water, and no way of finding the Hollow Shaft. She certainly wasn't going for a swim. Winded, she sat on a big gray boulder to look out over the beautiful water, forgetting the cold for now.

The glossy water—spelled cold—was gray and reflective as a mirror. A thick bank of fog slowly encroached from the far side of the lake toward Ivy's shore. She opened her bag half-heartedly, and then smiled to herself when she saw yesterday's drumnuts. Though shorehorses were only mythical, Ivy couldn't help but let a wish form in her mind as she bent to the water and tossed drumnuts in one by one, flicking her wrist and letting them lightly skid across the surface. She sighed, imagining a shorehorse ascending from the deep depths of the dark lake. It didn't seem much less likely than a scaldrony maid discovering her own, blood-born magic after all. The sky above now had a hint of lavender, reminding Ivy of her time in the slurry fields and of Rimbrick. How she longed to ask Rimbrick for advice, to see him, to share her stories, now that she had some really good ones.

Ivy was startled to hear a groggy voice from over her shoulder. "What are you doing out at this hour?"

Ivy nearly fell off the rock. Fyn's shadowy figure emerged from the murkiness of the trees. He had a look of curiosity on his okay-maybe-he's-handsome face, head cocked to the side.

"Are you following me?" Ivy accused, less annoyed than she would be if she had the energy for it.

"I wouldn't be doing my job if I hadn't come looking for you. You're not hard to track, anyway; you're about as quiet as that scaldron of yours. Are you determined to get expelled?"

Fyn edged closer and Ivy looked back out over the lake.

"Well, what are you doing out here? You shouldn't leave the school grounds unless you plan on not coming back. And at such an hour? Shouldn't you be sleeping?"

"I couldn't sleep."

Noticing the bag of drumnuts on the ground, Fyn said, "Breaking two rules. First years aren't supposed to leave school grounds, and secondly, they're not supposed to be fishing for something they shouldn't be fishing for in a place they shouldn't be in the first place."

"I wasn't fishing! I'm, I'm looking for the Hollow Shaft, not a shorehorse," Ivy admitted the half-truth. She was *looking* for the Hollow Shaft, *hoping* to greet a shorehorse.

"The Hollow Shaft?" Fyn laughed. "You're a bit early for that, aren't you? Not planning on dying anytime soon? Or maybe you thought your life would end when the Selector found out you've been outside of school without a chaperone. What do you want with the scrivenists' dying place?"

Ivy was spared from having to answer. A small boat—powder blue with silver edging and two seats—was drifting toward them. No waves pushed it along; only the bank of fog seemed to propel it. The boat cut silently through the still water leaving the tiniest wake that rippled across the Loch's smooth surface. It was almost camouflaged by the mist and the water, its color a precise match to the waterline at the horizon. A single, free-floating hairie propelled the vessel; entirely silver, the hairie's light shone like moonlight as she sat at the tip of the bow on an inverted spiral that hooked back toward the boat like a beckoning finger. Fyn and Ivy sat hushed. As the boat slid onto the beach, its hull crunching softly on the sand, they were both overcome by an urge to climb aboard. Fyn helped Ivy and her satchel into the boat and they sat side-by-side on the small bench.

With the small vessel's arrival the approaching fog enclosed the pair. Ivy was grateful for the lunar-like light of the hairie. It helped her notice something stored beneath each bench. *Of all things, books!* She read the titles:

Parting Potions: A Carefree Guide to Traveling Lightly
Turning Tome: The Transition
Rare Remedies: Should You Change Your Mind

"My goodness, even on our way out we scrivenists find new study material. As in life, so in death, I suppose," Fyn noted.

"All right, well, since you are on this little dinghy too, I suppose that means you'll keep quiet about all this."

"You mean your breaking the Code of Conduct? Remember, I'm no stickler for rules. Plus, I'm just trying to get you back to the Halls safely," Fyn grinned, clearly as eager for adventure as Ivy. The hairie smiled at the pair as the boat moved out over the gray water noiselessly. Ivy unfolded the Loquator again: it showed the Hollow Shaft in the lake's center, a small dot floating in the middle of the water—no island, nothing.

"So why are you looking for the Hollow Shaft anyway? You do know you have to be on the list to get in, don't you? You have to sign up a few years in advance."

"You have almost as many questions as I do."

"Like what?"

"Like, what were you doing removing paintings from the walls and delivering them to the Selector the other night?"

Fyn paused, turning away before answering. "I don't know what you're talking about."

"Maybe I should remind you? You, the Selector, and Ivory Lucky locked away paintings inside the Forgotten Room. What were you doing there?"

"How can you remember the paintings?"

"Don't you?"

"Only that there were paintings. Can't remember much about them."

"Is the Selector making you do it?"

"I'm supposed to report strange occurrences to the Selector. The portraits have been changing ever since school started."

"What do you mean changing?"

"It's like the subjects of the paintings have come out of hiding. The mist is gone, and they're coming closer. They're back to being normal portraits, where you can actually see their faces. The Selector's real weird about it."

The lake appeared to have turned into a galaxy made of fog and darkness, punctured by the pinprick lights of stars. The boat guided them for what seemed like a long time, but Ivy couldn't really tell. She was overcome by a sense that the silence was sacred, that if she or Fyn spoke any louder they would be thrust from this dream-like boat.

"I might have something in here to brighten the journey."

Fyn reached into his bag and pulled out a cloudy glass cylinder. He gently uncorked it and tapped the side: out came delicate brum-sized butterflies, glowing warm as candles. They were mesmerizing, flitting around and above the boat, highlighting the boat's small wake and the dark ominous water below.

"They're remarkable. What are they called?"

"Flutterlights. They like others to appreciate their beauty so they stay close."

Fyn held his finger out and one landed on it, opening its gilded wings. Ivy did the same and a second landed near her fingernail. Looking closely, Ivy could see veins running through its wings. They glowed a vibrant orange.

The Lonefellow Loch narrowed and Ivy could now see that the beach they departed from was the exception: most of the shoreline abutted the forest, making the waterline swampy and wooded. She could spy silhouettes of castles in the distance and she wondered who lived in them.

Then at the center of the water rose a dark shadow, slowly growing larger. Ivy gripped Fyn's arm.

"What is that?" she whispered with a twinge of fear tightening her voice.

As the shadow grew, its sound carried to them: shouts of enjoyment, loud arguing, laughter, and energetic conversation.

"It's not the Hollow Shaft, is it?"

"It can't be. It's too noisy. The only talking at the Hollow Shaft is the tomes, though of course they speak through the Translator."

"You've been?"

"Er, only read about it."

The shadow was now more clearly emerging from the fog. It was not at all what Ivy had expected to see in the middle of a lake. A grand dame of a mansion had been upended and somehow hovered upside down over the water. The mansion's weathervane just touched the lake's surface, and a widow's walk perched just above it. Each of the floors, ascending away from the water, grew more somber and grand, stretching past where Ivy could see in the hairie's light. The lower floors (though they would have been the top floors in any other situation) were not somber at all, however. The shingled exterior barely contained the jubilant raucousness.

"What, is someone celebrating something?"

"This must be the Old Carriage House. It's supposed to be a tavern of sorts. You know, for one last hurrah for scrivenists on their way to the Hollow Shaft."

"What's it like in there?" Ivy asked as they drew closer.

"Don't know. Never been in. I did try, though. Last year." At this, Fyn's eyes got distant. "But no one's allowed even close to the Old Carriage House nor the Hollow Shaft. Not unless you are on the list or an official school trip. Which we are not, Ivy."

"What time is it anyway?"

"Time doesn't matter when you've only got a few more hours left to live."

As Fyn spoke the boat drew near enough for Ivy to touch the weathervane, which she did almost instinctively. At her touch a ladder was extended down into their boat, latching into divots in the vessel that Ivy hadn't noticed before. She grabbed the ladder's rung and started climbing.

As Ivy stood Fyn protested, "You're not going in there, are you?"

"Why not?"

"We will stick out like sore thumbs! They're old and dressed in their finest, ready to cross over for all time. I'm dressed in yesterday's uniform and you," Fyn blushed, "you are ready for bed! And more than that, we aren't on the list and what if we get thrown out? Or reported to a professor?"

Ivy set her jaw. "Fyn, I appreciate you following me, but as you can see, I'm safe and you can go back and report me if you like. But you invited yourself along. I'm going inside. Besides, I've never been to a party," she smiled, turning away.

"Ivy!" Fyn called after her. But after a moment, he followed.

They walked up narrow stairs through a dark, musty attic, pulled a hatch and climbed up into the light. Somehow, the room they entered was right side up—all as it should be except for the books strewn across the ceiling. The walls were covered in sketches of varying vintages. It was a drawing room that had been adapted into a tavern with only ancient scrivenists for customers. As they crossed the threshold an ominous hush fell over the crowded room, but it was shortly shattered by a roar of laughter.

A shrunken, completely bald man squealed, "They get younger and younger every year!" He slapped his knee and nearly spilled his pint.

Fyn ushered Ivy up the stairs to the next level. Portraits hung on the walls of the stairwell, busts of scrivenists painted in black-and-white except for the subjects' vibrant quills. As Ivy passed by, she saw the painted quills quivering at the sight of her, some vibrating more than others inside their pockets. Fyn noticed, too.

"Are you going to take these with you?" Ivy teased in a whisper. "Add it to your collection inside that horrible room?"

"Very funny."

The next room was both a bindery and showroom for books. A small handful of elders browsed the selection, asking questions and feeling books—their heft, the sheen of the paper, and the strength of the spine. Some books seemed not large enough to hold a collection of poems and others were so powerful and massive they required several buckles to hold them together.

"They're picking out their editions," Fyn said in a hushed voice behind Ivy. "They'll turn tome soon. These are the books into which the lives of the most notable scrivenists— every lesson, mood, spell, and episode—will be gathered together for all time."

Ivy sat on a stool to take in the strangest shopping experience she'd ever seen. The older men and women seemed content, happy to do this errand and intent on selecting the right book. The dim light of elderly hairies illuminated the looks of peace and accomplishment on their faces.

On a stool near Ivy and Fyn sat a woman in a cloche hat with a black veil and quivering coque tail feathers. She seemed entirely uninterested in the books, and even with her back to them, Ivy could tell that she kept checking her timepiece. As they watched, a fellow entered and sat down next to the woman. The collar on his immensely oversized jacket was buttoned to his chin and stood stiff around his neck. He wore a wide brimmed felt hat that was pulled down tight.

"A good place to meet, Selector," he said in a hushed tone.

Selector! Ivy nearly fell off her stool. She silenced Fyn with a finger to her lip. Now she could see the woman's signature braid peeking out from her cape. The Selector nodded her head with the air of a woman who just simply had better things to think about.

"Yes, well, by now if anyone were to overhear us, they won't live long enough to share the dreadful news."

Please don't turn around. Please don't turn around.

The Selector whispered, "She's coming along well, you can see that in her Individualis, but the curse, it's so strong." Ivy leaned in, focusing her magic on eavesdropping.

"And yet the school year is nearly over and you haven't helped her? How can I trust anything you tell me?"

"I just don't think she's ready. Looking at her Individualis—she's so impulsive. Clever, but what she will face..." the Selector shuddered. "But I can feel it. I swear on my skill and quill. It's going to happen and it's going to happen soon. She's coming for her."

"And what should we do? Lock the girl away? Just like *him*?" he said disapprovingly.

This was met with silence.

"Selector, you cannot keep that man locked up any longer!"

"The time is not yet right. Even if I release him, he's still trapped."

"If you don't, I will! I promise you."

With that, Ivy leaned an inch too far. Her elbow knocked over a display of books, which fell to the floor in a series of thumps.

"Let's go!" Fyn grabbed Ivy and hurried her out of the bindery and downstairs into the bar before the Selector and her conspirator could get a good look at them.

"Did you hear that, Fyn?"

"They were talking about someone. A student? Didn't sound good."

In a fervent whisper she said, "This is going to sound crazy. The one who is in trouble, I can't help but feel that it's me."

"Don't be silly, Ivy."

"Who do you think that man was? That man with the Selector?"

"I don't know. All I care about is getting you back to the Halls safely."

"Do you suppose they'll know we were here?"

"I'm certain if we're not back soon they will. We've got to leave now," Fyn said firmly.

Ivy couldn't move. She watched glassy-eyed as the female barkeep yanked the tap to fill an enormous pewter tankard with an old man's heady brew. The barkeep was young. Ivy heard the customer address her as Coton. Coton had a slender figure, pupils as green as emeralds, and carmine-red hair.

"We're closing early. Drink up," she told her customer hastily, tucking mugs and tankards in cupboards below her rough wood bar. She worked quickly, putting odd contraptions away and removing half-full, lurid tinctures from the counter. She placed them securely above in unique pulley systems strung from the beamed ceiling. Turning to wipe the counter around Ivy and Fyn hastily, Ivy noticed a look of growing anxiety on her olive face. "Up and out. Don't want to have to lock you up with the brews!"

"Why? What's happening?"

"The Queen. She's near," Coton whispered. "She's not meant to approach the Old Carriage House, it's part of the Selector's treaty."

Ivy looked out toward the glass window. Like the goblets and antique crystal hanging from the low-slung ceiling, the window's red-tinted glass both obscured the outside and illuminated it. At the distant shore Ivy could just make out shadowy, giant torchbearers.

"Is that the Cloaked Brood?" asked Ivy in a tiny voice. No one replied.

"I suppose that's our cue to head up to the cellar," chirped a tiny, ancient man, straightening his quill in its pocket. "Cheerio!"

On the whole, the scrivenists appeared largely unexcited by the Cloaked Brood's presence and Coton's rush. They leisurely made their way out of the bar and up the stairs. In contrast, Ivy could feel the color drain out of her face at the thought of the Cloaked Brood and Fyn could feel his heart pounding all the way down in his fingertips.

"I guess when you are about to turn tome, nothing's that

scary," Ivy whispered, trying to stuff down her own fear. "What's in the cellar?"

"Not sure exactly, no one is. Some kind of transport to the Hollow Shaft. The Hollow Shaft only appears momentarily and heading to the bottom floor is the only sure way to get in. But Ivy, we've got to get out of here!"

The racket of scrivenists hurrying to leave was penetrating. Coton shuffled Ivy and Fyn out of the main room with one final push of her broom, slamming the door behind them. They ran down the stairs against the current of scrivenists headed to the upstairs cellar. When they reached the weathervane trapdoor, they jumped straight down into their little boat.

THE
HOLLOW SHAFT

A BOARD their small dinghy, the water was as glassy as ever as if the lake itself were unconcerned by the Cloaked Brood's appearance. Ivy unfolded the map.

"Ivy, you can't be serious! You heard Coton yourself. The Queen is near, which means we should get out of here. We're going back to the Halls! No Hollow Shaft for you today."

"I haven't come this far—"

"The Cloaked Brood is on the shore, for heaven's sake! This is no longer about getting to class on time!"

"Fyn. There is information that I'm sure I can only get from a tome. I have to go on. If you want, you can swim back," she said, only half joking.

Fyn sighed. He looked back toward the Cloaked Brood, their lanterns flickering in the distance. "Fine. What does that map say?"

Ivy smiled with relief and turned the map toward him. Its compass spun. "It's pointing to the center of the Loch." She squinted into the fog. "But I don't see a thing."

"You'll have no problem seeing it when we get there. Rather, when it gets here, though I still don't think we can enter. I'm not sure what this is all about, Ivy, but I can say a morning jaunt with you isn't boring." He flashed a grin and Ivy was grateful for his sense of humor. "Let's go. But if the Hollow Shaft doesn't emerge in ten minutes, or if the Cloaked Brood comes any nearer, we are going back to shore—got it?" Fyn spoke to Ivy and the hairie. The little creature brightened its glow in response and Ivy nodded eagerly.

The sky was three shades darker than anything they had traveled through that morning. The hairie flew ahead by several boat lengths, illuminating the water.

Then the hairie stopped. So did the boat.

"It's waiting for something," Ivy whispered, sure of herself.

They waited. Ivy chose to focus on the hairie and the water but Fyn couldn't help sending furtive looks toward shore. All at once there was a cataclysmic sucking sound and a dark cliff began to emerge from the deep waters. Its jagged crest, topped with a tuft of greenery, speared the surface first. The rock face spiraled up higher and higher. The thickest part, at the top, was about the diameter of the ballroom. Fyn and Ivy watched with their mouths agape.

Once it stopped spiraling, the top now impossible to spot, Ivy saw that the bottom was extremely narrow, almost narrow enough for Fyn to wrap his arms around. With a dainty splash, a dock popped up like a cork. The hairie moved forward, bringing them closer to a water-stained, antique door at the base of the Hollow Shaft.

"Have you ever seen anything like it in your entire life? I'll bet from the top you could reach the stars," Ivy said, mesmerized.

"If you're daring enough to be that high up."

"Not daring. Only thinking how amazing it must be all the way up there. To see everything, all of Croswald. Of course, if I wasn't badly afraid of heights."

"A bad time for dreaming, I'd say!"

"It doesn't matter, not today anyway. Our business is inside."

The hairie pressed its small hands against the door and pushed it open with a wet creak to reveal a dark chamber. Ivy scrambled from the boat to the dock, leaving her bag on the boat's bench.

"You leaving these behind?" Fyn said, holding the bag of drumnuts in the air. "You'll get hungry for breakfast eventually!"

"Leave them there," she replied distractedly.

As they walked through the rock-walled tunnel on the other side of the door, it shrank until it was barely wide enough for Fyn to walk through. Ivy was struck with a sense of both welcome and unwelcome: an easily opened door, tumultuous water, access to the Old Carriage House, a foreboding Brood. She shook off the feeling. Fyn put a reassuring hand on her back.

A small door at the end of the tunnel opened up to a room that had more in common with the bottom of a well than an entrance, which is what it was. The chamber was larger than appeared possible from the outside and it was silent except for an echoing drip that Ivy couldn't locate. Everything in the cavernous room was hewn from a gray stone, from the hexagonal tiles on the floor to the rough cut stone of the Hollow Shaft's walls. The gray tone was without warmth, like ashes. Strange glowing embers flitted about the dark air of the room, which seemed to not have a ceiling. The hollow chamber extended up toward a pinprick of light at the very top where the Hollow Shaft must have scraped the sky. A ray of daylight shone down like a blue-beamed spotlight.

A small clearing of a throat echoed behind them. They spun around to find a desk, hosting a fanciful display of old pocket watches showing different times. A woman behind the desk motioned them toward her. Fyn and Ivy looked at each other. The woman's hair was a balloon-sized nest—a literal nest with a small bird perched on top. Her eyelids were painted the exact shade of the two teal eggs that rested under the lark in her hair.

"Do you have an appointment?" she asked without introduction.

Before they could answer, an elevator they hadn't noticed deposited a scrivenist in the room with a shrill *ding*. Again, Ivy and Fyn turned in surprise.

"I'm LaVera Wand. Here to turn tome," she said in a tiny voice that matched her figure. She held an enormous leather book with gilded pages, selected at the Old Carriage House.

"Ah yes, LaVera, I've been expecting you. The taming of the Von Gund Dragon, was it? Fine work there. Also, deciphering the hairie language? Tell me, does it have its origins in the ancient troll language?"

She nodded, a little proud, but all business. Without hesitation, the spry scrivenist stepped directly into the shaft of light with her book and turned to face Ivy, Fyn, and the receptionist.

Clenching the book tightly, LaVera's body began to tingle

and sparkle, as if made from jewels. The scent of ink filled the air. The book she held in her hands remained solid, even as her figure disappeared into a rainbow of light. The book, hovering, now embodied the scrivenist's glitter. Then it floated safely into the receptionist's welcoming hands. She held it, admiring the book's form: one of the thickest Ivy had ever seen, practically bursting at the seams. It still sparkled as she sent it back into the shaft of light where it traveled up, up, up, disappearing through the open ceiling.

The bird-coiffed woman turned to Ivy and Fyn who stood staring at the spot where LaVera had disappeared. Subconsciously, they both inched away.

"Now, that tiny little voice will be hilarious coming out of the Tome Translator!" She chuckled. "As I was asking, do you have an appointment?"

"Um, no but we should be on the list," Ivy lied, looking at Fyn guiltily.

"Name, please?"

"Um, Ivy Lovely. And this here, this is Fyn."

"Fyn Greeley," he inserted and nodded his head.

"Yes. Very good."

Ivy and Fyn glanced at each other, surprised the woman had been expecting their arrival. She led them to the bronze elevator door set into the rock wall. The lark flew from her hair and pressed a gigantic green button that let out a loud *ding*, followed by a *rattle* and *whoosh* that could be heard one hundred flights up. While the elevator came, the woman unrolled a map so large that it covered over Ivy's and Fyn's feet on the stone floor. Ivy saw at a glance that they weren't at the bottom of the Hollow Shaft; there were still several floors below.

"This is where you are. Your allotted two hours begins the moment you step foot in the elevator, which will deliver you precisely where you need to go and only there. Here's your timepiece. The Hollow Shaft contains 179 floors, 989,322 tomes, and only one Norman Wrinkles. Of course, keep your talking to a minimum."

"Norman Wrinkles, that's the fellow I told you about," Fyn murmured to Ivy. "He translates the tomes."

"A minimum," she reiterated. "Any questions?" The elevator dinged behind them, announcing its arrival.

"Um, yeah. Derwin Edgar Night. Looking for his tome?"

"Never heard of the man. Good day."

"Wait!" Ivy wedged her foot in the elevator door, preventing it from closing. "One more question. What if we run out of time and we're still upstairs? What if a scrivenist hasn't finished sharing his story?"

"Best be good at swimming. Off with you!"

The elevator groaned and shuddered as it began its ascent. In any other place, this ancient elevator would have been long abandoned. Here, it looked well used.

"So who's supposed to give us that information you're after?" Fyn asked.

"Derwin. Derwin Edgar Night," Ivy repeated.

"Never heard of him."

Ivy pointed to her map. "These floors, the ones marked confidential. I wonder what's there?"

"That's the insignia of queens."

"Ugh, I'm not sure I want to know more about her."

"Not the Dark Queen, the queenly line. Isabella, and all that."

"What do you mean, Fyn?"

"Isabella was the last in Croswald's original line of queens."

"Original?"

The elevator had steadily been gaining speed as it shot up, up, up. By the time they reached the 70th floor, Ivy's face had taken on a green hue. She grabbed Fyn's arm, fearful that yesterday's dinner was soon about to make a reappearance. As they shot upwards, rattling as they journeyed, each numbered button lit up as a reminder of just how high they were headed. As lights flashed the bell dinged louder, each note growing shriller. Ivy closed her eyes and held Fyn with one arm and a brass rail with her other.

"Still want to see the stars?" Fyn teased.

Finally, with an ear-piercing *screech* and a *ding*, they arrived on floor 122. Fyn opened the cage-like door and they stepped into a rounded room. It looked like a combination of library and ballroom. The beam of light was here, too, stretching from the center of the floor to the ceiling. It was wider and almost vibrating. While still blue, Ivy could swear she saw a rainbow shimmer running through it. But it was only visible from the corner of her eye; the shimmer disappeared when she tried to look directly at it.

In the middle of the room near the shaft of light was an open circle, like a dance floor. Rows of floor-to-ceiling walnut bookcases, filling every square inch of the room, radiated out from the dance floor like a sundial. A giant nautical wheel marked the end of each bookcase near the light. The rows were crammed so close together that shelves pressed into each other. Ivy couldn't imagine anyone squeezing a book off a shelf, let alone finding the book they needed. And in time.

Her heart sank.

A giant of a man was cranking one of the wheels. It was the size of a carriage wheel but looked tiny in his hands. As he spun the wheel, the shelf moved to the side, groaning as it pressed into the others and making room enough for the giant to hobble down the aisle. When he turned toward Fyn and Ivy, who were standing at the edge of the circular floor, they got a good look at him. His bald head nearly rubbed the ceiling as he shuffled slowly toward them. Though his frame and head were massive, it seemed as if his legs were far too short for him. He held an enormous pipe between his ruddy lips, his face framed by bushy, white sideburns and even bushier white eyebrows. His woolen pants and cashmere vest were brown and he had the air of a librarian about him.

"You shouldn't be on this floor," he said in a gravelly yet quiet voice.

Ivy looked at her Hollow Shaft map: they were on a confidential floor.

"So sorry!" Ivy stuttered, quite intimidated by the man's size. "Are you, are you Norman Wrinkles?"

"Who asks?"

"Ivy Lovely, sir. This here is my friend Fyn. Fyn Greeley."

"Pleasure," Fyn said quietly.

"Ivy Lovely? Oh yes, old man Winsome sent a mendlott. Said you'd be on your way for a certain insight. Didn't say you'd be bringing a fellow."

"Winsome? I believe I'm looking for Derwin Edgar Night's tome."

Norman's booming laugh shook the room. "You'll not find him here, Ivy. You need Daryl Debnick, scrivenist to our beloved Princess Isabella so many years ago. It's Debnick's tome that's twitching to talk to you."

He rolled back yet another shelf, and with his quill called out a tome. It was thick—at least as thick as LaVera's—and covered in warm chestnut leather. Gold chevrons were emblazoned on the spine, reminiscent of the Queen's emblem on the Hollow Shaft's map. The already open tome floated into Norman's arms. He was right: the tome was twitching to talk.

THE DOUBLE MOON

IVY sat entranced, everything outside of the room forgotten, while Norman Wrinkles embodied Daryl Debnick. Her anticipation was at an all-time high and so when she heard the voice of the long-gone scrivenist, who was meant to give her the most meaningful information of her life, she was crestfallen.

An embittered, sarcastic voice rang out from Norman: "Oh, would you get on with it now!"

Norman replied in his own voice, looking like a loony who had one too many tankards of Spinner's Foam and was conversing with himself. "Winsome Monocle says that these two are seeking information about the double moon."

"The doub—" Fyn interjected before Daryl cut him off.

"Winsome? Never heard of him."

"No need to be tetchy! The double moon, Mr. Debnick. Tell us what you know." Norman sounded positively gruff.

The tome cleared its throat or rather, the Tome Translator cleared his throat for the tome. Then Daryl's voice spoke again, "This is a tale that begins before I came to work for the temperamental Princess Isabella. To me, she was too irreverent to be a proper Queen. Couldn't follow a rule to save her life!"

Fyn and Ivy shot each other a look.

"Isabella was the kind of princess who took every opportunity, since she could first walk, to adventure. She spent most nights wandering with her unicorn by her side to places that her parents forbade her to explore. Unfortunately, her father died young, leaving her in the care of her stepmother who believed that it was beneath Isabella's station to wander alone and interact with commoners and creatures. Absolutely true, if you ask me.

"After her father's passing, it was her stepmother who helped influence my selection as Princess Isabella's scrivenist. She knew that we were of the same mind when it came to the proper behavior for a princess in the queenly line. When I arrived, Isabella didn't trust me because of my kinship with her stepmother. So of course, I had to resort to privately reading her journal to fill in the blanks.

"I discovered she had cultivated a friendship with a dwarf! Appalling! Can you imagine? One of the most notorious creatures in the woods, capable of powerful magic, yes, but often for nefarious purposes!

"In her journal, Isabella revealed that she flew by way of night while the town slept, masked by the dark, gray clouds. It was on one such night that she found the dwarf, beaten to the bone. A pixie's light captured Isabella's attention; she followed it and found a little crowd of pixies hovering over his helpless body. He was battered and bruised and lay motionless. Despite her stepmother's warning to keep to her own kind and stay away from trouble, she instinctively cradled his bruised head and convinced the pixies to let her take him home. The pixies were rightfully very worried about sending the reclusive dwarf, their guardian, into the castle where dwarves were loathed.

"Despite her initial shock at how dirty dwarves are—and they are!—Isabella managed to strike up a mentorship with the dwarf, and more than that, a friendship. She referred to him as 'her only friend,' but really she had only herself to blame—it was not our fault that she didn't like afternoon tea with other princesses! And then Rimbrick showed his gratitude by opening the world of magic to Isabella in a way no one else could."

"Wait! Rimbrick?!" Ivy interjected. "You didn't say Rimbrick, did you?"

"Ivy?" Fyn looked at her in concern.

"He's a friend of mine," she replied quickly, more interested in what Daryl had to say. But the scrivenist, rude as he was, lost sight of the story.

"A bit like Isabella, isn't she?" the nasally voice complained to Norman, "Doesn't she know the rules?"

With a wave of his left arm, Norman opened the left side of his vest. Lovely scripted words floated out: it was the Hollow Shaft rulebook, transcribed in hovering letters. In a croaky voice, as if Norman had just woken from a nap, he read, "Rule number 292: Do not interrupt a tome, for the tome then has the right to A. Continue on; B. Choose to end his or her story; C. Change accents or languages so as to be impenetrable; D. Wander off topic; or E. Start all over again. I know because of the nature of this story, you will be curious. Please limit speaking, Ivy, and remember—though it seems like he himself is in the room with us—it is but Daryl's tome. Meaningful conversation with you or knowledge of events that occurred after his death are both impossible."

"I'm so terribly sorry, Mr. Debnick. No need for the accent today, Daryl. Or starting over. You were say—"

Norman put his finger, the size of a sausage, to his lip. After a sullen silence, Daryl Debnick's ego and desire to be heard got the better of him.

"Well, as I was saying, a deep friendship was born. But most importantly, Isabella's stepmother was fortunate to acquire me at just the right time. Shortly after I arrived, Isabella's evening ventures were forbidden. Instead, her attention was directed to my expertise on beastly betrayals—emphasis on dwarf betrayals. I did write *Don't Dare Depend on a Dwarf*, after all. Isabella dreaded my lectures and was always late. On one such evening I visited Isabella's room to remind her of our lecture appointment only to discover that she was gone. The light wind from the open window made the sheer curtain sway. There was a letter cast aside on the floor.

My future Queen,

Your friendship has been the greatest gift in all my years. You have promise to be Croswald's most enchanting queen in history. I know that you are no longer permitted to come out and adventure with me—remember when we used to roam these hills?—but I know your desire to discover and learn about magic must still thrive. I have the perfect gift for you. Something you will find most useful. Meet me in Grimlock's back room.

Rimbrick

"I even had to look up where Grimlock was. And *what* it was. Where those dirty dwarves live, it's not even a town—just a cluster of little, shingled shacks they call homes scattered in a wooded hamlet. The overgrowth there is so rampant rain can hardly fall on their paths. Grimlock is a gathering place, you see, where all manner of dwarves dwell—bohrs, dwelling dummers, and dwindles. Can you imagine? The future Queen of all of Croswald, cavorting in such a place? She would surely have been the only human there. As her dutiful scrivenist I bravely followed her, hero that I am. I tracked them in the dark for the moon hadn't yet risen.

"From the outside, Grimlock looked like a rundown tavern, sized just right for dwarves. I couldn't very well walk in, could I? So I snuck around back. Peering in through a tiny square window I saw a back room far more sumptuously appointed than I expected. Brick walls fortified the small cottage and arches held up the structure. The pint-sized furniture was upholstered in rich, red velvet and circled around little conversation corners. In one plush armchair sat a dwarf—it could only be Rimbrick. Across from him sat Isabella who took up the whole of a little loveseat with her trim figure. Her nut-brown hair was hastily pulled back into a knot and her blue eyes were wide.

"I leaned in: what gift could a dwarf give? They can barely afford the clothes on their backs. The table between the two was a rugged piece of wood atop an old barrel of boysenberry liqueur. On the table rested a package wrapped in brown paper.

"'I didn't think you knew when my birthday was! And I've so missed our nocturnal explorations,' Isabella said as she unwrapped the package happily. It was a glass bottle the size of a fish bowl. The viscous liquid inside glowed a hazy silver.

"Cocking her head to the side, Isabella asked him, 'What is this?' She tipped the bottle from one side to the other—it was quite mesmerizing. I had never seen anything like it. The bottle had to be dwarf magic. They spoke in low tones and I could see Isabella's excitement rising. This kind of magic, new and forbidden, was her favorite pastime and I could tell she was anxious to experiment. The dwarf appeared to be giving some instruction, but Isabella couldn't wait.

"'This is a—wait, Isabella, don't!'

"Before Rimbrick could finish his warning, Isabella popped the stopper off the round bottle, and a cloud puffed out. It circled her and she was swept up into the small glowing jar. The moment Isabella disappeared, I charged through the back door. I knew that dwarves couldn't be trusted. When I came in, Rimbrick knew exactly why I was there.

"'Don't touch the bottle!' he shouted.

"I asked him if he expected me to just wait while my charge had been cursed away, perhaps killed.

"'She's not gone forever; we just have to wait. Oh, she didn't finish listening to my warning! This is powerful magic and needs to be treated with delicacy.'

"I made a move for the bottle. When he blocked me, the tip of my quill sparked. I directed that energy towards the bottle, summoning Isabella from the glowing vessel.

"'No! You can't tamper with a bottle when there's life inside!' he screamed. I knew he would try and prevent me from helping. But what happened next was too much for even me to fathom. Yes, my summoning magic brought out Isabella, but something else, too. The absence of light came with her. It is impossible to sketch the details of such blackness. It was something entirely not of this world and its shrill scream penetrated my eardrums as it escaped the bottle and barreled through Grimlock's open door with such force that it blew out the side of the tavern.

"Before I could even process what was going on, Isabella's limp body returned, spilled out on the floor in the bottle's water.

"'Noooooo!' Rimbrick screeched, his body buckling in agony. I dropped to my knees and heard Isabella's low moan, barely audible over the crackling of the fire and the thumping of my own heart. She lay motionless in Rimbrick's arms. I could tell from his face that grief and guilt had shattered his heart.

"Rimbrick blurted, tears streaming, 'Isabella, please, please don't go! This wasn't supposed to happen! I cannot bear to see you die! Especially not because of me! It wasn't meant to be this way!'

"Before he could finish, Isabella's eyes closed for what I feared would be forever. The slowly-rising moon cast light on her beautiful face.

"'We have to do something!' I shouted.

"Rimbrick gritted his teeth and nodded. He kissed her forehead. Then, closing his eyes, he held his stubby arms outstretched over her body. I could sense magic, more powerful than any one quill, passing from his palms to her heart. A vibrant light formed above Isabella's chest and her body rose off the ground slowly. Her whole chest began taking on the brightness of the magic, which formed something hard and gleaming. Then a bright light—so many colors that it appeared white—burst wildly out from her heart and towards the sky through the ruined side of the tavern. At first, I thought the light was following that, that *thing*, but it shot high over the treetops, feeding into the moon. The moon grew to twice the size and brightness than it had just been.

"Then some unearthly, non-human magic shook the ground. A dark cloud swept through Grimlock's back room. Rimbrick and I froze. And then everything was still and quiet.

"In the light of the giant moon, there lay on Isabella's chest a solid, shining stone. It was the exact color of moonlight, and it shimmered vibrantly. I—"

Suddenly the ground shook violently. Ivy and Fyn were jolted back to reality and Norman's voice returned to his natural grumble.

"Ah, two hours is up," he said regretfully. "I'm sorry."

The tome floated back to its shelf; Norman tucked the books in tight, securing them, and the tower began to shake and sink, dust rising up from the rock floor and walls. The initial jolt gave way to creaks and groans. Books trembled in their shelves and Norman spun the wheels expertly, cranking everything tightly together. The wall sconces shivered and gave off a vibrating light. It seemed that the whole structure was sinking back down, sliding back into the bedrock underneath the lake.

"What's happening?" Ivy hollered over the rumble. "What happened to Isabella?"

"The Hollow Shaft is going back underwater, Ivy! We have to get out of here!" Fyn shouted.

She ran to the elevator, but Fyn grabbed her arm and shook his head.

"Too late for that! We have to jump!"

Ivy's stomach dropped. As much as she loved adventure, she was terrified of heights.

"Fyn! Are you out of your mind? We are on the 122nd floor! I can't. I can't do it! We won't make it."

He practically dragged Ivy to the narrow window, barely wider than his shoulders but twice as tall as he was. Ivy looked at the water below: it was roiling as the Hollow Shaft sank back into the water. The dock and their little boat were like pin pricks. No, grains of rice. Now they were the size of her palm. They were sinking fast.

"Ivy, listen. We have to jump. It's the only way. Wait until I say so!"

"There has to be another way, Fyn!"

"Are you ready?" Fyn shouted, crouching at the edge of an open window, preparing to jump.

"I can't, Fyn! I can't!"

"You can, Ivy. Trust me. Okay?"

It was the longest three seconds of Ivy's life. When the dock was close, Fyn yelled, "Jump!" and they flung their bodies from the window onto the sloshing dock, smashing against the splintering wood.

The force of the Hollow Shaft being swallowed by the lake pulled the two off the dock and beneath the water for a terrifying few seconds. It was bone-chillingly cold. They resurfaced to silence, startling after the rumble of rushing water and groaning rock. The only noise was the fizz of tiny bubbles popping. Besides that, the Hollow Shaft left no trace. Fyn dragged them through the water to what remained of the dock. Ivy's crash landing had knocked the air from her lungs and she rolled onto her back gasping.

For minutes, there was complete stillness. Neither made a sound.

Then Ivy found her shivering voice. "That," she gasped, "was absolutely terrifying! Don't ever make me jump from a height like that again. Don't ever let me *be* that high again!"

"Not exactly my idea to be out here, Ivy." He shot her a glare. "Guess we'll never hear the end of *that* story."

"Argh! I need to know what happened! I imagine Isabella died, after all. But what was that thing? That apparition Daryl spoke of. And Rimbrick? It couldn't be *my* Rimbrick, could it?"

Fyn was quiet.

After a moment, she turned back toward him, grateful. In the drama of their jump, she had somehow forgotten what he did for her. "Thank you. Thank you for saving my life."

"You're welcome. Now let's get you back. I need a good meal after that jump. Something other than wet drumnuts."

Ivy groaned and rolled away from Fyn. Something bright in the dark water caught her eye. Like a shimmering shadow, it flitted away. She saw it again, swimming underneath the dock and far below the surface. It was big. And then it was sinking their boat.

THE
BEARDED CLOUD

ITH a splash, a giant creature breached the water and landed on their tiny boat, half submerging it. It was part horse and part seahorse with hooves encased by flippers. The iridescent creature buried its maned head in Ivy's knapsack, chomping away at day-old drumnuts. Its muscled flank twitched and stretched as it attempted to lick every crumb out of the boat. After a moment of scavenging it looked up, peacefully sated, with big, heavy-lashed eyes. Its silver skin matched the school of silver divers now circling the boat on the Loch's surface.

"Fyn," Ivy whispered, following its every movement with her eyes—at that moment, her eyes were the only part of her she dared to move. She kneeled down beside him slowly and whispered in his ear, "Fyn, is that, that's not what I think it is, is it?"

"It's a shorehorse! And it's a hungry one! He must have followed us here."

Ivy was half excited, half panicked. "I'll be sure to make a note of it in my Startus when we return. Professor Wheeler won't believe it!"

"And what? Admit you're guilty of venturing off school grounds all on your own?"

"But I'm not alone. I'm with you. Remember?" Ivy spoke through chattering teeth.

Fyn inched closer to the beast as it started to slowly sink deeper and deeper, clearly unfazed by the numbing coldness of the Loch's water, which was now sinking the boat and dock.

"Don't scare it away, Fyn," Ivy muttered as he drew nearer. "And remember, they're not supposed to be very friendly."

"I'm not going to scare it. Are you kidding? It's our only chance to get out of here alive. We'll never make it across the Loch on our own. It's a long swim, that's all I'm saying. I've heard the Loch freezes over when it feels threatened. I'm not dressed for the winter, you know. And I'm already freezing!"

"Like I'm not?"

"No sympathy for you. You are officially the one who got us into this mess."

The boat's bow was pitching upward but the creature didn't flinch. Finding a stray drumnut, he snacked happily, like Woodley Butterlove on a stick of butter. Fyn crept closer, trying not to scare the beast off.

"You're okay. Come on. You like those, don't you? I've got a whole bag of them back at the dorms. All for you! If you'll just take us home. Take us home and they're all yours. I promise."

Fyn extended his arm and the shorehorse thrust upward, swinging its long snout rapidly to the right and knocking Fyn from the edge of the dock. The shorehorse dove down.

"Fyn!"

He swam like a champion through water. Silver divers pecked at his clothes before deciding they didn't like the taste of him. Ivy reached for his cold hand and wrestled him up. The two fell back, Ivy on her bottom and Fyn on top of her. He nearly crushed her. She quickly shoved him off and the two attempted to catch their breath while watching the boat sink and the hairie flit away.

"Well, that wasn't awkward or anything," Ivy muttered. "When are you ever going to start listening to me?"

"Me? When am I going to start listening to *you*? You're unbelievable." Fyn tried to storm off but found he couldn't walk far on the barely floating dock.

"I told you shorehorses aren't the friendliest creatures," Ivy went on.

"Right, because you know them so well, I'm sure."

"Well, I've read a little about them. I'll make sure to make a note of what I've just discovered about the silver divers: they can't stand the taste of Fyn Greeley's sarcasm and rudeness. I can't blame them."

"Are you done insulting me yet?"

The two turned away from each other, equally annoyed.

"You nearly got us killed back there, Ivy! How are we going to get back?"

Suddenly, the wind grew stronger and even colder than before. The shorehorse reemerged, breaching onto the end of the dock and tilting them toward the water. It whinnied and gazed at the shore, snorting in fear. The Cloaked Brood had not disappeared as Ivy had hoped, and now she realized they were making their way to the lopsided dock in small boats. Their massive bodies were terrifying in the light of the boats' lanterns. An ominous black carriage tethered to black unicorns waited on shore.

In that moment, Ivy couldn't determine what was true even as she watched the large bodies moving nearer. Her lip trembled as she felt fear welling up in her heart.

"It's them. They're here," said Fyn.

"They're after me."

"You don't know that."

"What else would they still be doing here? They have no business being here. Their business is me."

"We have to get you out of here."

"Let me try talking to it."

"What?"

Fyn had no choice but to watch as Ivy turned her attention to the great creature before her. She focused her thoughts on how lovely the animal was, how powerful. The creature seemed to relax and began to look at her. Ivy leaned forward to stroke its mane and iridescent cloak while she whispered to it. It responded by nuzzling her hand and lowering its giant head.

"Really?" Fyn scoffed.

"What's the matter, sweet thing? You don't like Fyn? I know. He can be irritating at times. But we need your help. Please."

Fyn rolled his eyes.

With the Cloaked Brood on the horizon, Ivy climbed onto its back, using the slip of seaweed around its neck to hold onto.

"Good girl. That's it. Gooood girl."

"Girl?"

"She's sensitive. Look at her. Sweet girl. She—"

"No time for lectures. Here. Catch this!" Fyn tossed Ivy

her satchel and jumped on, too; his large frame felt protective behind her. The shorehorse tucked its huge hooves back under its fins and curled its tail like a giant seahorse. The cold seemed to energize the beast; it whinnied as it tossed its head and kicked its front legs. With a splash, they were off. The shorehorse arched smoothly in and out of the water. On the one hand, this was a much faster ride than the Hollow Shaft's hairie boat. On the other, they were soaking. Ivy was getting used to feeling drenched, though she would never get used to the cold.

When they reached the shore, the creature unfurled its hooves and sped through the forest, knocking over saplings and trampling brush underfoot. They clung to its back desperately—the shorehorse clearly sensed the danger of the Cloaked Brood. As they pushed through the thicket, leaving a soggy trail behind them, Ivy looked over her shoulder to spot the dark figures pursuing them at a distance. Lanterns flashed off their helmets' facemasks. Fyn yelled over the sounds of hooves, "We have to get you to the Halls. Fast. C'mon!"

A roaring sound closed in on them. A stampede of vicious-looking unicorns was running beside them, dipping in and out of the frosted trees. Ivy kicked the shorehorse in its flanks and the shorehorse led on, tossing up mud on the way. Then ahead of them, in a clearing, Ivy saw the Cloaked Brood lining their steeds to form a wall, forbidding their exit from the forest. The shorehorse screeched to a halt and turned back in the direction they'd come. But behind them rose a great bank of black cloud—the angriest storm that Ivy had ever seen. Before they could change direction, the three were swept up into the tempest.

The shorehorse thrashed in the air like a helpless butterfly. Ivy gripped the luminescent mane tighter and screamed for it to turn back. The shorehorse used all her strength to fight the strong wind that trapped them. But even a beast as powerful as the shorehorse couldn't push through. Ivy tried to use her magic to steady it, but she and Fyn were barely able to cling on, let alone ride out of the storm.

The deeper into the storm they were dragged, the more frightening it became. Bolts of lightning flashed around them. Sheets of rain soaked their already drenched frames. The storm gained power by the moment, becoming darker, windier, and louder. Ivy and Fyn could see nothing. Then there was a horrible jolt and Ivy was thrown to the left, rolling over the beast's flank. She screamed, flailing her arms and grasping for the shorehorse's mane. Fyn reached down and grabbed her, hoisting her back up just in time.

Then they reached what felt like the center of the storm—a dark and dreadful hole. The wall of black cloud writhed with terrifying shapes. Ivy buried her face into the beast's mane. Ivy screamed and she turned to see a carriage barreling straight at them, chased by the Cloaked Brood. It seemed impossibly real, but right as the carriage crashed into them, it evaporated into smoke.

When Ivy looked up again, a larger-than-life Helga was chasing them down, waving a heavy iron pan. Her scream was inhuman and unbearable: "Ivyyy! I'll throw the cages at you!" But again, as she reached them the figure was absorbed back into the storm with a puff of smoke.

Still screaming, they dug their heels into the shorehorse to strain away from the eye of the storm, but the wind carried them straight into a huge tidal wave that crested and wrapped its darkness around them.

"HELP!" Ivy screamed. "Fyn! Turn it around!"

"I can't! I can't see anything!"

Next came a pack of wolves now circling the three like prey. Their growls matched the growl of the thunder. Ivy forced magic toward them in a beam of light: it was useless, though she tried over and over. The light only illuminated more terrifying shadows lurking in the storm. Then a matte black carriage careened toward them—could it be real? It was impossible to tell.

The shorehorse suddenly dipped dramatically, narrowly escaping the crash.

"What's happening?"

It dropped another ten feet in the snap of a finger.

"Oh no!" Something rose to the top of Ivy's memory. "Fyn, shorehorses only have twenty minutes at a time out of water! Then they go back to being aquatic! It won't be able to breathe soon!"

The beast dropped again. But this time, it kept falling.

"AAAAAAAAHHHH!" Ivy lost her grip on the shorehorse. Fyn was holding tight to her waist. They fell a very, very long way, picking up speed as they went.

"Fyn!" Ivy screamed.

"Ivy!"

Then Fyn's grip loosened and they lost each other. As they plummeted out of the bitter storm, she could see it still swarming angrily above, full of debris and terrifying shadows.

o   o   o   o

That was the last thing Ivy remembered. That is, before waking up from a deep, still sleep neatly tucked underneath a mound of comfortable, sweetly scented linens. The sun's bright light seeped through the window. Her eyes opened just wide enough to see the honey-blonde Rebecca returning the pot of tea to her bedside table and plumping the pillows that surrounded Ivy.

"About time you woke up! How do you feel?"

"All right, I think. I've got a massive headache though. And a cold. How did I get here? Why am I in your bed? What happened?"

"You tell me. It's lucky Professor Wrigley's class was out hunting beasts when they spotted you and Fyn. By now the entire school has heard about the two of you outside school boundaries. And alone! What were you thinking? You could have been hurt! You had me worried sick."

"I'm sorry," Ivy groaned. "Where did they find us?"

"On the edge of the Bitter Forest, freezing cold, even though it was a beautiful morning."

"I—wait, where's Fyn? Is he all right?" Ivy asked weakly. "The shorehorse?"

"The what? Fyn's off with the Selector. Making a case for you probably. I've heard he's all right. Though his position may not be after today. I heard he told the Selector you simply had a bad case of the sleepwalkers. That was before she gave him a confessiper. He's been beat up pretty bad. Looks like he got into it with something; bruises above his eye and all. His lies were hardly believable. So dangerous what the two of you did. Really Ivy, what were you thinking?"

"I wasn't. I just—I went looking for Derwin. I thought

maybe if I found him, I could stop looking for him. Focus on school, you know."

"Focus on school. Now that's a good idea."

Ivy shrugged. "How does everyone else know what happened?"

"Confessiper."

"The what? Oh wait, the tea?"

"Not a tea you usually want to drink. Troll oil—straight off its slimy back! It's supposed to force truth from whoever imbibes. The side effect is deep, restive sleep. But the smell!"

"Gross. Sounds almost as bad as the rest of my morning."

"You mean your morning two days ago!"

"Ugh. I've been out that long? So, did I tell you all about what happened?"

"It wasn't me that gave you the confessiper. It was the Selector herself! In this very room."

"Oh no, that's terrible! What did I say?"

"Well, you might have admitted a few things you hadn't planned."

"Like what?"

"Like you have a small crush on Fyn."

"I—what? I could never. He's so irritating." After a short pause, Ivy spoke more calmly. "He didn't hear, did he? I mean, you didn't tell him that?"

"I'm only kidding. Got you to confess though, didn't I? With or without the troll oil. No, the confessiper didn't work on you. So strange. The Selector left in a huff. You were of no use to her without a confession." Rebecca paused then said, "But you spoke of the Hollow Shaft in your dreams last night. That you had to leave too soon. You were there with someone named Isabella? Couldn't make out much of what you were saying after that. I'm just happy to have you back and safe."

"Thanks. Me, too."

"Here. Have some more," Rebecca insisted.

"And confess something else? No thanks."

"I told you, it didn't work on you. The Selector actually threw down the vial and said that she might have expected as much. Do you know what she might have meant by that?"

"Not a clue."

"Well, drink this." Rebecca handed her a cup of broth. "This will just make you feel better. Get rid of that nasty cold."

Ivy felt like all her thoughts were trying to escape at once and though she had only been sitting up for a few seconds, she needed to lie back down again.

"My head is throbbing." She rubbed it softly, feeling a matted haystack of hair on top of her head. "My hair must look dreadful."

"I wouldn't worry about your hair. Only some much-needed rest."

"I can't. I have to find Winsome! I have to find out if he knows the end of the story!"

"Simmer down! The Selector said she'd send for you when you woke."

"Ugh, I can't even imagine what my Individualis has to say about yesterday."

"The day before yesterday, you mean? That's the strange thing. Nothing. It says nothing. All that was recorded was a giant scribble, almost blacking out the page. That's why she had to resort to the confessiper. So, what really happened out there?"

Once Ivy gathered the strength to sit up in bed again she spoke slowly, the day coming back to her in fragments.

"When Fyn and I left the Hollow Shaft, there was a shorehorse in our boat, sinking it."

"Oh, Ivy. You don't know what you're saying."

"Do you want me to tell you or not?"

"Of course I do."

"Then listen. There was a storm; we got caught in a terrifying storm riding the shorehorse. The Queen was there with her Cloaked Brood. I thought, I thought she was trying to kill me."

Ivy took another sip of broth, warming her throat. Rebecca placed the almost empty cup on the bedside table as Ivy remembered more details. "Everything I've ever been afraid of was in that storm. Or maybe I was just seeing it that way? I don't know. It was loud and frightful…so frightful! The clouds were wild. Oh, my head! I lost my grip of the shorehorse's mane and we fell. That's all I remember before waking up here."

"You must have hit your head harder than I thought to think a shorehorse could fly! But it sounds like you ran into the Bearded Cloud," Rebecca mused.

"The Bearded Cloud? That illusion from Professor Fenix's class? I never got to see it."

"Right! Because you went somewhere else. The ship, right?"

"A glanagerie gone wrong, I suppose. When you saw it, the Bearded Cloud, were there ghastly visions in black clouds thicker than mud?" Ivy relayed her experience.

"Yes, that's it. Its power is in wrapping you in your biggest fears."

"Is that what all those ghastly shapes were? Helga? The Cloaked Brood? A tidal wave?"

"Well, some might be Fyn's fears, some yours, and some future fears. The Bearded Cloud forces you to relive the most frightening moments in your life but it also forewarns you of the future and what you will soon fear."

"That's awful! Lucky for us we made it home safely. The Cloaked Brood was inches away from us before it struck."

Now Ivy stood from bed to get dressed.

"And just where do you think you are going now?"

"To class."

"You can't possibly—"

Rebecca's protest was interrupted by Damaris barging in.

Quite pleased with herself the princess said, "Ivy Lovely, your presence is requested by the Selector. Now." She spun on her heel and left.

Ivy exchanged looks with Rebecca, afraid of what was to come. Seeing Damaris was never good news.

When she entered the Selector's office, Fyn stood quietly in the far corner avoiding eye contact with Ivy.

"Selector," Ivy greeted her nervously. "Fyn."

She looked him over—he looked bruised but well.

"It seems as if you enjoy time in my office," the Selector said. "We've certainly never had a student who is quite so, shall we say, exploratory. Your Compass Individualis is taking up more than it's fair share on my shelf."

Ivy stood silent, listening.

"You know, I understand your need to know things, Ivy. The best scrivenists are that way. It's what makes you a true candidate to further your studies. What you've uncovered over the year is quite impressive, I daresay. Tell me, how is it that a girl like you, who has excused herself from more classes than she has attended, receives the highest marks of any first year?"

"Luck, I suppose. Being in the right place at the right time."

"Being in the wrong place at the wrong time is more like it. And for that, I regret to inform you that you are forbidden to attend this year's Ball, despite your grades."

"What? Selector, you can't!"

"I can."

Fyn finally looked up at Ivy like he wanted to speak but thought it better to not get involved.

"And him? Fyn?"

"Rewarded for keeping you safe as he so willingly shared with me moments ago. It was a brave thing he did, following you."

"So, the confessiper worked—" Her question was interrupted.

"Ivy, it's simply not safe for you to attend. Not for you or the other students. We don't know what your presence at the Ball could attract. It's been an interesting year to say the least."

"But I—"

"And if you continue to disrupt the student body as you have—setting balding hairies loose, drifting away from school grounds, skipping class—you will be expelled from the Halls of Ivy. Not just suspended, but expelled permanently. Do I make myself clear?"

"As crystal." Ivy's heart welled with sadness.

"Venturing off to the Hollow Shaft on your own, honestly, Ivy. I want you to know that I will be reviewing your Individualis

on an hourly basis from now on. And I've extended the scope
of the spell to include conversations you have outside of class,
in the dining halls, and in your dormitory. Suffice it to say,
I am watching you. The story that you seek is dangerous, Ivy.
For you and for others."

Ivy shivered.

"You are dismissed."

THE
WANDERER

o   o   o   o   o   o   o   o

THE next moon passed in a blur. Ivy went about her schoolwork, but her mind was elsewhere. She couldn't get the strange story of Isabella and her dwarf out of her head. Ivy felt cursed by the Selector's warning: she'd never had more questions for Winsome or more to talk about with Rebecca, and she couldn't say a word. She didn't know if she could make it to summer without bursting.

Ivy's last final of the year was for her glanagerie class. She walked into Professor Fenix's room nonchalantly. It was a noisy group, celebrating the end of school term and looking forward to the end-of-year parties. While Professor Fenix waited for things to settle down, he stood behind a beautiful glanagerie. From what Ivy could see, it held a miniature castle, green fields, and a lovely lake in the distance.

"Good morning, everyone!" called Professor Fenix.

"Good morning," replied everyone except Ivy. It wasn't a good morning for her so far—it hadn't been in a while.

"Thought we'd finish this year off with a momentous glanagerie experience! If you all gather around, you'll observe a happy little castle. Happy except, of course, that they have not had a scrivenist in many many moons and all of the royal heirs have lost interest in their stones. Some have actually lost their stones altogether. Their library is in terrible disarray, their land not producing the harvest that it should, and the minds of the royals have grown dim. The harvest, mind you, is one that should be of particular interest to you future scrivenists. Nixbeans are the primary ingredient in the scrivenist's favorite drink, Spinner's Foam.

"Your challenge is to set the castle right. As future crown-bearing royals and scrivenists, this will be your life's work! And I bet not one of you has had an adventure like this one before." He beamed proudly around the room.

It sounded pretty domestic to Ivy, but she was relieved to avoid more adventures today. The entire class moved to see the castle up close. When Ivy approached, she got a whiff of salt air. *Odd*, she thought.

"I know you're all very anxious to work together, putting those porcupels and crowns to use. Your task is to support the castle and the royal family of my imagination, make it fulfill its purpose, and engage the inhabitants in the pursuit and care for magic. When Didley passes through, you will all return safely in time for supper." Professor Fenix chuckled, "Forgive me, lunch. You'll arrive in time for lunch. The evening landscape has me thinking of supper!"

Professor Fenix called off every name in class and the students lined up. With a whoosh, they were swept inside the glanagerie's world. The professor's instructions transformed into a gruff voice.

"Welcome aboard *The Wanderer*, mates." The sound was hauntingly familiar and Ivy's eyes flew open. There stood the captain, the same one from her first glanagerie experience. He was as imposing as she remembered, with daggers tied to his waistband and a long, whiskery beard. He wore a loose white shirt tucked into snug leather pants. His voice was rough like the water, and his hair was long and straggly. Ivy made sure to tuck herself away in the shadows, not sure of what might happen if he saw her again. Her classmates were in varying states of surprise, amusement, interest, and fear.

"Where is the castle?"

"Oh my moon, we're pirates!"

The captain's voice boomed, "*The Wanderer* is me own ship. You may all refer to me as, well, simply Captain will dooooOOOoo—" He stumbled as an enormous wave rolled under them and tilted the ship.

"There be a rare treasure—hang on!" The deck of the ship made a sudden drop. The crew lost their footing on the slippery deck, and Ivy's classmates reached for whatever they could grab hold of. Eventually, the ship righted itself and the captain continued, "A rare treasure that I lost meself."

Ivy's classmates were bewildered. This certainly wasn't the tame final that Professor Fenix had described. It looked like she had pulled them into her own personal world. Was her imagination driving this? But Ivy could swear she'd never even thought of a pirate until she met this one last time.

"Stay steady, mates! Looks like this is going to be a large one! High as the masts. Hang on," he yelled again as a large wave neared. They held on tightly waiting for the ship to keel over. Luckily, Quincy Fryer was aboard. He ran to the ship's port side and used his Hoarfrost Stone to freeze the wave: it solidified instantly into a wall, as high as the ship's masts. But another large wave barreled through the ice-encased one, knocking everyone off their feet including the drunken captain. The rush of water knocked Hannelore Lawler flat against the boat's starboard side. Ivy nearly fell over the railing and Gregory Gershwin went right over.

"Gregory!" Ivy shouted.

"You okay?" Hannelore yelled to Ivy lying flat against the floor.

Ivy could finally stand long enough to reply, "I'm okay. And you?" Ivy hoped Gregory was okay. The fall looked a long way down.

"I'm going to steady the ship from below!" Rebecca shouted. Using her Hellexor Stone, she transformed into a giant orange octopus and leapt into the deep, blue water. Meanwhile, Elaina Portal attempted to steady the ocean waves with her Wagua Stone. It was a shame that she was the worst magic practitioner that the Halls had ever seen. Within minutes, the water below lay calm even though the storm thundered above. Then lightning struck the ship's main mast, setting the rigging on fire. Bobby Willcock hurried forward with his Flameral Stone and condensed the fire into a flame small enough to blow out. Woodley Butterlove had remained completely paralyzed this whole time. Ivy slid across to where he was gripping a rope tied to the bottom of the mast with white knuckles.

"Woodley! C'mon! You can help us get out of this mess," she shouted over the rain. "You are the only one who is still holding a potions kit! C'mon! Let's do it together."

"Can't! Wa-was only pre-prepared to send rain over c-c-crops," he stuttered in fear, his potions kit gripped uselessly in his fist.

Ivy bit her lip. More lightning was sure to come. Taking a breath, she plunged on. "I heard the Jester say he was making hot, buttered rolls for lunch."

Woodley made eye contact with her for the first time.

"Yes, and I'll probably need help eating mine, Woodley. Don't you think we ought to be getting out of this bottle and heading back to the Halls for lunch?"

With the image of butter melting down the sides of hot rolls seared in his mind, Woodley helped Ivy cast the calming spell that she had learned from Winsome with his unlocker. They managed to roughly crumble the copper cocoon and shake it into the louie pollen's vial that had been waiting in Woodley's kit. *Rest, rest, this storm shall pass; calm yourself, peace surpass.* It took both of them and they had to try twice before Woodley got it right, but it worked. A great pink haze stretched out in the softest *poof.* The thrashing of the ocean gradually subsided and the black clouds lightened to gray misty ones. As soon as she was sure that the storm was ending, Ivy quickly scurried back into the shadows, anxious to avoid the captain's notice.

The storm was nearly gone and only a light rain kept their heads wet. The captain thanked all still aboard for their services. Reenie Wallow made rounds with her Healite Stone, making sure that anyone who was seasick or banged up was cared for. Hannelore put everything loose back in order in no time. Ivy mended the cracked hull and splintered floorboards as best as she could without being seen.

"I've been through terrible storms but not one as dreadful as this. Gather around the quarterdeck," the captain ordered the students. He opened up a map for the entire crew to see. There were three large Xs on the map but they floated around, not tethered to any one spot. Their shapes were hard to spot because the parchment seemed more ink than map.

"This treasure. It's in three places."

"Is it pirate gold?"

"No, matey. Better than that!"

"You say you lost it? Was it stolen?"

"In a way, lass. 'Twas stolen through a curse! Not mine to keep either—was meant to be protectin' it." The captain looked mournful.

"You—what's your name?" His eyes suddenly burned with intent. His thick brows were nearly hidden beneath his jewel-encrusted bandana.

Ivy realized he was calling to her across the deck. She bumped up against the main mast as she tried to back away from the captain's piercing gaze. Her heart began to pump uncontrollably.

"Me?" Despite yearning to know who he was, she wasn't quite sure she could trust the man. After all, she had stolen his journal.

"Yes, you! What's your name?"

"I should ask you yours."

"A captain is supposed to know all aboard his ship, is he not?"

She hesitated. "Ivy."

"Ivy..." he repeated slowly, shock and understanding both creeping into his voice. He sounded as if he were waking from a long dream.

"Come with me," he ordered, regaining his faculties and

losing his pirate accent for an instant.

"Ivy, are you sure about this?" Hannelore stopped her with a hand to the shoulder.

"I'm not sure about anything anymore."

"Then be careful, my friend."

Ivy gulped and nervously followed him into a room that was far too familiar.

Behind his weathered door and heavy velvet drapes were heaps of treasure. It looked the same as when she'd seen it last except the treasure had been tossed about by the storm. Gold was piled high and jewels were strewn recklessly on his antique silk rugs. Open books lay thrown on the floor. His desk was covered with maps and markings, scrolls and ancient timepieces. But no journal.

"You're probably wondering why I asked you in here, aren't you? Please, bear with me. I'm not myself." He shook his head as if trying to slough off a cloud of unhelpful thoughts, then picked up a letter from his desk.

Ivy gingerly nodded her head and bit her lip. *This isn't real,* she tried to remind herself but the warm cabin, her wet clothes, and the intensity of the captain in front of her certainly didn't feel like an illusion. She eyed the porthole warily. The conversation she had overheard in the Old Carriage House coupled with what Daryl Debnick had told her about glanageries set her on edge.

"I wrote this for you when I saw you the last time. You see, Ivy, I've been aboard this ship for some time now and—" He grabbed her hand to put the letter in it, but Ivy shook him off and backed away.

The captain's face flushed. Ivy saw anger but truly it was

frustration and desperation. He advanced toward Ivy again.

"Listen, girl! There's no time—"

"Take your hands off of me! I don't even know who you are! This can't be real! You're a character in a bottle."

In her fear, Ivy's electric energy shattered every porthole in his living quarters and water flooded in as the thunder grew louder and the rain fell more heavily. Ivy fell with the ship's dive and flew across the room, nearly falling out the open porthole. She gasped for air as she looked below, the long drop leading to rough sea. The captain remained where he was, looking stunned, as she stood ready to jump. Then with another lurch, the ship took her decision away. It tossed her from the porthole and she fell into the surging water.

She sank down, despite her thrashing efforts to swim in her uniform. Ivy felt like she was drowning. She was frantic for air, desperately willing Professor Fenix to bring her back out.

She felt another splash. She flipped and saw the captain swimming toward her. Trying to keep herself from panicking, she kicked away furiously. He held both hands up, a gesture of peace, kicking powerfully down to her. In one hand he still held the letter. He swam directly to her and pressed the letter into her palm.

"Squawk!"

The sound of Didley's obnoxious honking was unmistakable, even underwater.

"Wait!" Her words bubbled through the waves. "Not yet!" She closed her eyes, almost out of air, and then she was back in Professor Fenix's classroom along with the other students.

Ivy stood shivering, drenched in salty water. She breathed

a deep sigh of relief to be back safely but she felt uneasy. Had she done the right thing talking to the captain? She didn't know. What if he knew something she needed to know? Professor Fenix's long-haired expeller mopped the floor underneath her and dried Ivy with forceful blows. Within minutes Ivy was dry and put together again.

"Welcome back," Professor Fenix grinned. "Most of you faired well! Better than Gregory here who was out in the blink of an eye." Gregory Gershwin looked a little disappointed.

Then he frowned. "But why are all of you wet?" Doing a double take, he peered into the glanagerie bottle. "Oh my moon! That's not the castle of my machinations! Where did that ship come from?" He looked suspiciously at Ivy.

Quincy returned with his hands frozen solid—his stone's magic had gone awry. The expeller moved over to thaw them. Ivy still felt like her lungs were opening up, catching breath. She noticed her left hand was tightly closed around the piece of mushy, folded vellum. She could still feel the touch of the captain's hand on hers. Ivy quickly hid the letter from the professor's view and unfolded it secretly when his back was turned.

> I am locked in by the evil one's imagination.
> We need each other to end this.

Ivy started to hyperventilate. Perhaps the captain was real. Make-believe or not, whatever was inside this bottle seemed to be chasing after her, like her dream, and could return to this world just like the journal had. Like the letter had. It sounded like the captain knew he was in a glanagerie bottle. But how did he know of the real world? How did he know her?

"Class is dismissed! Er, I'll let you know how you fared on the final as soon as possible." Then Professor Fenix mumbled to himself as the class filed out to lunch, "What a year full of nonsense! Am I testing my students or are they testing me?"

As soon as she could, Ivy rushed to the Den.

"Wait up!" Rebecca shouted from behind. "Where are you off to in such a rush?"

"The Den."

"What for?"

"Those glanageries. There's something to them. Read this."

"Read what?"

Rebecca looked curiously at what appeared to be a scrunched up, soggy scrap of parchment and then expectantly back at her.

"It's from the captain. The captain of the glanagerie ship."

"I can't see any writing, Ivy. Only soggy paper." Rebecca knew better than to doubt her friend at this point, but a blank note was a blank note. "What did he want from you?"

"I think he knows he's in the bottle, not like an imaginary person. He's trapped. I know, it doesn't make any sense, does it? I visited his ship earlier this year, accidently, and this time I think I pulled all of you with me. What if it's him? Derwin Edgar Night?"

"What if he's who?"

"I forgot. I forgot that you forgot who I'm talking about. That room! It's so annoying! I think I'm supposed to help him: 'We need each other to end this,'" she said, folding the letter into a tiny square, rolling it in her palm thoughtfully.

"End what?"

"I don't know! If he's real, why is he trapped in there? Who would have put him in there? Who would have the power to do such a thing?"

After a short pause, Ivy asked, "Hey Rebecca? What are your feelings about our Queen?"

"Feelings? I don't believe I have any. She's been such a mystery for so many years," Rebecca said. "It's hard to develop feelings in such a way. She could walk the streets of Ravenshollow and no one would ever know it. Of course, I've always wondered what she looked like. I'm only human. Although I must say, the rumors I've heard are terrifying. Are we supposed to be talking about this?"

As the two walked the quiet aisles, Rebecca transformed, clearly not taking Ivy's conversation seriously. With a rush of white wind, her periwinkle pullover turned into a black silk taffeta gown emblazoned with white pearls, crystals, and fluffy feathers; her hair towered above her head in tight ringlets and a white, porcelain mask hid her face. Ivy couldn't help but giggle.

"Is that you in there? You look like you're going to a party wearing that thing. It's horrible! Take it off."

"Undress myself in the middle of the library? I wouldn't dare. Besides, I am going to a ball later this week. Trying out my options, you see. Maybe I should go like this? No one would be able to take their eyes off me."

"They couldn't miss you."

Rebecca's hugely voluminous skirt knocked down a stack of books. The two giggled.

Ivy scanned the aisles until she found a glanagerie section:

Glanagerie: A Menagerie in the Mind by Filbert Fenix

Glanageries Gone Wrong by Filbert Fenix

"So this is the infamous *Glanageries Gone Wrong.* Apparently a lot *has* gone wrong."

GLAMagerie: Glanageries in Style by Filbert Fenix

"What, is he the only man who uses those bottles?"

Rebecca's voice distracted her. "Er, Ivy."

"Yes?"

"I'm, well, I'm stuck."

"You're what?"

"I'm stuck!" Rebecca's ridiculous dress was too large to fit through the narrow corridors and she had become wedged between the potions and praxis aisles. Ivy crawled underneath Rebecca, pushing through mounds of velvety brocade, and pulled her forward from the other side.

"You know you're not supposed to be practicing magic outside the classroom," Ivy admonished as she grunted.

"Look who's talking!"

"Don't want you to be banned from the Ball, too."

Suddenly, the girls heard Mistis's clunky footsteps from around the corner and did their best to act like all was normal. Rebecca quickly removed the mask and hid it behind her back.

Mistis rounded the corner. "Is everything all right over here?"

"Of course, just browsing for books."

"Good girls. Anything I can help you with?"

"Er, um, we were just on our way out."

Mistis nodded. "Lovely dress, by the way," she said to Rebecca. Rebecca's outfit did indeed look like something Mistis would be happy to hang in her closet.

They waited until the librarian was out of sight before laughing. They sputtered behind their hands, trying to keep quiet.

"I needed a good laugh. Thanks, Rebecca," Ivy said as her roommate transformed back into the form Ivy was so fond of.

"Where are you headed now?" Rebecca asked.

"Lunch. I'm starving."

"I'll see you back at the room. I'm going to work on a few ideas. So many choices for Ball outfits. But nothing like that dress, don't worry!"

A
MYSTERIOUS GIFT

IVY sat on a bench in the garden gazing up at the medley of color circling in the sky. She hadn't sketched freely in moons. It was the one thing that made her feel completely calm. A vibrant purple light was all that remained of the sunset. It reminded Ivy of the slurry fields, where her journey started. As the school year came to an end, she couldn't help but worry about the summer ahead and wish she were back with Rimbrick. She remembered all the times that he had nudged her awake, pointy hickory boot to the ribs, after she dozed off sketching. But then she thought of the oppressive power the slurry fields had held for her, and what secrets Rimbrick must have kept. Maybe she didn't want to go back at all. Things might have been different had she known everything she knew now.

She took a deep breath, closed her eyes, and pictured the slurry fields. The image before her rose in her mind in a flash. After a flurry of her porcupel, she held the parchment with a perfect replica of the lavender field in front of her. With a small smile, she stared at the two figures in the drawing on their treasured hilltop, imagining a year's worth of stories missed.

The hairs on the back of Ivy's neck stood up. And then she smelled a spicy soap, used by only one person she knew. Fyn's voice sounded doubly loud as it broke the silence. "Is that your friend there? The dwarf you told me about? Beautiful place, beautiful sketch."

"Could you please stop doing that?" Ivy pleaded, annoyed.

"Doing what?"

"Just showing up out of nowhere! You're like a fly; you're always around."

"Sorry. I went for a stroll and saw you sitting here. I could leave if you want me to? I do have to get ready for the Masquerade."

Ivy sat silent.

"Is something bothering you?"

"You mean other than the fact that I can't go to the Ball? And that I feel bad about being grumpy with you?" Ivy sighed.

"Yeah. I think we've been grumpy with each other, actually. Here to say I'm sorry about confessing."

"I know you wouldn't have told the Selector if you could help it. I didn't mean what I said. I'm sorry. I just, I just have a lot on my mind and was just trying to work through it. Though I should start anticipating your arrival wherever I go. I wasn't kidding when I said you're always around."

"Well, great minds think alike, don't they?"

She smiled and waved her hand at the stack of parchment. "I figured if I can't go to the Ball, I'd sketch my own party."

"That looks too peaceful to be a party," Fyn teased. "Quite the opposite of what's going to happen in that ballroom."

"Won't someone be waiting for you?" Ivy asked glumly.

"I don't have a date, if that's what you mean, and I enjoy a good sunset, too. I'll sit with you for a few moments longer if you don't mind." Fyn smiled and then redirected Ivy's attention to the sketch. "Your home, it's a beautiful place."

"Well, I wouldn't call it home but you should see it in person. The way the slurry glows at night…it glimmers like antique crystals. It changes colors with the season—sometimes a shade of orchid, other times almost blue."

"Sounds surreal."

"Ethereal too, but you'd quickly change your mind if you spent more than a minute there. No magic and, really, no light in anyone's eyes. How could a place be so magnificent and yet so deceiving at the same time, you know? I don't understand it."

"Looks can be deceiving. Must not be that bad if you're still sketching it."

"I guess."

"I could do it, though, you know? If it meant visiting you this summer," Fyn smiled at her. "I'd like to come visit you."

Ivy blushed. "I'm not going back there, Fyn. I'm definitely not welcome back at the Castle Plum. I would give almost anything to see Rimbrick again, but he's probably gone. We usually met on full moon nights, like tonight. He'd share his stories…I longed to hear them after a long day's work. I never had anything to tell him then but now I have a story of my own to share and I can't. And I can't ask his advice."

"You can tell me your stories. Not sure I'd have much in the way of advice, but still."

"The thing is, you're part of the story. I'd tell him about you."

"What would you tell him?" Fyn raised a brow.

There was an awkward silence as Ivy paused, leaving her thoughts unsaid. Fyn punctured the silence with a change of subject.

"Listen, I know you're forbidden to attend the Ball tonight, and I'm sorry about that, but I wanted you to know, I was going to ask you to accompany me. Be my date. So if you change your mind—"

"You know I can't, Fyn."

"I know, I know, but if you do," Fyn shot Ivy an impish grin, "if anything changes, I'm going alone. Hoping you'll break the rules or something like that. Judging by the past year's adventures, I've concluded that you're no stickler for rules, either."

She looked up at him, grinning from ear to ear.

"Fyn, I—" and then she stopped as her eyes caught a glimpse of something strange in the distance. It was Winsome's window, a high point where her eyes often wandered. She cocked her head as she watched a light inside his room. Ivy knew Winsome normally activated a spell to keep his windows dark to maintain his secret quarters.

"I—I have to go," Ivy stumbled, tripping over her words.

"So soon? Have I scared you away?"

"I'll see you later, okay?"

"I sure hope so."

As she rushed off, Fyn inhaled a long breath, gazing in the direction Ivy had looked. He saw nothing but a stone structure with wild ivy growing up the round turret and windows beautifully lit as the sun dipped below the horizon. Strange shadows stretched across the school garden.

Ivy dashed up the stairs, through the empty Den, and

through the passageway into Winsome's private lair without being seen. It helped that everyone was either setting up or getting ready for the Ball. When she opened the door to his chamber the air was eerily still though the hairies were still glowing bright.

"Winsome? Is everything all right? It's me, Ivy."

The room was silent, cold. No sound of explosion, no rifling parchment, no penetrating old man snores—nothing could be heard. Something was wrong.

"Winsome, where are you?" she called, convinced he should be there.

Where could he have gone? Ivy wondered as she snooped around. Everything was just as disorderly as usual. It seemed as if he had stepped out for a moment, but how could that be? He never left. Never.

Ivy peeked into his private nook and saw the door of his mendlott open—a huge spill of unopened letters had piled onto the desk. One was propped up on its flap, its antiquated wax scrivenist seal torn open. The envelope was stamped *FINAL NOTICE* in red ink. She knew then. She didn't want to know, but she knew. It was Winsome's End Letter. He was being summoned by the Hollow Shaft.

"No," Ivy gasped. "He can't go yet!" She ran down the stairs, through the library, hoping to catch him. She ran through the halls—passing early partygoers, tables carried into the ballroom, cheese platters floating by—and out a side entrance. A sudden breeze blew at the leaves. The air had the cool feel of a storm nearing, yet there wasn't a cloud in the sky. She ran toward the Bitter Forest, looking out over the path to Lonefellow Loch.

"Winsome," Ivy whispered. He was gone. What was she to do? She still had so many questions!

Ivy walked glumly back toward her dormitory, taking the long way. In the grand entry she gazed over the balcony railing, watching as waiters and workers set up the Masquerade Ball. The nosy hairies in a nearby lantern tittered and spied alongside her. Inside the ballroom the three massive crystal chandeliers were glowing their brightest, helping the army of party preparers as they rushed about. Translucent gold balloons hovered in the grand room, filling the air like so many champagne bubbles. Enormous floral arrangements ensconced in gold wire crowns passed Ivy on plush cushions.

A sense of wistfulness overwhelmed her. She knew she could visit Winsome in the Hollow Shaft, in a way. But she wished she had him now to tell her what to do. If she was honest with herself, she was also more than a little disappointed to miss her first Ball. Who could say whether she'd get a chance at another?

"It's a shame you can't attend such a grand affair." The Selector had snuck up behind Ivy unexpectedly. It seemed that she was awaiting her arrival. "Lovely, isn't it? You can't imagine it looking more inviting than it does now, but it will."

Ivy hardly acknowledged her. What could she say? She watched sidelong as the Selector walked away. She rolled the words around in her head as she made her way back to her dorm. Why, it almost seemed like the Selector was tempting her to come. She arrived at their room just in time to see Rebecca off.

Rebecca had her mask on—a half-mask made of thick black-and-purple brocade and long, elegant purple feathers held in place by an elaborate gold brooch. The shape of the eyes was vaguely minx-like and Rebecca looked mysterious in it. The dress complemented the mask perfectly. Then she sighed and put her hand on her hip in her familiar way, and all mystery vanished.

"Should I wear this one—" she gestured to the delicate gown she wore, a lavender two-piece dress encrusted with jewels, "—or this one?" She waved her hand and was instantly dressed in the flowing organza skirt and dainty cap-sleeved crop top that had been on her bed. The effect was like lilac-colored ice. She placed a few matching stones in her hair, spun into a simple chignon. She smiled at Ivy. "What do you think?"

Ivy looked at Rebecca in awe. "You'd knock any prince off his horse wearing that one."

"Do you think so?"

"It's beautiful. You look like a slurry fairy."

Ivy's head began to ache and she lay on her bed, cradling it in her hands. Humboldt cuddled up by her feet.

"Are you all right?" Rebecca asked.

"As good as can be expected. I've just been asked on my first date. I think. By someone I like."

"That's wonderful! Fyn? I knew he liked you. That boy watches you like Didley watches the clock!"

"But I've been asked to attend something that I'm forbidden to go to! What makes it worse is not only do I have the perfect date, but I also have the most perfect dress that I can't even use. It's been sitting in my closet for years. My Compass Individualis has me labeled as the most disruptive student in the entire school and that's not the worst of it."

Ivy started to cry. "As of thirty minutes ago, Winsome is gone. How is everything falling apart on the very same night, my last night here? The last night! It's awful, just awful."

"Gone?" Rebecca repeated. "What do you mean Winsome's gone?"

"I found his End Letter inside his classroom. He didn't even say goodbye, Rebecca. Something about it doesn't feel right. Why would he just leave without saying goodbye?"

"And come looking for you in the Halls? In plain daylight? A man whose very existence is not existing? For everyone to spot him?"

"He would have said goodbye, Rebecca. A letter. Something. I know him."

"And what makes you think word won't come? Ivy. I'm certain there was a reason. Maybe he wants you to come visit him at the Hollow Shaft? I'm sorry to cut this short, but could you hand me my shoes? Yes, those. Thanks. I've got to go." She hugged Ivy. "I'm so sorry you can't come—I'm sure it'll be boring without you. I hate to remind you of what you're not invited to by leaving. Take care of yourself, okay? I'll tell you everything when I come back."

As Rebecca turned to leave, Ivy stopped her.

"Wait! Do my eyes deceive me or are you voluntarily wearing your crown?"

"It's not so bad, is it?" Rebecca smiled. "I guess I'm kind of starting to like it after all. I'd still be forgotten if it weren't for this flimsy thing. But don't tell anyone, especially my mother! I'll never hear the end of it: 'Oh, if only you had listened to me…yada, yada, yada!'" Rebecca smiled. "Don't think I'll be giving up my porcupels anytime soon, though."

The door closed and Ivy lay back in her bed staring at the gray ceiling. Humboldt whimpered in empathy. She was thinking of Winsome's disappearance. Wishing she could attend the Ball. As she rolled over to face the stone wall, a strange memory—one she hadn't seen clearly in real life, but that came to her with perfect understanding now—hit Ivy like a pile of bricks, intense and forceful. The man in the Old Carriage House. It was Winsome the Selector had spoken to. Had Winsome been the Selector's collaborator all along? Like a puppet, had Ivy done everything the two had planned? Ivy sat bolt upright and set her jaw. Humboldt fell off the bed, startled.

What were the two of you up to? What are you up to now? Why don't you want me at the Ball? Her thoughts swirled frantically.

"Time to put that forever-fitting dress to use!"

Ivy jumped from bed, threw open the closet and put on the only thing she owned that was appropriate for anything besides adventuring or class: her forever-fitting dress. The dress she had owned for as long as she could remember, one of the few items she lugged aboard Lionel's cabby, sent up to the Halls through Warwick, and then stuffed into the back of her dormitory closet.

After putting it on for the first time since she left the Castle Plum, she stared at herself in Rebecca's full-length mirror. Ivy's hair was soft and shone like it had just been washed. A few short tendrils hung down the sides of her face in gentle twists.

Her hazel-eyed gaze had deepened.

Her eyelashes had grown longer.

Her eyebrows had thickened.

Her face had a soft, bright glow and her pale complexion glistened.

The stones that embellished her dress beamed like her entire appearance suddenly did.

Not bad, she thought, as she swept her long hair up and away from her neck. Ivy's nerves settled and her smile relaxed and widened. For the first time in her life she truly felt like a princess. Yes, Ivy: the same girl who spent her days below the grimy ground that royals walked upon. Rather than mingling with scaldrons Ivy would soon be mingling with royals and soon-to-be scrivenists. Standing in front of that mirror, Ivy felt more alive than ever before. She hadn't smiled like this in a very long time.

Then an unexpected knock on the door sounded.

"Rebecca?" Ivy was excited to go down with her friend. "Did you forget something? You're just in ti—"

Ivy opened the door to find a primly wrapped package on the threshold. It matched exactly the color scheme of the Ball downstairs—satiny black paper, a glittering gold bow, and gossamer ribbon.

"What is this? Who could this be from?" she asked Humboldt. "Not another pie, I hope."

She lifted it, feeling its lightness, and tentatively untied the silver ribbon. The box fell open easily and on the black velvet interior lay a bright-white masquerade mask. It was elegantly composed of intertwined branches as delicate as glass. It reminded Ivy of an aspen in winter. She held it to her face and it fastened itself magically over her features, shaped perfectly to her eyes and brow. When she looked in the mirror, the effect was stunning. Even she didn't recognize herself.

"You don't suppose Fyn sent this, Humboldt?" Ivy paused for a moment. "One more reason to go!"

She pulled on shoes and noted the time—the Ball had been in full swing for an hour now. Holding the thick layers of satin and Chantilly lace with one hand, Ivy put her other on the door—was she doing the right thing? She felt as if she had no choice. Did the Selector really have her best interest in mind? She sighed. If nothing else, it would be nice to spend one night free from worrying about the future or why she was different. It would be fun while it lasted.

THE BALL

○   ○   ○   ○   ○   ○   ○   ○

T HE Masquerade Ball was a long-standing tradition at
the Halls of Ivy. The feats of magic performed there
were legendary—some said that the masks were a
guise for the few scrivenists who were powerful enough (and
mischievous enough) to try magic the Dark Queen herself
had forbidden. Just the year before two fourth year royals had
intertwined their crowns, each with its own Weatheritall
Stone, to make a beautiful, light snow fall over the Masquerade.
The Selector had quickly escorted the two out; the Dark
Queen hated nothing more than compounded magic and it
was the Selector's job to keep the Dark Queen out of the
Halls.

Inside the packed ballroom, Fyn paced. In the dim light
he couldn't see his timepiece, but he kept checking it anyway,
hoping Ivy would show. The high ceilings were draped with
overlapping layers of heavy black fabric intertwined with impossibly long strands of white pearls. The terrace encom-
passed the entire northwest side of the room and looked out
over all of Croswald. The terrace doors—two stories tall—
were open and the night air felt tropical thanks to a spell

from Professor Petty. Light shone both from the moon and from the candles—and there seemed to be a million of them. Each round table was topped with a candelabrum taller than any student. Its finger-thin candles tapered to warm flames. Along the aisles and around the large dance floor at the center of the room, giant glass bottles and vitrines sat in clusters, each holding several candles and tabletop hairies. Fresh from the Hall's gardens, enormous golden and cream louies floated in shallow dishes on the tables, releasing their intoxicating aroma. *Ivy's favorite*, Fyn thought with a smile.

Royals and sqwinches buzzed with excitement, their laughs and titters mixing with the band's music.

"Well, I heard that last year Alianna's dress was a sight to be seen! I can't wait to see what she wears this year."

"A Miss McCorkle original, I'll bet."

People arrived in groups, descending the red-carpeted stairs with *oohs* and *ahhs*. Bright, metallic confetti rained down upon the crowd, evaporating as it touched the ground. Each dress seemed more elaborate than the last. One royal was dressed like a swan, complete with a full mask covered in feathers and glitter. Another girl wore a dress with silk embroidered wings that attached at her wrists. Even the boys had cleaned up quite well. Their double-breasted Regency suits were of various jewel tones and embroidered in gold thread. Each jacket's collar was turned up and tapered into long tails. Unlike in their beast classes, the boys all smelled fresh. Everyone wore masks—even Fyn couldn't tell the students apart.

A hush fell over the crowd and everyone turned toward the top of the stairs: Damaris was sashaying her way down the steps, her dress a cacophony of changing colors. She waved to a crowd of princes at the bottom of the stairs with her mask's stick, proudly letting everyone see her perfectly applied makeup and immaculate hair.

But it wasn't Damaris that they were gazing at. Just behind the preening princess stood a stunning young woman, biting her lip. Her dress's long lace sleeves and bodice clung to her lithe figure. The cream of the dress was as pale as her bare skin, offset by the hundreds of glittering gems sprinkled across it. The skirt was full and lavish, taking up half of the grand staircase. Her mask's frosted branches intertwined with her rich-brown hair. She tentatively stepped down the stairs as if unsure if she should continue. Damaris looked back at her, annoyed to be sharing the spotlight. Though the mysterious girl was clearly uncomfortable with the attention, she inched closer to the dance floor, scanning the room.

Fyn gasped—Ivy! He was sure it was her behind the glittering mask. She was so beautiful. He'd somehow lost track of that on their adventures. As if under the influence of Celebratease he walked toward her in a trance. The two locked eyes and then smiled at one another. Ivy's knees buckled. Fyn jumped to greet Ivy with a welcoming bow, bending over with one white glove pressed neatly against his stomach and the other tucked behind his back.

"Knew you weren't one for following rules."

"How can I be when I'm friends with you? Besides, it's a Masquerade Ball, isn't it? Perhaps I won't be recognized. By anyone but you, anyway."

Fyn chuckled and held out his hand. "Happy to see you. I'd know that lip bite anywhere. Your hand, my lady?"

Now the ballroom was full. Classical music resonated throughout the space. Crimson gowns pressed against black ones against gold against mint. The air was warm with excitement and the ghostly trio's many unseen waiters flew flutes of bubbly elderberry nectar to the crowd. The Jester's food—he was allowed to cook but not to attend—wafted up through the halls, filling the air with a delectable scent. A bright, strong moon shone over the Halls. The Selector glided confidently to the center of the dance floor and cleared her throat.

"Welcome to the annual Masquerade Ball! Each of you has finished a year of course work at this esteemed academy of magic: our Halls of Ivy. My colleagues and I agree there is no greater calling than to hone your magical ability, whether by stones or by blood. So congratulations! We celebrate you!" With a wide smile she swept her arms wide and a burst of sparks rained down gently on the attendees and illuminated the tables set for dinner. Each plate was customized to its guest, the favorite foods of each person piled high on gold dishes offset by the black tablecloths. Dinner was marked by cries of enjoyment, long conversations, and, finally, empty plates.

Full and happy, Ivy looked around. "Have you seen Rebecca?"

"Not yet. I'm sure she's around somewhere. Mingling and flirting, probably! What made you decide to come after all? Was it my invitation?"

"The mask? Yes! Well, I'd decided to come before, but the mask didn't hurt. It's lovely."

"Your mask? It's absolutely stunning, but I didn't send it."

"No? Strange." Ivy wondered who could have sent her such a gift.

"Let's dance. Come on!"

Fyn held the small of Ivy's back and whirled her around the room. She laughed and threw her head back as they spun, watching the lights and confetti float above. Fyn was a natural dancer, helping lead her through the most difficult steps, and Ivy couldn't remember the last time she felt so free. The lively waltz tapered to a slower number, and the two danced in perfect synchronization. Ivy couldn't say anything, nor could she look away. Fyn's warm, green eyes held hers. They spun and as they turned, a hand tapped Ivy's shoulder.

She swung into a prince's arms as Fyn danced away with Spinna Jolly. The dancers laughed and cavorted. Woodley spun a second year as thin as a beanpole. Ivy spotted Rebecca laughing with a prince from Minor Magic. Soon she ended up in the arms of a stranger. Now Fyn danced with Ivory Lucky, but not even he could make that one (those two?) look graceful. It seemed Ivory's right side only wanted to shimmy while the left only could box step. Ivy was winded—she must have changed partners a dozen times.

"You don't mind, do you?" A woman in a midnight black gown gestured toward her. Ivy didn't recognize the student, but then again she wore an elaborate black lace mask that resembled a mourning veil. That was the only thing about her that was modest; her formfitting dress had daring cutouts and she moved with authority. Her wild curls, platinum blonde, cascaded around her mask and down her back. *Maybe she's a fourth year,* Ivy thought as she adjusted her mask to ensure her own face stayed hidden.

They danced, Ivy's hand clutched in the taller woman's icy, almost clammy grip. Something didn't feel right. And then the music switched songs to a much faster tune. "You're holding on so tight, please. Let go of me," Ivy yelped as she tried to get her hand out of her partner's grip. The hand that held hers was heavily ornamented with onyx jewelry and manicured nails filed to a point. The woman muttered something under her breath. She seemed less and less like a student by the second.

"Excuse me? But did you say something?"

"Calling forth the waters that be, from the depths of the glanagerie; spin and twirl and masquerade, in my hands all power be laid." She repeated this over and over, first in a whisper, then in a voice loud enough to drown out the music. Ivy's mouth fell open. She looked around, but those who danced around them were locked into a blissful trance.

Do they not hear what I hear? The band is quiet and this woman is uttering curses! Ivy saw that the band still played, but the room was as silent as a morgue. The woman in black finally released her hand and as Ivy backed away the woman watched her with a strange smirk. She grew taller by the second, much taller than Ivy. Then she raised her lace-clad arms and Ivy heard a trickle. The sound became a rushing and then a roar. A cascade of water, starting at the entry and flowing down the stairs, began to fill the ballroom. The smell of mountain spring water was overwhelming, its pleasant scent at odds with the terrible thing unfolding before Ivy's eyes. The water had reached the dancers and was lapping around their ankles as they waltzed, waltzed, waltzed. Other students went back to sipping nectar, gossiping, or flirting as if nothing were the matter despite their dresses being soaked and cream puffs floating out of their hands.

Then down the flooded staircase, its red carpet now hidden by the rushing water, came the Cloaked Brood. Their chest and arms were exposed, revealing hulking muscle. They had no necks—their massive shoulders sloped straight up to their bald heads. Their gloved hands carried maces and they wore strange, menacing smiles, anticipating a long-awaited treat. *Where is the Selector? Isn't it her job to protect us?* Ivy felt an icy grip on her heart. *Could her worst fear be true? The Selector must have had a hand in this,* she thought. *Gone at just the right time.*

Ivy felt a cold breath on her shoulder and turned to face the woman—the woman who could only be the Dark Queen.

"You! It's you, isn't it? You sent the mask," Ivy demanded, her voice shaking. "A good way to find me among the crowd?"

"A clever guise for those disguised."

Ivy ran to Hayword Nesselton who was awkwardly dancing through the water with another sqwinch, laughing and smiling while the two discussed his newest pet. Looking around at her swaying classmates, professors, and friends, Ivy had to quickly move aside to avoid being knocked down—nothing was going to stop them dancing.

"What did you do to them?" she yelled in fear. "Have you cursed them all? My friends! What have you done?"

"They're in a trance. They can't see you." The Queen took a step forward. "They can't hear you." And another. "They can't help you," she whispered with unsettling pleasure, an arm's length away from Ivy. She made a powerful arc with her right hand and Ivy flew backward ten feet. Her facemask flew off as she landed on her back with a thud.

The Queen let out a malicious laugh. "So that's what you

look like! Pretty little thing, aren't you? Not dressed in your muddy smocks and clogs, like the slurry girl you once were. You should have remained a slurry girl. A slurry girl is far better than a dead girl, don't you think? Your family's scrivenist was quite clever to dispose of you so quickly."

"I'm not scared of you." Ivy coughed, getting her wind back. "What do you want? Why are you here? Please, just leave my friends alone. Whatever you want, whatever it is, you can have it!"

"You're so willing to give up your own life. And your birthright. A queenly instinct, no doubt."

Ivy was speechless at the threat.

"You've caused me a lot of trouble, do you know that? And now, how will you save your life and your crown?"

With a wicked grin exposing pointed, sharp teeth, the Dark Queen raised her hand and began mumbling words over Ivy. But Ivy's first thought wasn't to save herself. She half ran and half swam toward the bandstand. The water was now up to the chins of the shorter girls. She racked her brain for charms from Winsome, minor magic spells from Professor Royal, even some swimming creature she could conjure from Professor Wheeler. She knew nothing of how to counteract magic this powerful and cruel. Her panic rose in her like a bubble of vomit, clogging her throat.

Ivy faced the water and summoned her magic the best she knew how. She pushed back against the water, straining her hands out toward the waterfall that was overtaking the stairs. The flood slowly stopped and walled up. Ivy blinked— she couldn't believe it was working! But then she was knocked back by another of the Queen's shoves. This time it sent her flying into the water. As her body slapped the surface and she sank, she watched in a daze as the surface grew farther away. She sank down toward her classmates, already underwater by several feet. They continued to dance and enjoy a party that was no longer happening.

"Let them go!" Ivy yelled, surprised by the power of her voice under water.

"Are you certain it's what you want? They'll all die. It's only my spell that's keeping them alive. Like it's keeping you alive. But if that's your request, it's perfectly all right by me." She could hear the Queen's voice in her head, as if it were part of the water itself. The Queen herself walked through the water without getting wet—a bubble of icy air protected her.

Ivy kicked to the surface and as she tread water, she locked eyes with the Queen. Her dress was heavy and catching around her legs.

"Stop this. Please!"

"Give me what I request and I'll drain the ballroom, rather than let them all drown. A simple snap of my finger and they are as good as dead. Swimming won't save them now— far too deep. All I want is two things. The first is the magic in your veins—the blood of Isabella's line." The Dark Queen spat as she said Isabella's name. "Well, it won't be your blood for long. I'll spill it the old fashioned way, no magic required." She pulled a dagger from her dress, its bejeweled hilt covered in the same onyx crystals as her mask.

As she continued to speak, Ivy swam slowly backward toward the stairs, not taking her eyes from the Dark Queen.

"The second is your crown, which I see you've hidden.

I thought I killed you when I killed your parents, like I killed Isabella so long ago. But now that the last of the Wandering Family and the last of Isabella's line has returned, I've got business to take care of. It does me no good allowing you to live. So it's only your fault, you see, that I'm here. Rightfully ending the Wandering Curse—I should be thanked for such an honorable act, a favor to you and your miserable family!"

"Don't you dare talk about my family that way. Don't you dare!" The Dark Queen remained perfectly calm as Ivy spoke.

"Oh, how terribly sorry of me. Terribly sorry to even speak of your wretched, cursed family! I'll see to it that no one will ever speak the name Lovely again. And now, brat, you must die."

The thought of having parents—people that were hers—gutted Ivy. Anger rose up in her and she suddenly felt strong. With a cry of anguish she raised her hands and knocked the Queen to her back on the balustrade with a burst of magic, reciprocating the Dark Queen's force. Swimming fiercely for the stairs, she finally reached them and ran up: there had to be someone in the Halls not at the Ball who could help her. The weight of her wet dress slowed her steps, but she ran, determined to get away, even with the Cloaked Brood guarding the perimeter. As she turned a corner, past the Den, much to her surprise, she saw someone scurrying down the hall. She'd know that white mane anywhere!

"Winsome! What, what are you doing here?"

He turned, met her eye, and then kept running. He was holding a box—the unlock box!

"What! Where are you going? I need help!"

He disappeared down the hall shouting behind him,

"Sorry, dear! Just have one last thing I need to get to—no time to chat!"

Ivy shouted after him, "Winsome, the Dark Queen! She's here! She's here and she's just downstairs! The whole ballroom is flooded! Like a monsoon, everything is covered in water! She's cursed them all; they're dancing, they hardly notice what's going on! She's trying to ki—"

Ivy stopped short when she heard a door slam. She stood dumbfounded. Betrayed. What could possibly be more important than helping her? Helping every student at school? She felt tears well up in her eyes.

"Your presence is requested in the ballroom, Ivy Lovely." The Dark Queen's wicked laughter ricocheted down the hall.

The water had reached the second level and Ivy ran through the ankle-deep water, looking over the balustrade, desperate to help. The clear spring water had a faint glow. The Ball was just as beautiful as it had been an hour ago but everything was fully submerged. The water distorted the people waltzing at the bottom, but she could still identify her friends.

Fyn. Rebecca.

Ivy glanced up at the long strands of pearls swagged from the ceiling. She stretched out her hand and coaxed a rope of pearls to her, simultaneously happy that she could perform magic and angered that it wasn't enough. She tied the loose end of the strand around her waist—she didn't want to get caught in a trance underwater without a way out. Ivy climbed the banister, ready to dive down.

The Dark Queen's snarl echoed around her. With it the water darkened and rose in front of Ivy. A monstrous wave reached for her with watery tentacles. She turned and ran, the wall of water chasing her back toward the hall and crashing in wild waves against the walls. At the top of the stairs she was wrenched back by the strand of pearls.

"No!" Ivy shouted and tore it off, beads spilling across the floor. She got up and kept running. The tentacles of water were like creatures themselves: fast and slippery, burbling and hissing after her. One shot out and gripped Ivy by her tattered dress and legs. Ivy's dress ripped and she wriggled away only to be caught again. The water pulled her back under. She thrashed, gulping its sweet taste. The force pulled her around the bend, down the stairs, and to the balustrade where the Queen was waiting, shielded from the water.

"Now, tell me where your crown is!"

"I—I, I don't have a crown! I'm a sqwinch!"

"How pathetic, little liar! We will see if you choose to lie as you watch your friends drown!"

With a wave of her hand, the Queen sent the thick tentacles of water and the girl they carried down, deep into the center of the now-aquatic ballroom. Ivy was pulled to the bottom, past the floating masks, thrashing Broods, sunken pearls, and flutes now filled with spring water. She suddenly remembered the familiar taste of that water—it was glanagerie water. She couldn't breathe, but fought to remain calm. Her only comfort was seeing her classmates carry on, dresses and tux tails floating gracefully around them.

Though the water was darker, Ivy could see the Dark Queen easily. The beautiful yet terrifying woman swept her arm again and woke one student from his trance. Woodley Butterlove stopped eating a soggy macaroon in his desperate

CHAPTER TWENTY THREE

realization that he was underwater. He sputtered and
thrashed, inhaling water and swimming wildly toward the
surface. Ivy racked her brain. The Dark Queen was waking
the students one at a time. Hannelore, Bobby, and then
Rebecca and Fyn were among the panicking students.

Ivy squealed, unable to breathe. Bubbles rose from her
mouth rather than words.

Again she heard the Dark Queen's voice in the water:
"It'd be easy to end this, you know. Just tell me where that
crown is. That stone can't be that special to you if you aren't
wearing it," she reasoned. "I, on the other hand, have great
designs on that stone."

Her friends couldn't speak either. Rebecca's crown had
floated down under a table and she swam after it. Fyn grabbed
the nearest princess, weighed down by her dress, and swam
for the ceiling.

"Care to say goodbye to your friends? Or your crown?
Let's have a little fun while you decide, shall we?"

The water was now so deep that Ivy felt crushing pressure
in her ears. The girls were struggling especially—what had
been the best outfits of the night were now the worst and
most dangerous. Ivy again wracked her brain for magic. She
closed her eyes and cleared her mind. A picture of Winsome
on a sunny day flashed into her mind. He had been sending
out spelled bubbles—leftover from his bath—from his air ducts
for fun. She opened her eyes, ready to cast the spell, but hundreds of bubbles already ballooned from her fingertips,
stretching wider and wider as they inflated. Ivy directed the
bubbles to each person's head, enclosing them with a pocket
of air.

288

Meanwhile, Rebecca had retrieved her crown and swam by as a silvery purple mermaid; Fyn was hanging onto her back. With a nudge from Rebecca, Ivy did the same. Rebecca kicked hard and brought them to a half-submerged, swaying chandelier. They clung to it.

Rebecca dove back down with a powerful kick of her tailfin and began pulling students up one and two at a time. As soon as she caught her breath Ivy sent magic down to the bubbles, expanding them so that they rose to the surface, pulling the students up gently. Once on top of the water the bubbles were sturdy enough to cling too—they formed lovely, shimmering rescue rings.

Ivy and Fyn watched as the water level continued to rise to greet them. Ivy's body convulsed with shivers and she couldn't tell if it was fear or cold or both. She slumped against Fyn, who held her tightly to the chandelier. His knuckles were white. Rebecca the mermaid flopped up and transformed back into Rebecca the royal sqwinch.

"What do we do?"

"What can we do? She's too strong! She'll kill us all."

This was no glanagerie world—Didley's squawk wasn't coming to save them at the last second. *The glanagerie world. Not just any glanagerie, but the one that I keep being pulled to! That's it.* "We need each other to end this," Ivy muttered. "Rebecca, tell me again what a glanagerie world is?"

"An imagination come to life."

"Exactly."

Feeling Fyn's strong arm around her waist and the freezing metal of the chandelier at her back, Ivy closed her eyes, thinking.

"All right. I've had enough fun!" the Dark Queen yelled from across the room. It was almost as if the shield that kept her dry magnified her voice as well. She stood partially obscured in a cloud of swirling black mist. Her mask still in place, she stamped her lace-up stiletto and the cloud whirled up behind her. Then it swept forward, racing across the water and engulfing the chandelier. A cold, wet force wrenched Ivy away from Fyn's grip; then her own hands left the slippery metal. She grasped at the crystals of the chandelier but missed. The Dark Queen dragged her toward the balustrade across the surface and Fyn dove after her. Ivy's nose filled with water and she sputtered as she fought against the Dark Queen's pull. When she was within arm's reach, the cloud threw her down at the Dark Queen's feet. The impact on the stone floor nearly shattered Ivy's elbow.

Looking at Ivy pitilessly the Dark Queen smiled, revealing her menacing, pointed teeth. "Isn't it funny that the only person in this room with the power to make this right is the same person I'm about to kill?"

She raised her dagger. Ivy held her hands up. The only thing she could see was the Dark Queen and the cloud that obscured everything else. Ivy closed her eyes, willing time to slow down. She thought of her parents, who they might have been; of Winsome; of Rimbrick; of Isabella. She thought of the man hidden in her dreams, the one who she felt calling to her from beyond the slurry for those many years. Her mind stuck on him. She suddenly knew that the man in her dreams and the captain were one and the same. *Help me: I'm about to help you*, she thought. *Please work, please.* She summoned the scene from her dream and allowed it to resurface in her memory, as if she was about to make a sketch. Focusing on the dream image, she followed the man from the Den, the beautiful library that she loved, past the portal to Winsome's classroom, out into the Halls. Ivy gave herself completely over to the dream and followed the man, whose face she still couldn't see, into the Selector's office. He pointed to the door, beckoning her to open it. Ivy felt fear rise up in her again.

The Dark Queen jolted her from her reverie, "I never thought that magic, no matter how petty, should be distributed to students—" she spat out the word, "—even if the royals' paltry stones only have one facet, one power, of the stone I desire." She bent low over Ivy's crumpled figure. "But you can imagine a stone like that, can't you? A stone with all of the magical powers in the hands of a single individual? And to be left to you, a silly girl! Give me your crown, Ivy. If not your crown, then your blood."

Rather than deny the evil woman's claim again, Ivy focused on the dreamscape. She dove back into the vision; the Dark Queen's words had convinced her that she needed to open the Selector's door. She felt something heavy on her head and, reaching up to touch it, she found a crown. But the shadowy figure beckoned her forward and pressed something hard into her hand: a key. Under the watchful gaze of the entry dragons, Ivy opened the door to the Forgotten Room.

But what lay behind the door wasn't the storage room of forbidden ideas Ivy remembered. Dozens of gems floated out to meet her, their magic humming and thrumming around her. It was as if every stone from the crowns of those on the dance floor had dislodged and were gently floating through the air. Directly in front of her, a stone the size of a plum glowed the exact color of the moon. It had strange, deep cuts on its sides, not as fine as the facets on its face. The stone lit up Ivy's face, almost too bright to bear.

Ivy jerked herself from the dream, terrified.

"What's happening?" screamed the Dark Queen.

The Dark Queen hovered over Ivy with her dagger raised, her terrible mist enclosing them. Then there was a terrible cracking noise—as if all of Croswald were being split in two—that startled even the Dark Queen. A huge sucking noise like water in a vacuum followed, and the Dark Queen's black cloud dispersed, her magic diminishing. A giant ship cresting a wave of salty blue water hit the ballroom, splitting the entry and stairs in two. The creaking and splintering of wood was deafening. The surge carried the tranced students to the far edge of the room. The ship's final wake careened through the room, spinning the chandelier and sweeping the Dark Queen toward the veranda. The ship lurched all the way to the balcony and cracked the boundary that had kept the water in: glanagerie water mixed with salt water spilled out of the ballroom, down the castle walls, and flooded the courtyard. The waterfall carried the Ball's tables and decorations, which had remained sunken on the dance floor, with it over the balcony.

It was a full-sized ocean schooner, captain included. Winsome was wrapped around the bow like a figurehead, looking as if he had narrowly avoided being run over by the ship. Hurricane winds whipped around the vessel. The water was draining from the gala quickly and people soon found themselves on the ballroom floor, shivering and coughing and spitting out water. All the candles had been extinguished and now the only light came from the moon outside.

"Nooooooooo!" a blood-curdling scream sounded from the veranda.

"I'm not finished with you! I'll be back and when I am, there will be no captain to save you. I will have your blood, Ivy! I will have your blood!" The Dark Queen dragged her Cloaked Brood to her with a sweep of magic and disappeared into the night.

Winsome was ecstatic. Clinging to the bow of the ship he yelled, "You harnessed it, child! It's you who have set him free!" The wind thrashed his white hair. Without another word a burst of gold light exploded around him. When the light faded, all that was left was shimmering metallic dust and the ship's prow.

The stones in Ivy's mind had vanished back into her imagination and she looked at the destroyed room around her. Her dazed classmates coughed and spat up seawater. Rebecca's eyes were wide and for the first time in her life she had nothing to say. Fyn was shaking his head in disbelief, helping classmates to their feet. And where had Winsome gone? Had Ivy imagined him?

Professor Wheeler, apparently in shock, called out from the dance floor, "Rebecca, be a dear, rather be a unicorn, and help your classmates down again, would you?" She obliged and transformed in order to ferry down students that hung from the balustrade, chandeliers, pearls, and sconces. The professors called forth their expellers and those with Healite and Fixeen Stones joined the work of restoration.

The ship was wedged in at an improbable angle, if there were such thing as a probable angle to crash a ship through an old castle. Now that Winsome had vanished, it seemed there was no crew—only a captain. A rope was thrown down on the starboard side and he climbed down. It was the same ship from Ivy's disastrous first and final glanagerie adventures. The captain, who had been so surprised to see her that first time, now strode to her purposefully. He looked decidedly different than he had only that morning in the bottle; same outfit, same beard, but a face she did not recognize.

"You're not going to jump this time, are you?" There was no trace of the pirate speak now.

Ivy was too nervous to reply.

"Been pent up in that glanagerie bottle for far too long. The life of a captain, while interesting, doesn't compare to my true calling," he said, shaking water out of his ear. "Now, would it be possible for a gentleman to get a bubble bath?"

"Your true calling?" Ivy repeated, weak at the knees. Fyn stood beside her, helping to hold her up.

"I'd know a Lovely anywhere." His voice softened as he looked at her and he took a deep bow, "I was your parents' scrivenist. They call me Derwin Edgar Night."

THE TOWN
HAS A NAME

FOR the first time in her life, Ivy's mind was quiet. She gazed out her window in silence, arms folded. The events of yesterday were a blur—she was thankful for the night's sleep and to be in fresh, dry clothes. *That poor thing*, she thought, looking at her shredded, stained, and still wet forever-fitting dress. She doubted that it would ever be wearable again.

Rebecca rolled over in her bed and groaned, "Did that really happen? Last night? Ugh, I'm so sore. All that swimming. Are you okay?"

Ivy drew in a long breath. "I guess. If you set aside the fact that we were all nearly killed last night. Then yeah, I'm okay. Your swimming last night was just amazing! Thanks for being a hero."

Rebecca smiled, "No, *you* were the real hero. Amazing what you did. Don't know how you did it but, really, amazing. In other news, I heard most of the students left last night. As soon as their parents caught wind of it, they were summoned home. I have to admit, being in my safe, cozy bed at home sounds pretty good. Even though the Selector said we were safe to stay, I still have the chills."

"I just have so many questions. Hoping to have some of them answered before we leave later this morning. I guess that's what this is for." She fingered the letter Derwin handed her the night before. It was just a quick note inviting her to tea in the library, just the two of them.

> Meet me where you always pictured me.
> There's much to say.
> D.E.N.

There was a knock on the door and Rebecca rolled out of bed to let Fyn in. His face was weary but kind.

"Brought you pie. Just one, but it's blueberry—your favorite. Thought you might need a little something sweet after last night. And before your conversation with—er, the captain?"

"Derwin Edgar Night, the man that I used to dream about."

Fyn looked a little miffed. "Well, if it's like that..."

Ivy rolled her eyes. "It's not and you know it. Now give me that pie."

The three settled in and ate in silence—too tired, too overwhelmed to talk about the Dark Queen, the flood, and the ship in the ballroom. Despite her exhaustion, Ivy felt exceptionally glad to have friends with whom to eat in peace.

"How are you doing?" Fyn asked once he was full.

"Pretty freaked out by the whole thing to be honest. And you?"

"All right. I heard Professor Fenix is taking next year off.

He's already packed up his things and left special instructions for Ivory Lucky. To watch over his, er, bottles."

"Good luck to her."

"Poor guy, he'll probably never be the same again."

"Will any of us?" Ivy added.

"Can't believe it's the end of the year," said Rebecca finally, licking her spoon.

"Nor can I."

"Where will you go, Ivy?" inquired Fyn. "You sure you're not headed back to Helga and the slurry?"

"Are you kidding? I'd rather sleep outside in the Bitter Forest than see her. Rather have it out with the Dark Queen again. Says something, doesn't it?"

"You can't mean that."

Ivy looked up guiltily, her eyes tearing up. "I'm so sorry to put you all through that."

Fyn reached out to rub Ivy's back and Rebecca shouted, "Don't say that, Ivy! You didn't flood the ballroom! That horrible woman did." She paused. "I'm going to miss seeing you every day."

Before a few short moons ago, Ivy would never have imagined a royal expressing fondness for her. It made her heart feel warm.

"I'm going to miss you, too. There's always next year, right? I'm just sad this one has passed so quickly."

"You know you can always stay with me if you'd like. My mother would love you. I think."

Ivy smiled. "I just may have to take you up on that. I can't believe I passed this term, what with all the trouble I've caused. Hopefully they don't uninvite me next year. Thank you, though. For everything. Both of you." Ivy threw her arms around Rebecca and then Fyn.

Fyn pointed to the little scaldron who was licking the pie tin clean. "I think Humboldt's going to miss this place, too. Look at him. He's probably put on a few pounds eating all that pie this year. I hope you can still carry him."

Ivy laughed as she packed her meager belongings into her bag. With a start, she realized that the three books from Rimbrick had been restored—no longer blank, the spines read, *The Whiz and The Weasel* by Derwin Edgar Night; *Wanda Wetzel The Wise* by Derwin Edgar Night; and *A Scrivenist's Guide to Quills* by Derwin Edgar Night.

"I'm looking forward to finally finishing these," she mused, flipping through the pages of lustrous illustration, spells, and more.

"Look at that! The guy does exist, I guess," laughed Fyn. "And I can remember his name. I'd like to read that quill one, actually. When you finish."

Ivy picked up her Startus from the shelf. "Ooof," she grunted. "So much covered in one year. I have Winsome to thank for most of these pages." Waving her hand, she shrunk the book to a tenth of its original size.

"Look at that! It's about as thick as Damaris's now," Rebecca joked. "Really, you can't leave me with her as my nearest neighbor all summer long, Ivy. Cruel and unusual punishment."

"I'd love to come."

"Wonderful! Glad that's settled." She set to making a hot cup of tea. Ivy sat bolt upright.

"Tea! I've got to run."

She felt emboldened to use her magic freely, dorm room

or not. With a few flicks of her finger, the room started tidying itself up. In minutes the place was as neat as when she first found it, pie crumbs swept and belongings packed—no Loshes Washes required.

When Ivy reached the library, she pushed open the lead glass doors for what she thought must be the thousandth time. Only a year had passed but it felt like a century. And then Derwin Edgar Night stood before her, exactly where she left him so many times in her dream but now solid, discernable, real. He was small framed and had impeccable posture.

"Greetings."

Ivy smiled timidly. She didn't know how to feel or whether she'd wake from a dream in minutes. It was a strange feeling to finally meet him. She had so many questions that tumbled around her head, tripping over each other to get out.

"I must say it is an honor, truly it is."

"An honor? I'm sorry, but what is an honor?" Ivy asked.

"Meeting you, of course, Your Highness." Derwin welcomed her into the empty library and Ivy followed his direction. They walked past Mistis's desk, past the study halls, and toward a wing that Ivy had never noticed before. *How can that be?* she wondered as she automatically slowed her pace.

"Because it was forgotten, along with the rest of me," Derwin answered her unspoken question. "This was the section where my writings were held. And when the Dark Queen cursed me into one of those wretched bottles," he shivered, "the Selector decided to hide away my musings and work so that the Dark Queen would lose the scent. I'd rather not be killed, you know. Though I can't say I completely trust the Selector's reasoning."

The room they entered was a combination of lovely, striking, and inviting. The hearth was warm and an old silver mirror above the fireplace magnified its light. A deep, dusty blue, the room made Ivy want to cozy up and read while watching a storm through the leaded glass. She could barely keep from taking off her shoes and digging her feet into the silken carpet imported from a far-off land. In fact, she would have if it weren't covered with old trunks and boxes. Purple drapes hung heavy around the windows and soft, moody music played in the background. The room smelled comfortably of pipe smoke. There was an assortment of oddities on the shelves, fighting for space.

"After you had rescued me this wing restored itself. Please excuse the state of all these boxes; I haven't had much time to unpack," Derwin said. "Time inside a glanagerie certainly moves at a much quicker rate than the outside world."

Ivy nodded. "You look different than you did in your days as a pirate. Sound different, too." Gone was the weather-beaten skin and gray beard. In the crusty old pirate's place stood a man that could have been his trim younger brother. He moved spryly and his long curls were shiny if a little unruly.

"Is this your office?"

"It would have been my home," he said quietly. "Long ago, before the castle was taken from our line, before it became a school. But first, I'd say the day calls for a celebration? Doesn't it?"

"A celebration of what?"

"You, of course! You're alive! And me! I'm out of that bottle. And the Lovely family, restored to their rightful home. I've got the perfect swill: a bottle of boysenberry bubbly, a blissful brew to toast the many good moons to come! A bit of an antidote to all that happened last night." Derwin now began opening and closing cabinets as he searched for the bubbly.

"Ah, here we go!" He grinned, popping the lid, and sweet smelling fumes sizzled up.

"None for me, thanks," said Ivy. "I'm still processing it all."

"Well, more for me then!" Derwin sipped at the foam bubbling over and poured himself a generous glass, crying out as he sipped, "Delectable! None of this to be found in that wretched world dreamt up by the person who thinks she's Queen."

He set up Ivy with a cup of tea after searching for the teapot in a similar manner.

"You said," Ivy ventured, "you said that you were my family's scrivenist? I have so many questions. I hardly know where to start. All of this, it just can't be! I'm not royal?"

He guffawed. "Royal in the most royal of ways. The last time I saw you, however, Miss Lovely, well, was never. Winsome, the man who served as your grandparents' scrivenist, pushed your bassinet into the slurry fields before I arrived. Your parents thought the life of a scaldrony maid would be the last thing anyone would expect."

"Winsome! Where is he? Is he okay?"

"I'm sorry, Ivy. He passed on."

"He's at the Hollow Shaft, you mean?"

"No, Winsome died saving you. It was he who opened the door to the Forgotten Room last night. Well, he opened it in real life, and you opened it in your mind—which was more important, I think. Your imagination was the thing that summoned me out from under the curse."

"He...he died?"

"He should have been at the Hollow Shaft but stayed behind to help you. His time was up...and then poof! A good man," he said sadly, raising his glass in a solemn toast.

"You mean I'll never get to hear his voice again? To thank him? And here I've been thinking he was betraying my confidence. No tome?" Ivy whispered. "The unlock box. Why would he do that?"

"A promise to your parents, of course! And allegiance to the blood of rightful Queens. And affection for you, I'm sure. I've gathered that you've been under his tutelage? I came along just as you were born to serve your parents, to replace Winsome who was bound to turn tome, but you see how he's put that off for quite a while. Seventeen years he's been denying that invitation." Derwin gazed out the window somberly. "An unfortunate bit of luck, that Wandering Curse. For the Lovely family *and* your scrivenists."

He drifted off and Ivy took the opportunity to wipe the stray tears from her cheeks. *Winsome was dead.* After a few moments of quiet she asked, "Why have you been in my dreams?"

"Ahh." Derwin nodded. "Scrivenists are connected to their families in many ways—a good scrivenist can often be in sync with a royal's mind, just like a quill is in sync with its scrivenist. It allows us to sense what our royal may be thinking, or to have a hunch when they might be in danger. The connection is even stronger when the royal has the bloodline of a true Queen.

"Here." Derwin pushed two sketches across to her. "Look what I found."

"Are these by Winsome?"

"They are."

One sketch was of a handsome couple, healthy and regal looking even though their clothes appeared ragged. The scene was dusky and stars dappled the darkening sky above them. They held hands, keeping warm on two stumps pushed together around a fire. Ivy's heart caught in her throat and she let out a little whimper.

"Your magic, it comes from your mother. But your smile and eyes favor your father," Derwin said softly.

The second sketch was of the man holding a tiny baby wrapped in a blanket so big you could barely see her face. The father gazed down at his child, enraptured with this new creature. Ivy didn't trust herself to speak.

Finally, she asked, "May I have these?"

"Of course, you can. You know, I remember perfectly the day I was sent out to meet the family I'd be serving. If only I had paid attention to all that was going on around me, I'd have had a clue. The headlines! 'Wandering Family Still Lost.' I was so focused on the achievements that lay ahead, who I would become, and how I would make my family proud." Derwin tickled his chin with his quill, now rusted from years of briny air.

"Here, might I show you something else? Sit. Sit. Please." He cleared off a velvet wingback chair and then opened a rusted, salty trunk. Ivy hadn't realized she was still standing and found she could not move. He pulled out a scroll, unfurling yards of timeworn vellum. As he unrolled and unrolled the scroll, Ivy saw small black silhouettes in profile dotting the document. Small connections ran between some of the silhouettes—marriages, children, lone progeny, grandchildren.

And Derwin kept unfurling—certainly this was hundreds if not thousands of years. Finally at the end of the scroll, Derwin landed his boney finger on a feminine silhouette.

"That's you," he said. "This is your family tree—the magical bloodline of Queens. We don't know many details, only how many of you there are at any given time. Isabella was up here. That evil woman—the Dark Queen—exterminated every other Queenly branch so as to ensure her rule. Your family—the Wandering Family—was cursed here, seven generations ago. But what was a terrible burden, Ivy, is now an incredible gift to Croswald. Because your family was cursed, the Dark Queen couldn't find you and the line of true Queens survived."

"I can't, I just, I…" Ivy stuttered. "It's a bit much to take in. My family was—"

"The Wandering Family. You are part of that family, and I, well, I belong to a select group of scrivenists who served them. We call ourselves the Seven Wandering. You are she." He pointed to the last figure on the list. "The one all of Croswald has been searching for. Waiting for, whether they knew it or not."

Ivy could not speak.

He gestured around them. "This is the ancestral home of the Lovely Family. For seven generations we suffered the same curse and in that time the Halls of Ivy were turned into the fine academy that it is now. But that curse was broken when you returned home, Ivy. Surely you noticed the portraits of the wandering scrivenists becoming more clear as they emerged from their curse?"

Memories of portraits and then the blank spaces where

the portraits had hung flashed in her mind.

"So who cursed us?" Then Ivy remembered Rimbrick's story of the lost castle—he was telling a story about her family! Bits of Rimbrick's letter dashed across Ivy's mind: *I need to repay your family a debt of sorts...This, and watching over you, in no way atone for my mistakes, but I hope that you'll remember me with fondness...Trust the magic in you...*

"Rimbrick. Rimbrick cursed my family, didn't he?" Ivy muttered, disbelieving, knees growing weak and forcing her finally into the chair. "He was trying to tell me about it before he left." Struggling for breath, she said, "If I'm, if I'm a royal..."

"Not just a royal. Heir to the throne," Derwin corrected, holding up his finger.

"Heir to the throne, how did I end up living in the slurry fields with horrible Helga to look after me?" She thought of all the years she spent fighting the cats for food or shivering herself to sleep, never once getting a day to spend outside.

"You are the repository of powerful magic, magic that passes through a lineage of Queens alone. Your kind of magic is the kind powerful enough to be sensed—if Winsome hadn't hidden you, our dangerous Dark Queen would have known you were still alive and well. You are the only thing standing between her and the throne forever."

"So, the Dark Queen isn't from our line? That's why Winsome directed me to the Hollow Shaft..." She was now speaking to herself, "To learn of Isabella's death. The Dark Queen took her life and now she wants mine."

"She's not human, Ivy. She's a perversion, a mistake that came from a glanagerie experiment. That's why she's lived so long."

"So even while you were in a glanagerie bottle, you could feel my magic the day I crossed the slurry fields?"

"Yes! I felt your magic awakening. All of Croswald and the heavens above, Ivy! The only thing that compares to the tremor caused by your crossing out of the slurry fields is that of your birth. There is something from Winsome's old journals that I'd like to show you..." He shuffled parchment and books until he found what he was looking for.

The child was born on the double moon—a lucky and fortuitous birthdate, especially as it relates to the prophecy. Also fortunate as we had happened upon an abandoned cottage and had a roof over our heads for the birth. Only minutes old, the child changed the color of her blanket to match her mood as we watched. When she let out her first cry, the little cottage shuddered—but it wasn't just the cottage. The whole world quaked. I ran to the window and threw it open wide.

The double moon filled the entire horizon, growing steadily. My measurements showed it was not only growing larger— eight times the size of a typical double moon—but it was growing closer. It was captivating. When it had filled the whole sky, it descended toward the cottage. It seemed as if you could reach up and hold it. Shimmering moon dust sprinkled the garden, the cottage, and us.

The newborn was as enthralled with the magnificent moon as we were; her eyes lit up with delight. Then something extraordinary occurred. A point on the orb began glowing with special intensity and soon the moon rays consolidated themselves into a single spear of light that was directed into the room and right at the baby's heart. The moon collapsed in on itself, as if imploding. The moonbeams whirled around the child. In an instant, the double moon shrank to a pinpoint of brightness that could have been mistaken for a star.

Ivy's breath caught in her throat. "The double moon! That's when it disappeared?"

"Yes. It had been the repository of Isabella's magic, in part at least, and upon your birth, a suitable heir was found." Derwin drew a deep inhale. "The magic restored itself to your heart."

Ivy sat in shock, clenching a fist at her chest. "I almost don't know how to feel." Her eyes filled with tears at the thought of her own birth, her family, her life before the Castle Plum...the responsibility of her gift of magic.

"Did you know them? My family?"

"I wish I could say I did. Winsome knew them very well. But the carriage accident." His voice dropped to a low undertone. "It happened right before I was transported to your family. They were rushing to hide you away. They were attacked. The Cloaked Brood thought that you had perished with your parents and grandfather, as they could no longer sense your magic."

He gave her a moment to process.

"When I came upon the wreckage, Winsome had already pushed you into the slurry fields, the only place where you could come of age safely. He came back to the Halls to finish out his years working on the prophecy in secret. Waiting for you, I suppose. He then shared his secrets with me. He had been released from the curse because his charge, your grandfather's generation, had passed away and he was summoned to the Hollow Shaft. When I came to the carriage's wreckage, I found something. Something very valuable. Something that dates from far before the crash. Something I was meant to give you."

Derwin handed her a letter and wooden box. The letter was ancient and barely legible.

To the One to Whom This Box is Entrusted:

Today our illustrious Isabella has been murdered and her blood still soaks into the ground. She was taken from us too early by an evil force not of this world. This is a desperate time, the dawn of many moons of evil rule.

What magic remains of a beloved heart is safeguarded by the double moon. The only thing that offers hope to this world lays within this box: a stone pure and bright. A fraction of the powerful queenly magic reverberates in this crystal form.

The one who guards this box guards the future of Croswald.

In protection,
The Hand That Left Her

"What is in the box?"

"One way of looking at it is that it's what the Dark Queen

wants. It's what she's after. Another way of looking at it is that it's your destiny. Open it, Ivy."

Ivy opened the box to reveal the bright, moon-colored stone that she had seen last night in her vision. Or rather, part of the stone.

"Before I was cast away, I broke the stone into three parts—if the Dark Queen gets her hands on this, who knows what she could be capable of? I hid the other two pieces but kept this with me because I hoped to one day give it to you myself. That's been the worst part of being stuck in the bottle for sixteen years, besides the seasickness: not being able to give this to you."

Ivy held the stone in stunned silence.

"It is the first magical stone that ever existed. It marked the beginning of the moon's light forming magical stones underground all over Croswald. Surely you remember the sketches of this stone from the journal you borrowed." Derwin cleared his throat. "I know this is more information than you can process at once, but we haven't got a lot of time. Experienced scrivenists and those who have honed magical detection—like the Dark Queen and her Cloaked Brood— sensed your arrival into this world. And after last night, they know exactly where you are."

"And what exactly am I to do now? Run? Keep scaldrons at another castle? Wander in the woods like my family? She saw me. She knows who I am. She knows."

"Trust me when I tell you, the Dark Queen is weakening. She's rightfully scared and she's coming for you. She knows her only chance to maintain power is to prevent you from possessing and reuniting the Kindred Stone's triad. Your blood called forth the magic of the double moon and is now connecting with the royal jewels that belong together in the crown. You're alive. Despite Isabella's murder, the Wandering Curse, my banishment, and the murder of all others in your line. You are Croswald's only hope. This is your destiny. But here," he gestured around the office, "is safe no longer. Someone in this school allowed the Dark Queen access to our Halls. Until we uncover who the perpetrator is, it is no longer safe for you to remain at the Halls of Ivy."

Ivy looked up. "Then where do I go?" She steeled her nerves.

"The Town. The center of the scrivenist world. We call it Belzebuthe."

ACKNOWLEDGEMENTS

First, I thank my husband for being the sounding board for countless ideas and especially for being the recipient of many random text messages, holding bits of Croswald conversation and character names when I don't want to forget an idea! I dedicate this book to you, Z, because there is so much of you and me inside of it. I would like to thank my parents for always encouraging me to chase my dreams and for introducing me early on to the most magical place, a place that surely inspired my wild imagination. And a big thanks to my editors, Jessie Chatigny and Miriam Lacob Stix. Jessie, you're a gem. The best way to put it is you're as special to me as bread is to Butterlove! And I think only you will ever understand how special that is. I'd also like to thank Resn Global, specifically D, Dan, David, Cam, Charlie and Wade. Thanks for bringing my world to life in more ways than I could have ever imagined. Also, thanks to Jeniffer Thompson at Monkey C Media, Rachel Street, and Annelise Jolley. And lastly, I want to thank my grandmothers: your stories have unwittingly inspired my own and will do so forever.